# MIAMI
## SPY GAMES RUSSIAN ZOMBIE GUN

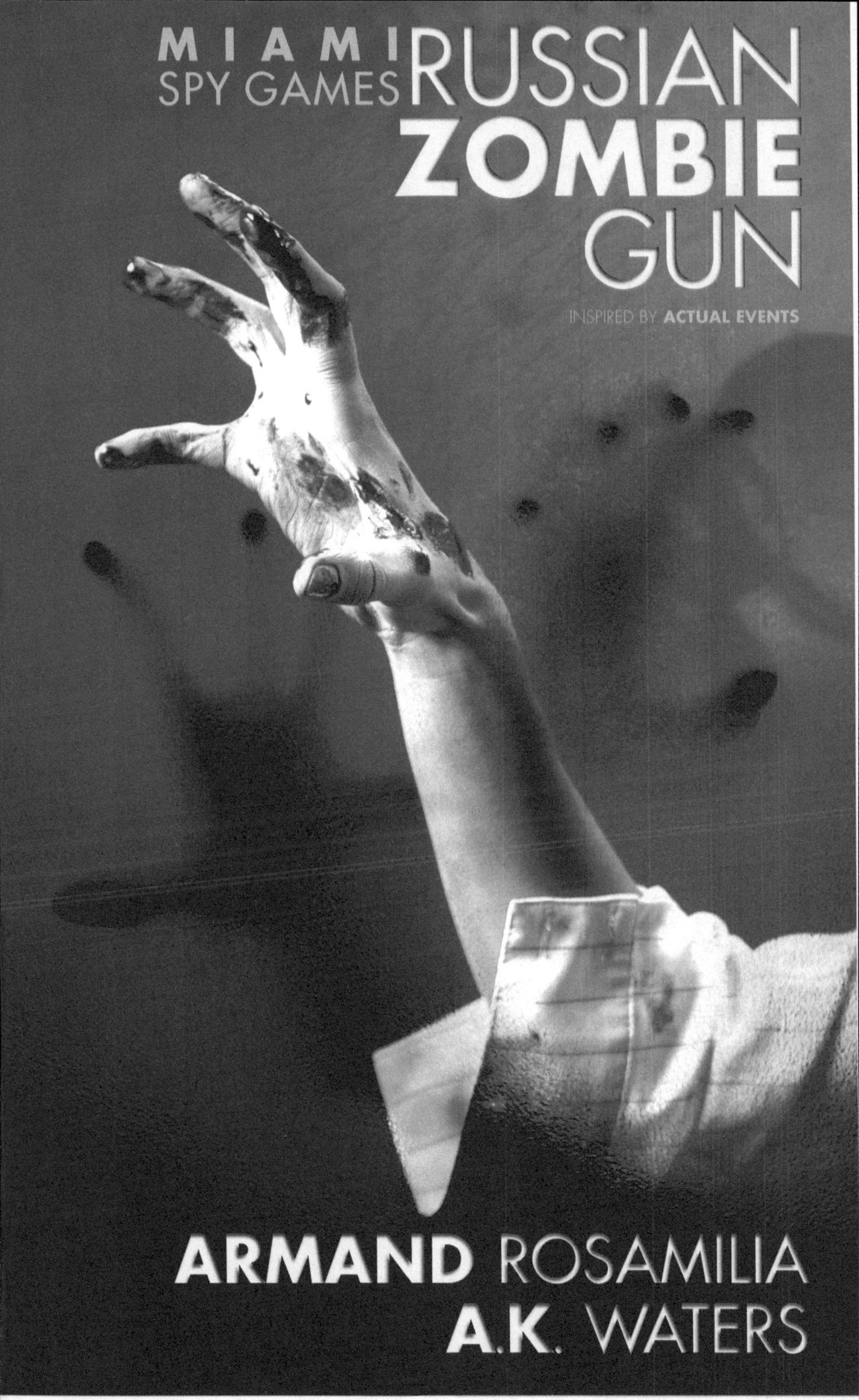
MIAMI
SPY GAMES
RUSSIAN
ZOMBIE
GUN
INSPIRED BY ACTUAL EVENTS
ARMAND ROSAMILIA
A.K. WATERS

Miami Spy Games: Russian Zombie Gun
Published by Hobbes End Publishing, LLC, a division of Hobbes End Entertainment, LLC

1st Printing
Hobbes End Publishing, LLC: trade paperback, 2013
Printed in the United States of America

Author: Armand Rosamilia and A.K. Waters
Cover and Internal Design: Jordan Benoit

Written by
## ARMAND ROSAMILIA

Created and Produced by
## A.K. WATERS &
## ZULU 7 PRODUCTIONS, LLC

INSPIRED BY **ACTUAL EVENTS**

# EPISODE ONE
Asymmetrical Clandestine Elite Service

SVR FIRST DEPUTY DIRECTOR EGOR KOLOFF DETESTED THE WEAK scientist, Yuri, but held his tongue. "Enough with all the pompous talk. Show me the weapon." Koloff prided himself on not only speaking fluent English, but speaking it with no accent. In order to work under him, especially in the weapons division, meant you not only learned English, but learned to speak it like the enemy. In the old KGB days you simply despised the enemy and only a select few agents were taught to speak English or learn anything substantial about America.

And Koloff knew the Americans were still the enemy and had always been, make no mistake about it. Even someone like Yuri was effective in the fight, and his learning English might someday come in handy if they had to set him loose in America as an agent.

"Yes, brother," Yuri said before grimacing. "I mean, yes, sir," his English just a bit off.

"Work on your accent," Egor said to him. This man would never make it a week as an operative for Mother Russia. He was too weak, too small and had no discipline to learn. Egor had been speaking four languages fluently by his fourteenth birthday. This supposed great mind scientist barely spoke presentable Russian. "Now, show me the demonstration."

Yuri grinned and rubbed his hands together, his skin nearly as pale as his white lab coat. His team had been working for the last three years without a break, living in the bowels of the Yasenevo District without interference. Indeed, only Egor and a few loyalists knew the laboratories even existed.

"Well?" Egor finally yelled when the scientist wasn't moving fast enough.

Yuri punched in numbers on the wall keypad. The wall

before them split open, revealing another chamber beyond. Protective soundproof glass ran from floor to ceiling, separating the two men from the chamber.

Inside, a man was strapped to a table angled at 45 degrees. He was obviously in hysterics as two men in lab coats stood nearby at a rolling station, staring at Yuri.

"Is the sound not working?" Egor asked, clearly annoyed. "Do I have to spell everything out to you? Must you always make this a huge production when I come down here? Do you think I don't have better things to do with my time?"

"*Mne ochen' zhal'*," Yuri said. "I mean, sorry," he quickly added in English. He turned a dial and the man's screams filled the room. Yuri stabbed another button. "You may proceed."

The two men opened a black gun case on the rolling station, each using a key at the same time. One man stepped back as the other lifted what looked to be a short, thick pistol, set with an odd array of wires dangling from it.

Egor smiled. "This is the Mark Five?"

Yuri shook his head. "No, the fifth model killed the man. This is actually Mark Seven."

"What about the sixth?"

Yuri looked away. "The microwaves fried his brain immediately."

"I hope you logged and kept it."

"Of course." He nodded to the two men. "Proceed."

The bound man was begging for his life, frantically shaking his head and trying vainly to break free from the straps holding him down. One of the men took up position behind the table. The other walked quietly to the door before turning, slowly lifting the strange weapon in his hand.

"The weapon will short-circuit the executive function capacity of the brain, and either render him into a pliable state or turn him into a primal animal," Yuri said excitedly.

"Which is it?"

Yuri shrugged. "This is our first test, but I'm confident it will work."

Egor put a hand on the scientist's shoulder and grinned. "Let's hope it does, because if this fails and you've wasted my time again today, the next subject tied to the table will be you. Do I make myself clear?"

The worker inside pulled the trigger and a thin sickly yellow light flashed briefly on the top of the weapon. Egor was about to ask if it had failed when he saw the man strapped to the table stiffen.

Immediately the man behind the captive released the hand and feet straps and both men ran from the room, slamming the door behind them.

Egor pressed his hand against the glass partition and watched in fascination as the man stood, eyes now glazed over and mouth drooping. "He looks like he'll fall down at any moment. Is this the big reveal? We've created vegetables by scrambling their brains?"

Yuri grinned. "Not quite. You see, right now his system is in a sort of stasis. His senses are all fully functional, but he shuts down the ones that aren't being used. He will stand there for the next week if we let him, until his body runs out of food and water. He won't feed himself, though."

"I'm not interested in making the enemy docile. I'm interested in making them weapons."

"As am I." Yuri hit another button dramatically and the back wall on the far side opened, revealing a similar room. Inside stood two men.

When they saw the man they called out to him and rushed to his side.

Yuri laughed. "Now watch."

The man lifted his head, seeming to sniff the air. His mouth opened wide and he let out a shriek. He was suddenly animated, and he lunged at the man nearest him.

Egor put his face to the glass. "He's biting him."

"He won't stop until he rips both of them apart. Those people in there are his own family." Yuri turned away. "I can't watch anymore."

But Egor could, his eyes sparkling. This was the weapon he was looking for to conquer America. "I want four of these zombie guns manufactured and sent to our agents in Miami."

Yuri looked confused. "Why would we send them to America now? Should we not wait until we go to war with the Americans?"

"In the eighties we sent many suitcase nukes and buried them in America in anticipation of a war. It is much easier to have your weapons in place behind enemy lines before the fighting begins. Once the signal is given, our operatives will be armed and ready for battle."

Yuri left the room, leaving Egor to watch the slaughter.

≈

JENNIFER SANCHEZ PLACED THE FOLDERS NEATLY ON THE conference room table, making sure they were all set at perfect ninety degree angles to one another, as well as equidistant. She placed three pens to the right of each folder, each exactly two inches apart: red, blue and black pen, left to right.

"Good morning, ma'am," Mike Martin said as he entered the room and sat down in his usual seat, arms folded across his chest. He never smiled, or if he did, Jennifer had never seen it. He was thirteen years her junior at twenty-eight, with a military crew cut, steely gray eyes and a chiseled body he usually hid under over-large shirts and baggy khaki pants. He was former CIA SAD and before that on The Delta Force, but that's all Jennifer was allowed to know about him and his background. Even as office boss and team lead, there was only so much they knew about one another. For a reason.

"How are you doing today, Mike?" she asked, knowing his answer already: he would nod at her before settling back into staring at the wall in front of him, arms eternally crossed, until the rest of the team arrived and the meeting began.

The rest of the team only consisted of Mark Kostas, who was the polar opposite of Mike Martin. Kostas worked for the scientific directive of the CIA and made too many sexually charged remarks to too many females, but his talent had so far outweighed his personality. He was transferred to Jennifer's team at its inception. The Powers That Be knew she could handle him.

He wore a tight teal Miami Dolphins T-shirt, tight blue jeans, and he smiled constantly. He placed a large coffee cup on the table, not noticing when some coffee dribbled down the side and onto the folder before him.

Jennifer cringed but remained calm. To all outward appearances she was relaxed. *As cool as the other side of the pillow*, she said to herself. *Cool as a cucumber.*

Kostas pulled his chair out and dropped into it like a teenager. He was twenty-four but acted much more immature at times. He liked to play when he could, but Jennifer knew he would be all business as soon as she started the briefing. He was also the best tech guy she had ever worked with or studied. Kostas (he hated being called Mark, his last name worn like a badge of honor in the hacker community) was one of those guys who were book smart but not really street smart. He leaned back in his chair and grinned. "Guess what I just got? Two tickets to the Dolphins home opener. Fifty yard line. Third row. Two hundred a piece."

Mike stared at him. "Let me see them."

"No way, bro."

"Why not?"

"Because you always pee on my parade."

"He does it to help you, and because you're always doing something ridiculous," Jennifer chimed in, aware the can of worms she was opening by falling into the conversation.

Kostas smiled, staring brazenly at Jennifer's cleavage. "How are those babies doing today? Need some Kostas Time?"

"Up here or my thumbs will be the last thing your eyes see," Jennifer said. "*Es usted un idiota*," she mumbled under her breath.

Kostas laughed but kept glancing at her chest. "Relax, baby. I know you have to play cool in front of Mikey here, but how about we hook up later tonight? You can show me around *your* Miami, if you know what I mean." Kostas laughed and slapped the table. "Maybe I can see *your* South Beach. Get it?"

"Let me see the tickets," Mike said.

Kostas waved his hand at her and then pulled an envelope from his back pocket as he briefly stood. He threw it on the table in front of Mike, scattering the pens.

Jennifer nearly lunged to fix the items before closing her eyes.

"Are you really going to let me see them?" Mike asked with his arms still crossed.

"I trust you, bro," Kostas said nervously. He smiled at Jennifer. "I have two tickets. I can take you, babe. After the game we'll get a hotel nearby and the real game will begin. Get it?"

Jennifer ignored him.

Mike took his time opening the envelope and pulling the two large tickets out, his eyes on Kostas as he did so. He held them up to the fluorescent light and studied them.

"Well?" Kostas asked.

Mike glanced at him but said nothing as he turned them over and over in his hands. He finally put them neatly back in the envelope and pushed it back across the table.

"You're killing me, bro."

Mike looked at Jennifer. "They're fakes."

"You lie," Kostas said as he came out of his chair. "Please tell me you're busting my balls."

Mike shook his head. "They're decent but most people would be able to spot the fugazi seal."

"The what?"

"Fugazi, meaning fake. Sorry, Kostas. You've been duped.

And it looks like you're out four hundred dollars."

Kostas put his head down as he sat. "Damn, I paid four hundred a piece for them."

"So you lied to me," Mike said.

As amusing as this exchange was, they needed to get down to business. Jennifer hit the speed-dial on the central phone on the table and sat down.

"Miss Sanchez, is your team present?" a stern woman's voice said immediately. Jennifer had only met their Langley boss once, and that was more than she wished she had. Kim L was a strong business woman from the defense private sector side of weapons manufacturing. Kim understood both business and military and how to keep everything in check between them. She'd never been military, seemed to dislike the 'in crowd' of military personnel, and was firmly behind the CIA's directives, even though ACES (Asymmetrical Clandestine Elite Service) wasn't even on the CIA or any other agency's radar. Heck, few were aware of their existence, including Congress, the FBI, and most other counterterrorism agencies. Knowledge of this group's existence would cause further dissention among these various agencies, already withholding intelligence from one another. Only the top twelve Super Users (top level people cleared to view all intel) were aware of this team's existence.

"Yes. Agents Martin and Kostas are present. We can begin."

"Excellent. Is the video monitor on?"

"Yes." Jennifer dimmed the lights with a remote control as a fifty-inch TV screen lit up the far wall, showing a surveillance photo of two men carrying a crate between them.

Several successive photos showed the men putting the crate into the back of a black van.

"These pictures were taken three days ago in the city of Valencia in the State of Carabobo, Venezuela. The crate itself measures approximately six foot long by three foot wide by two foot deep," Kim L said from the speaker.

Jennifer clicked to the next picture, a close-up of the crate markings on the side.

"Russian," Kostas said. "Coming from one of the one hundred twenty-five raions of Moscow."

"The what?" Mike asked.

"Very good," Kim said. "Yasenevo District is an administrative district, or raion, of South-Western Administrative Okrug in Moscow. We are pretty sure it emanates from there. The last two intercepts we've had are from that area, some of the most powerful weapons we've intercepted from the Russians."

Jennifer went to the next slide, an aerial view of the Port of Miami. She pulled a red laser pointer from her pocket and lighted on a spot on the map. "We know the shipment arrives in the next twenty-four hours, and we know that it will come in at this general location of the international docks."

"There's been a slight change to that, however," Kim L said. "We now know there is an inside man for the Russians, a security guard. He'll be handing over the package to the Russians at Gate 7."

Jennifer found it on the map and highlighted it with a red mark. "Here."

Kim L continued. "You will need to intercept the Russians before they reach their destination, but not at the docks. We want to do this as quickly and quietly as possible and get the crate."

"And the security guard?" Jennifer asked.

"Osvaldo Rivera. He doesn't enter into this equation. Now that we know who he is, we can keep tabs on him. At this point, we have no idea how often he's helped the Russians or what his stake is in this. He might be just a low middle man, or part of something larger. For now we put him on the watch list."

Jennifer gave the thumbs up to Mike and Kostas. "We got this."

The phone call disconnected without another word, making Jennifer smile. Kim L was formal to the point of rude, parsing her words. There would be briefings where she would be silent for up to ten minutes before answering a question or after someone throwing in a 'funny' comment. She was all about ACES and nothing else. Jennifer didn't know how she ultimately got the job to lead this and other teams around the country, and she didn't care. So far, in the year Mike, Kostas and Jennifer had worked together in Miami, they'd completed every mission, gathered intelligence on dozens of Russian operatives working in and around Dade County, and done it all with complete anonymity.

"I'll see you at the game. I'll even buy the first round of hot dogs," Mike said to Kostas as he left the room.

Kostas looked at Jennifer, confusion etched on his face. Then he grinned and picked up the set of tickets in the envelope on the table. Only there was just a single Miami Dolphins ticket. "He got me again."

"It's better than the tickets being fugazi," Jennifer said.

"Not really. Have you ever been in a social setting with Mike Martin? He will literally sit in his seat for three hours, arms folded, taking in every player on the field. Every now and then he'll observe something that is purely freakish, like how a linebacker is winded and is going to make a bad play, or if the offense uses a certain pass option it will be a touchdown. And when they use it and they score, he doesn't move. Not even a smile for getting it right."

"Sounds like he missed his calling. He should have been a football coach."

"They'd all quit. He'd never say a word to anyone. Now that we're alone..." Kostas said before leaving the conference room when Jennifer turned her back to him.

Jennifer leaned against the table and stared out the window, overlooking the far runway for Miami International Airport. Her parents would be calling her any minute and she always looked forward to hearing about her hometown of Cartagena, Colombia, her family members and all the excitement that came along with it. Like a typically loud Costena family.

Of course, Senor and Senora Sanchez thought their little girl (even at 41 she was always their little *princesa*) worked in the movie business.

The ACES offices were situated here at Magic Productions to look like another big player in the Miami movie business. With so many great tax cuts, more and more movie studios were setting up companies and testing the waters with TV shows, independent films, all in the hopes they could film a steady stream of blockbuster movies in Miami.

To the casual eye, the first two floors of Magic Productions were genuine. Crammed with cameras, lighting rigs, microphones and other high tech gear, a glimpse inside would show you a company about to create some footage. Several people worked in the ground floor offices, and they were technically in the movie business. They were lesser operatives for ACES that did the filming of dozens of Russian SVR Operatives, mob presence (which often worked together or collided on a seemingly daily basis), and anyone else they were assigned to follow, film and report on.

Jennifer turned back to the table and began writing the next assignment for those working below: Intel on the security guard Osvaldo Rivera.

—

**"YOU CAN HAVE YOUR CAKE AND EAT IT, TOO," OSVALDO RIVERA** said aloud as he stood in the cramped security booth. He checked his watch. It was time for another routine patrol of the docks, but he was looking forward to it. An hour ago a shipment had come in from Venezuela he needed to get his hands on, although if the Russians he was in bed with knew his real plans they'd think twice about tipping him off to do their bidding. To them he was a grunt, a nothing middle man who intercepted important packages and handed them off to shadowy figures for an envelope of cash.

But Ozzie (as his friends would have called him if he had any) had bigger plans for himself. It had started with the cache of GP-25 Kostyor under barrel grenade launcher kits he'd skimmed off the top a year ago. From there, he'd been able to trade five of the six to the Pakistani ISI agents for a nice chunk of change.

He'd been a good boy since, even though the weapons and surveillance equipment being illegally shipped in were very tempting. But he needed to play cool, and he had. Until the money had run out, thanks to a few bad investments, like that stripper Jasmine. "Never again," he said as he thought of her. Ozzie wouldn't let a woman take advantage of him like that as long as he lived. He smiled when he thought of Krystelle, his newest girl, and the fun times they were about to have, depending on what was in this latest shipment.

Ozzie knew from past experience whatever was coming in was usually being held for the future. All the weapons and cool gadget stuff he'd seen never seemed to hit the streets, and never went missing. How would the Russians miss an entire crate of GP-25s unless they still hadn't used them?

He made sure he was doing everything he was supposed to be doing, like writing in his patrol times on the clipboard and checking the gates and everywhere else the cameras could capture his movements. This needed to seem like another boring night of patrolling, and just another shift.

"You can have your cake and eat it, too," Ozzie said again, almost singing the phrase. He didn't know what it actually meant or where he'd gotten it from, but he was sure it meant something important if it was still stuck in his head.

At this time of night it was quiet. He got into the golf cart and turned the key, the sound of the small engine sounding like an airplane in the stillness. Ozzie smiled inside, excited to be opening the crate and seeing what it was. Outwardly he yawned, shining his flashlight in dark corners of the yard as he drove for effect.

"Relax, take your time," he said to himself. There was no use rushing directly to the shipping container and doing something wrong. It was better to maintain his composure for the next half an hour and fantasize about what he'd do with the money.

"You don't even know what you're selling," he said and laughed. "Always putting the horse before the cart."

The thirty minutes seemed to crawl as he finally got to the far corner of the fenced-in lot, his flashlight quickly scanning for shipping crate 237. One thing he loved about doing this type of work: the Port of Miami was meticulous with their paperwork, and ninety-nine times out of a hundred, if a shipment was supposed to be in a certain spot, it was. Lot 237 was no exception.

"It looks like a coffin," he said with a laugh. Ozzie clipped a small light to his security cap, put his large flashlight back on the golf cart, and took his tool bag from under the seat. His trusty leather gloves were put on, as well as a pair of glasses, magnifying his sight. He'd been a petty thief since he was old enough to walk, in and out of juvenile detention. That's where he met most of his contacts, and got a name for himself as a go-to guy when you needed something lifted. Of course, his silence on the rare times he was pinched only added to people contracting him for jobs. A fake driver's license had landed him this gig, and he was hoping to propel it into something much bigger. And more lucrative. If the Russians trusted him he could move up as a solid contact, and then play them off of the Cubans, the Afghanistan agents and even trade key information with his fellow Americans. He just needed to get deeper into the Russian system, but this pickup and handoff was a nice, easy step in that direction.

Careful not to break the crate completely open so it couldn't be closed, Ozzie went to work. He used his small, silent electric screwdriver to get the shortest panel unscrewed. As he placed the panel onto the top of the crate, several clumps of packing material fell to the floor. He ignored them for now, reaching in with gloved hands and extracting a strange gun, a thick pistol with a fused ammunition clip. He gingerly touched the wires hanging off the front, thinking the gun was unfinished, but he noted they were part of the weapon.

Ozzie was a quick study of most basic weapons, whether foreign or domestic. His prized possession was a Desert Eagle made in Maine and with much better action than the Israeli ones he'd fired.

But this . . . he'd never seen anything like it, and thought he'd either been duped with fake guns or the Russians were about to be. There was nowhere for a clip to be inserted into the gun, and as he looked closer he saw it had a small battery pack on either side of the short barrel. "Maybe the Russians are making science fiction movies now," he said.

He was wasting time, and needed to be spotted by a camera in the next three minutes. He pulled another three from the crate. They were all the same. He decided to take one and figure out what it was at a later time. Right now he needed to get this coffin moving.

Ozzie stuffed the strange weapon under the seat of the golf cart, put the three weapons back inside the crate and screwed the panel back on, careful to get the stuffing back inside as well. No trace evidence anywhere. For all intent, nothing had been touched in this area and it was ready to be shipped. It was hell to lift so he used the hand-truck he always kept on the back of the golf cart and maneuvered the crate onto it. He nearly ran two rows until he found the strategic cut in the chain-link fence he'd made months ago. From the outside perimeter you wouldn't see it because it was blocked by a patch of dense weeds, a perfect spot to get product out.

A short whistle from Ozzie and he heard the soft sound of a door opening and closing. He leaned the crate against the fence and watched two men struggle through the bushes.

"There's a path right there," he said as the two came to him. They were dressed in black loose-fitting clothes, their heads covered in black wool caps. Ozzie put his hand on the crate and put his other hand in his security jacket pocket. He wasn't allowed to bring weapons to work, but these two probably didn't know that fact. "The envelope, please?"

"When we get the package secured," one of them said in a thick Russian accent.

"That's not how we play this game, brother. I think you know that already." He moved his finger-gun in his pocket for effect and hoped the bad lighting would emphasize his point without making him look stupid. Stupid would lead to dead right about now.

The second man handed him a small manila envelope.

"Nice doing business with you," Ozzie said and stuffed it into his other jacket pocket. He'd have the rest of the shift to count it but knew ten crisp one hundred dollar bills awaited him. And Krystelle and Ozzie would be painting Miami red tomorrow night.

The Russians ignored him, already lifting the crate and walking right through the weeds to their van.

Ozzie shook his head. *Who hired these two idiots?* "Again: there's a path around so you don't have to do that." *And destroy my little natural fence so I can't use this spot again.* It didn't matter right now. He was sure he could find someone to take the Star Wars gun off his hands in no time, and he had the next two days off to do it.

He reset the fence so it didn't look breached and ran to the golf cart, stomping on the gas to get in line with the nearest camera. As he passed it he made sure to look in the general direction so they could see him intently looking around on routine patrol.

When he got back to the guard shack he quickly counted the money and deposited the bills in his wallet. He checked his watch. "Two more hours of this."

Ozzie stepped outside and casually leaned against the shack wall as he pulled his cell phone out and blocked the view of the camera trained on him and the gate.

"Krystelle? Honey? It's me . . . Ozzie. Yeah, Ozzie. Are you off work yet? Still dancing another shift? This late? That place should be closed already. Huh? No, no, baby, not fighting with you, just miss you. Uh huh. Uh huh. Are you off tomorrow night? Can you take off? Please? For me? I booked us a room at the Ritz-Carlton for tomorrow night." Ozzie wiped the sweat from his face. "The Setai? Sugar, that's three grand a night. Uh huh. I know how much money you make in a night. Uh huh. Fine, fine, I'll make it happen. Yes, I just told you I would. I love you. Hello?"

≈

**"I'VE GOT A VISUAL ON THE VAN," MIKE MARTIN SAID FROM HIS**
position on top of a building overlooking the Port of Miami
international docks. "They're parked just outside the fence."
He adjusted his night vision goggles. "I see at least a driver
and a passenger so far."

"Roger that." Jennifer sat in the ACES van, a non-descript
1999 Chevrolet Conversion Van Mark III, complete with a
dented side panel and the beginnings of flaking paint on the
hood. Inside, however, Kostas had his hands on every surveillance gadget known to man, and beyond.

"I have a lock on the Russians. Seriously, they're driving
around in a black van? I hope they're all wearing black turtle-
neck sweaters and knit hats as well. Damn cliché Russians,"
Kostas said. He tapped a button dramatically. "We're locked
on them. Tell Mike he can come back now." He turned to
Jennifer. "Unless you want to finally give in to your fiery Latina impulses and come sit on my lap. We can talk about the
first thing that pops up."

"We're good on this end," Jennifer said into her mic. Then
she half turned and stared at Kostas. "I have the authority to
break one of your fingers if provoked, did you know that?"

Kostas stopped smiling. "That can't be true."

Jennifer smiled. "Do you want to find out if I'm bluffing?
Keep it up." She cracked her knuckles for effect. Back to the
business at hand. She checked both side mirrors. The worst
thing right now would be a random police cruiser in the area,
wondering what they were doing parked here this time of
night. There was only one main road in and out of the port,

so it would be easy to track them by sight, but much easier once Kostas had them locked in his system.

Kostas began humming, something he always did once his first part was in place and until they started to move. He tapped on the control panel in front of him. "You like rock and roll music?"

Jennifer also knew he loved to chat, wasting hours with boring trivia and things she had no interest in. But she also knew to ignore him or to not feign interest only ramped him up more to ask another series of questions, or tell her innocuous trivialities. And it was better than the lame sexual innuendos he barraged her with constantly. "Yes, I do listen to rock and roll music on occasion."

"Cool. I figured you only listened to salsa music."

"*Calmáte*," she mumbled to herself as she closed her eyes and continued looking ahead. Kostas was egging her on, trying to get her to blow her cool. He was really bored right now, she could tell. It was never mean-spirited, but it was seeing which button to push to get the office boss and team lead to break a sweat, especially when she routinely shut him down with a threat of bodily harm. "I listen to all types of music."

"Meringue? All the different Latina stuff you can shake your big booty to?"

"Of course. I even listen to horrible Greek music if there's absolutely nothing to listen to. And I mean nothing," she said, hiding her smile.

"Hey, not funny." Kostas, who she knew was Greek on his father's side, nearly whined.

"Did I say something wrong?"

Before he could answer, Mike was back on the radio. "The

two targets are exiting their vehicle. I have visual."

"Roger." Jennifer casually checked her AA-12 automatic shotgun as she scanned around the van. In minutes they'd be on their way, and this was always the toughest part for her: the wait. Once you got into the action, it all fell into place and the training and mind took over, like muscle memory. While she wasn't as experienced as Mike Martin (he'd served three tours in Desert Shield and Desert Storm), she had honed her skills in the last year on the streets of Miami doing these takedowns.

"Just tell Mike the Snipe to shoot them, we'll drive up and grab the package, and I can be home to watch Sports Center," Kostas said. He mocked Mike sometimes by calling him Mike the Snipe, since he was an amazing shot when it came to the Tac-338 McMillan tactical rifle he used as his main weapon. But it was also said out of envy, because there was no better sniper than Mike Martin, and his services had long been sought by not only most branches of the United States government, but by many foreign as well.

The longest recorded confirmed sniper kill was made in November 2009 during the war in Afghanistan, using an L115A3 long range rifle and using .338 Lapua Magnum rounds (the same type Mike Martin used). The range was officially listed at 2,707 yards.

Mike Martin had beaten that record at least 5 times in his career, all unofficially, of course. Mike Martin and ACES didn't exist.

"They have the package and are loading it into the van."

"Come back and let's move. Kostas, you ready back there?" Jennifer asked as she started their vehicle.

"Born ready, senorita."

Within fifteen seconds Mike was in the passenger seat, stowing his weapon securely behind his seat but within easy reach.

Jennifer drove slowly, just under the speed limit. She was in no hurry because they knew who and what they were pursuing, and Kostas could easily track them. In cheesy TV shows and movies, you needed to place some small device under a bumper or behind the wheel of a car. In reality, they could follow wherever they were as long as they had a general idea of the initial coordinates. And Kostas has access to every computer system known to man, even the few ACES wasn't supposed to have access to.

They didn't want the Russians to get too far, and definitely not to their destination, but even in the middle of the night there were other cars on the road and potential witnesses and innocent bystanders that might get injured or killed.

"Make a right at the next intersection. They're driving slower than you are, which I thought was physically impossible," Kostas said.

Jennifer began to make the turn, using her turn signal.

"I have visual," Mike immediately said. Jennifer squinted. Even though her eyes were above average, Mike was like an eagle, and his mind could focus that quickly.

"How can you tell?" she had to ask.

"The right tail light has been replaced with a non-factory lens, most likely a Pilot brand."

"And you bitch I'm full of useless knowledge," Kostas said from the back but no one responded. "If I named the lead singer of Slipknot, you'd all look at me like I had two heads."

Jennifer knew Mike wasn't bragging, and she didn't really care where he came up with the crazy knowledge, as long as he knew it. Taking his word as law, she gave it a little more gas in hopes of catching up to the Russians before they got to the end of their ride.

"Corey Taylor is the answer, in case you were wondering," Kostas said from his perch. "They turned into a business up ahead. I'm sure Mike already knows which one based on the street light configuration."

"Days Inn a block up," Mike added humorlessly. "I can tell by the trajectory of their tires as they pulled in off the highway." He glanced at Jennifer and winked.

"Donovan Solano of the Miami Marlins was born on December 17th, 1987. Who does he share a birthday with?" Kostas asked.

Jennifer turned into the gas station right before the hotel parking lot and drove to the vacuum pumps and parked.

"Me," Kostas said loudly.

"Me what?" Jennifer asked.

Kostas sighed audibly. "Donovan Solano shares a birthday with me."

"I bet he makes more than you do," Mike said. "The minimum salary for a rookie MLB baseball player is $480,000. I don't think you make that much."

"I hate you," Kostas said as the three exited the van and moved quickly into the shadows and across the parking lot of the Days Inn, spreading out with weapons drawn but not in firing position.

It wouldn't be good to scare an early waking tourist or the maid service right now, and get everyone in a panic. "The van is in the rear lot. They're still inside," Jennifer heard Mike through her headphones.

"I have the exits," Kostas said immediately.

"We need a visual on the occupants," Jennifer said to Mike.

There was a long pause as she took up position behind a stairwell, the AA-12 automatic shotgun trained on the back tires of the parked van. If they started it up and tried to leave she'd have to keep them from doing it.

"They aren't in the front seats. They must be looking at the package. I'm going to approach," Mike said quietly.

Jennifer watched as Mike pulled a small smoke bomb from his pocket and lit the fuse, slipping it into the cracked open window of the passenger side. It wouldn't do much more than startle and confuse the Russians and perhaps make them cough.

Right on cue the two burst from the back doors of the van, and Jennifer fired twice, hitting both in the forehead with a clean shot before they had gone three feet. Mike was on them, waving his hands to clear some of the smoke as he lifted both men and tossed them back into the van, shutting the doors.

"That should clear out soon," Jennifer said into her mic. "You drive the van and follow Kostas and I. We'll get a few miles away before we get a good look at the cargo."

"Roger that."

Within minutes they were on the move, Mike following Jennifer as they made their way onto the 395, taking the NW 12th Avenue exit and pulling into a fast food restaurant parking lot.

Jennifer sat in the van and kept her eyes on the road. It

would be sunrise soon enough, and the morning shift would be pulling in any minute. "We don't have much time," she said into the mic.

"Bingo. Weapons secured," came Mike's reply. "I'll follow you back to Magic."

Jennifer pulled back onto 12th Avenue just as a clueless employee pulled in to start their job. Jennifer's job was over, and now she could sleep.

The bad guys had been taken down, another cache of weapons taken off the street before they could be used to harm an American civilian, and all done with two perfect shots to the head and no visible traces it had ever happened.

Mike would get rid of the Russian van, and it would appear as a blurb in the police blotter of the Miami Herald as a gang-related torched stolen vehicle. The Russians weren't going to report it stolen.

And the next time she spoke to her parents, it would be to tell them about the new spy movie she was working on for Magic Productions, and how the special effects look so real.

"It's still early. How about I make us some omelets and we watch the waves from my balcony? You know you want to. It could be meaningless sex if that's what you're in to. I just want to see that smoking body of yours naked. Is that too much to ask?" Kostas said with a smile.

Jennifer glanced at him in the rearview mirror. "Give me your middle finger. I've decided I'm going to start by breaking that one."

"All you have to say is that you'll take a rain-check. No big deal. I can wait, babe. Trust me, for you I can wait."

⚊

**OZZIE WAS STARTING TO FEEL THE PRESSURE. SO FAR HE'D BEEN** shut out from his main contacts, which meant he'd either been burned or he was just being paranoid. He needed to score with this weapon in the next hour, or he could kiss The Setai and Krystelle goodbye.

When his phone rang he nearly jumped. He relaxed and answered on the third ring. "Talk to me."

There was a pause on the other end. "Sally?"

"Nope, wrong number. This is Pete." In their street lingo, Pete was like Pistol Pete, which was saying he had a weapon he was trying to unload.

"My bad. I thought I had someone else. Do you know where Opa-Locka buys her oranges? Is it Sabur?"

Ozzie checked his watch. "No, but I have fifteen apples."

"Again, my bad. Double big tree heaven. Thank you."

He hung up. Ozzie knew the place mentioned—Sabur Apartments in Opa-Locka—and had told the caller he'd be there in fifteen minutes. Double big tree heaven translated to apartment 237. By the part of town he knew he was dealing with some lowly gangbangers, but they'd somehow gotten the word and were looking to deal. He didn't think they'd have enough to offer him but it was worth a shot.

Six minutes later he pulled up across the street and pulled binoculars from under his seat. The apartment was on the second floor, which he didn't like. Whoever was inside could watch the street, watch the stairs on either side of the building, and never be surprised. As if on cue, the drapes moved slightly. Someone was watching.

Ozzie picked up the blue backpack on the seat next to him and got out of his car, making sure his black leather jacket was zipped up despite the Florida heat. He was packing the Desert Eagle in his back waistband, a snub-nosed revolver in a shoulder holster under the jacket, and his Gerber Prodigy Survival knife in his boot sheath.

"And away we go," Ozzie said as he crossed the street and went to the stairs, flipping his sunglasses to the top of his head. Opa-Locka was a mean street area of Miami, and you didn't tread lightly here. Ozzie remembered reading somewhere in 2004 or 2005 that Opa-Locka had the highest rate of crime in the country. He didn't doubt it. The only reason he was here was to get rid of this weapon and make some quick cash.

He stood in front of apartment 237 and it suddenly hit him: this was the same number as the shipment. Ozzie didn't like coincidences, and was about to punt the deal when the door opened a crack. The security chain clanked. "Apples?"

"Oranges." Ozzie looked around to make sure this wasn't a setup, either from swarming cops or another gangbanger about to shoot him. He was the only one in view.

The door closed, the chain unlatched, and the door re-opened. A large Cuban man wearing a dark gray sleeveless shirt and baggy pants motioned for him to enter.

Ozzie flashed a thumbs up outside before he walked in, knowing what the reaction would be.

The man pulled Ozzie inside. "What was that?'

"Insurance. My partners are waiting for me outside. If I don't come out at a designated time they'll start to get worried. We don't want that. We all want to do business today, right?" Ozzie asked, staring at the man in charge on the couch, a smallish black man wearing a thick black T-shirt and khaki pants, his neck and wrists covered in thin gold chains.

He smiled through hooded eyes, and Ozzie thought he looked like a piranha. He didn't like this one bit.

"Heard a cracker had something neat to display, so took the liberty of getting your digits. You feel me?" the man said. "I'm Marcus and this is my boy Tiny."

"Who's the guy in the bedroom?" Ozzie asked without taking his eyes off of Marcus. Two against one if things got bad wasn't good. Add in a third potential shooter?

Marcus grinned. "Of no importance. Let's see what you got."

"Don't you want to hear my prices beforehand?"

"I'm looking for something powerful, if you feel me." Marcus pulled a wad of money from between the couch cushions and spread fifty and hundred dollar bills in a fan on the coffee table. "You feel me?"

Ozzie counted roughly six grand on the table, but knew this was a show of power and nothing more. Now the real fun would begin. He pulled the weapon from the backpack and held it pointing at the ceiling.

"What the hell is that?" Tiny asked.

Ozzie smiled. "One of the latest and greatest from the Russian arsenal."

Marcus didn't look as impressed. "What ammo does it take?"

"Huh?" Ozzie stuttered, his smile briefly dropping before he grinned again. "There's a self-propelling mechanism here. Notice the battery packs? It works on battery power."

"And shoots what, battery acid?" Marcus said. "Man, I was expecting something besides a movie prop. Cracker, you been all over town trying to pawn off what everyone thought was a new player in the game. You just a fool."

"Let me explain," Ozzie said, but he saw the glance Marcus gave Tiny and knew his time was up.

Tiny took two steps toward Ozzie when survival instinct kicked in. The intent was to use the weapon as a club to bash Tiny's head in before Marcus pulled a pistol from the seat cushion, but as Ozzie swung his arm around his finger touched the trigger and he pointed and fired, not expecting much.

And he wasn't disappointed, as a sparkly yellow light glowed on top of the gun.

Marcus laughed as he stood with a pistol in hand.

That's when Tiny growled.

Ozzie backed away as Tiny looked at him, snarling like a junkyard dog.

"Bro, are you all right?" Marcus asked.

Tiny turned at the sound of Marcus speaking.

Ozzie moved slowly to the door, keeping his eyes on the two men. At any moment one of them might notice him sneaking away and shoot him.

"Tiny, your eyes are messed up," Marcus said, his last words as Tiny lunged across the coffee table and clamped his teeth into the other man's shoulder blade.

Ozzie couldn't move as the giant Cuban began ripping his partner apart, biting and pummeling him onto the couch. The cash fell to the floor, scattering, and Ozzie had a brief moment of stupidity, wanting to reach in and grab some of it, but Marcus finally stopped screaming.

Ozzie slowly opened the door and walked backward outside.

"What's going on?" someone said close to him.

Ozzie turned and pulled the trigger, with the same effect. Without waiting to see the end result, he ran down the far stairway, across the street, and jumped into his car.

He heard someone scream from the apartment parking lot as he cut into traffic and sped away.

# EPISODE TWO
## The Thrill of the Chase

**JENNIFER SANCHEZ TRIED TO IGNORE THE DRAGONFLY DRONE IN** front of her as it caught her eye again. If you didn't know it was there it would look like nothing more than a bug flittering through the restaurant, but she knew. She also knew Kostas was trying his best to focus on her cleavage and not on the man currently sitting across from her in the crowded room.

Jennifer leaned forward and casually touched the emerald necklace she wore, a gift from her *abuela* (her mother's mother) on her sixteenth birthday. She casually covered her breasts. She was sure Kostas was back in the team van, ready to mark the spot on the video if he could get a better shot.

"Damn," he whispered into her ear as she straightened it out.

The man sitting across from her was smiling.

"So, tell me more about you and your travels," Jennifer said with a smile. "It seems so fascinating to see the world." *Even though I've seen it a dozen times over and most likely did more before you'd even had your first cup of coffee*, she reminded herself. Sometimes intel collections operations like this were so routine and boring, but she was a consummate professional. If doing her job meant sitting across the table from a boring Russian importer/exporter of women's real leather gloves, pretending he was interesting and laughing at his awkward jokes while he constantly stared at her boobs, so be it. *You can't have a shootout with the bad guys every day*, she thought. Gathering domestic intel for another ACES team (the team led by Hanneman in Dallas) was part of the job.

He was animated now, explaining the intricacies of buying and selling these 'super hot' items all over the world, and how there would be a glove revolution coming soon.

"Key in on the word *revolution*," Kostas said in her ear. "He's said it three times since you sat down."

"Revolution," she said evenly and stared blankly at him.

He stopped talking and smiled. "Yes . . . is, is that a question? I'm sorry. I talk so much. It must be driving such a beautiful woman like you crazy."

"Not at all," Jennifer said with another perfect smile. Unlike movies, where clandestine back alleys served as settings where agents handed one another non-descript documents and folders stamped TOP SECRET, quite a bit of the intel back and forth was made by assets who didn't even know they were assets.

Why risk shipping a handful of documents or having an e-mail unencrypted when you could literally use word of mouth to pass along something? These *assets* didn't carry drugs, they carried sensitive information you never wanted to fall into the wrong hands.

If Jennifer and Kostas could figure out the keyword imbedded in this guy's conscious, he'd begin to talk without even realizing it. They'd intercept the information and by the time he reached his destination and contact, they'd already have deciphered the data and would be one step ahead of the Russians.

But what was the keyword to open him up?

He was babbling again about gloves, and Kostas was breathing heavy in her earpiece on purpose. Jennifer took a sip of her water, putting the glass down slowly and continuing to give him her full attention.

"Hell, try *gloves* with him," Kostas finally said. "This dude is all over the place."

Jennifer sighed inwardly. "Gloves."

He was so caught up in his speech about how soft the Ukrainian leather was that he nodded and kept talking without missing a beat.

"Nope," Kostas said in her ear. "I'd rather be doing paperwork than these assignments. This could take us all day. I'd hate to have to see you and him getting jiggy with it under the sheets if we can't crack this."

"*Te puedes callar?*" she whispered, sure Kostas heard her. Her date was oblivious, leaning back in his chair and waving his wine glass.

"I love it when you talk dirty to me in Spanish," Kostas said.

"I said will you ever shut up?" Jennifer said a little too loud.

Her date's smile faded. "Excuse me?" he asked, his voice cracking.

Kostas laughed in her ear and swung the dragonfly drone closer to her shoulder.

"Nothing, just talking to myself." Jennifer swatted at the drone, hitting it and sending it careening out of view.

"Are you kidding me? You know how much that baby costs?"

Jennifer was going to hurt Kostas one day, and it might be soon.

"Enough playing around. Lean forward and say *boobs*," Kostas said.

"No." Jennifer smiled again but the guy was clearly unnerved.

"Seriously. Before he walks."

Jennifer sat up and leaned across the table, reaching for the salt shaker and making sure her date got a nice view. "Boobs," she said to him.

"*Strasveecha. Schto tee kareesh? Scoozeeta pushalsta. Buena e meer?*" Her date began rambling in Russian as she sat back and smiled. Most of the time it was random words or nonsensical sentences. Jennifer was positive he was talking about cigarettes, war and peace, and it didn't even matter. Her job was done. The tech team would pull it apart and figure out what it all meant.

"Damn, did I forget to tell you we knew the keyword already?" Kostas asked in her ear and chuckled. "One of these days I'm going to see those perfect boobs of yours."

When the man was finished spewing Russian he stopped and put his wine glass down. When they unloaded their message, assets were usually their most vulnerable because they never even knew they'd done it. To him, in his mind's eye, he hadn't missed a beat of this conversation.

"Excuse yourself to the bathroom," Kostas said.

Jennifer stood, preparing to exit. She'd gotten what they'd come for, and now it was time to slip away. Unwittingly, she'd upset the guy and now if she simply slunk away he would think she was a bit odd but nothing overtly wrong. "I need to powder my nose."

The man smiled meekly at her, clearly upset at the sudden turn in conversation.

*Poor guy. He probably thought this date was going great and he impressed me with his talk of gloves. Now I deflated his ego,* Jennifer thought.

"You can't leave yet, though. There's something else you need to do," Kostas said.

"I'm not falling for anymore of your crap. If you expect me to actually go into the bathroom with you watching, you are *loco.*"

"Nope. Straight behind your boyfriend there are two gentlemen sitting at the table against the wall. I need you to approach them."

Jennifer sighed. "This better be worth it, because people are staring."

"Then stop talking to yourself, crazy lady. The guy facing you with the bad toupee is Max. I need his last name and where he is from, as much info as you can get on him."

"Max? Is that you?" Jennifer asked as she bent down and smiled at him.

"Uh, yeah," Max said, staring at her ample cleavage. "Hey," he stuttered.

Jennifer turned to his friend and offered a hand. "I'm Jenny. Are you a friend of Max?"

"Yes, I'm Aaron Cole. Nice to meet you, Jenny," the man said. His toupee was even worse than the one Max had. Both men were in their early fifties but the hair made them seem older.

Jennifer caught Max giving his friend a dark look but he smiled when she refocused on him. "How have you been? Still living in Fort Lauderdale?"

Max looked confused. "Where did we meet?"

"At the Garcia party, of course." Jennifer leaned over the table and gave both men a great view. "You and I spent the night near that gaudy statue."

Kostas was in her ear. "Tell him he told you something about the nursing home he owned." He paused. "Wow, you have some great tits."

"You were telling me about the nursing home you ran. Remember?"

Aaron laughed. "The Beach View Nursing Home." He leaned forward and winked at Max. "I forgot you were the owner, buddy."

Max smiled. "I don't remember talking to you." He glanced again at her chest. "I'm sure I would remember you."

"Max Gamarro. Got him. Break off," Kostas said in her ear. "Bring those babies back to the van so I can see them in person."

Jennifer stood and shrugged. "Maybe it was someone else. Sorry."

"Wait, where are you going?" Aaron asked as she walked away.

She made sure neither man was stupid enough to follow her out of the restaurant. When she got around the corner, she slipped into the back door of the 1999 Chevrolet Conversion Van Mark III and wanted to punch Kostas when he looked up from his monitors and smiled at her.

"*Un Dia de estos te quiebro los dedos*," she said to him.

Kostas laughed. "Did you say something about my fingers being pretty?"

"Broken, actually," Jennifer said. "I can't wait to get out of this dress."

"Just say the word, my dear. It's only us today."

Jennifer smiled. "I'll start with either your pinkie or your thumb."

"The thumb isn't a finger," Kostas said.

"Then you won't miss it."

"You're so hostile because you need to get laid. You do know that, right?"

When Jennifer didn't take his bait and keep the conversation going he turned back to his dragonfly drone, sitting on his desk.

"What did you need that info for?" Jennifer asked as she moved to the driver's seat.

"While you were playing footsie with your boyfriend I was also monitoring that sleazy bastard. It seems he is a janitor at an old folk's home and he's been stealing their checks and cash and padding his bank account. He was bragging to his buddy Aaron over their fancy lunch. Aaron is his neighbor, which was also easy enough to find out."

"What are you doing about it?" Jennifer asked as she pulled out of the parking lot and began heading back to Magic Productions, the front of a Miami film studio but more importantly the base for the ACES team.

"I already did something. This guy had $27,000 in his account. I cleaned it out, and gave it to his friend Aaron Cole."

"Why?"

"So when the donation for $28,567 is added to The Beach View Nursing Home books, they'll know exactly where it came from: the generous Mr. Aaron Cole, who also added $1,567 of his own money for knowing Max."

"You always amaze me," Jennifer said.

"I amaze myself. It's so easy to do this stuff. Like shooting fish in a barrel."

"You probably shouldn't be telling me this stuff. I'm still

your boss and what you are doing is a crime on about fifteen different levels."

"Don't get all hard on me now. I expect that tone from Martin, but not you. I can't take two uptight partners, I'll go nuts," Kostas said.

Jennifer checked her watch. "We still have plenty of time to rendezvous with Martin at the Miamarina."

"Why can't we leave him there? We did the hard work today. He's watching babes walking around yachts. Not that I think he's into chicks."

"I'll let him know you said that."

"Why did I get stuck with watching some idiot eat, and he gets to check out chicks in thong bikinis?" Kostas asked with a slight whine to his voice.

"I don't trust you on your own to stay focused. Remember the incident on South Beach?"

"Not my fault."

"It's never your fault," Jennifer said with a laugh.

"If we have any time to kill before meeting up with Mr. Excitement Mikey, there's plenty of room back here to fool around. Just say the word. I'm ready to go. Or I could fly the drone up front and get the shot I missed when you covered up."

"If I so much as see it move, I will toss it out the window and have you explain to Kim why you lost their precious toy." Jennifer sped up, trying to get to Mike as fast as she legally could. The less time she spent with this *idiota* the better.

⁓

**OZZIE JUMPED WHEN HIS CELL PHONE RANG, SCATTERING THE EMPTY** pizza boxes on his coffee table. His heart was hammering in his chest, and the sudden glow from the phone in the gloom of his apartment, where he'd shut all the blinds, kept off the TV and shoved a chair under the doorknob, was like a bomb had gone off in his hands.

When he looked and saw it was Krystelle calling, he smiled. Ozzie wiped the sweat from his face as he answered, putting a smile in his voice despite his shaking. "Hey, baby."

There was a sigh on the other end. "Did you book the Setai for tonight?"

*Damn.* "I'm working on it."

"Working on it?" Krystelle yelled into the phone, her voice rising in pitch. "I need to know what my plans are. I'm at the club now."

"Your plans are with me, baby-girl. Tonight we're going to have a night to remember." Ozzie closed his eyes and tried to stay positive. *I'll sell this evil gun-thing and make some quick cash. Now that I know what it can do, I can up the price.*

"Not if you don't come through with what you promised me. I can easily find something else to do tonight. I was invited to a party on a yacht."

Ozzie opened his eyes. Maybe that was his way out of spending so much money tonight. "Hey, a party sounds like fun."

Krystelle sighed loudly again. "I was invited, not you. Personally by Souljack."

"The rapper?"

"That's right. He came into the club last night and dropped a grand on me for lap dances alone."

"I thought you were going to stop doing lap dances. You promised," Ozzie said.

There was a pause on the line. "I got another call. I'll give you two hours to get back to me, or I'll assume you didn't come through yet again."

"Yet again?" Ozzie asked, but the line was already disconnected. He didn't understand that comment. So far, in their short relationship, he'd given her anything and everything she asked for. Krystelle was so much different from Jasmine, his last stripper girlfriend. Jasmine was a money-hungry gold digger who only cared about his flash money.

"How is Krystelle different?" he asked himself. Ozzie began scanning through his phone addresses, looking for someone he might have missed on his first and second pass looking for a buyer. "She's much hotter than Jasmine," he finally told himself as he tossed the phone down on the couch next to him. He'd run out of realistic options.

He decided to take a nap, even though he'd only been awake for an hour. His night had been restless. Every time he'd closed his eyes he saw Tiny, the gangbanger's bodyguard, as he turned into a raging lunatic and attacked Marcus. He remembered the sight and smell of all the blood, and thinking he was going to be bitten next.

Ozzie also remembered the guy outside he'd shot, and how quickly he'd become a monster. He didn't know what to call it, but it was unnerving.

After twenty minutes of trying to get comfortable on the couch he gave up and decided to turn on the TV. Watching *Maury* or *Dr. Phil* always cleared his head, because he knew he was running out of time right now. He needed a master game plan and he needed it now. He was burning daylight.

Instead of couples arguing about paternity tests while the crowd cheered, there was a breaking news flash on. "Boring," he said and started switching channels. He only had basic cable and there was never anything else on this time of day. Three stations were playing the same news, so he decided to turn up the volume, wait for it to pass, and enjoy what was left of *Maury*.

Ozzie got up, intending to grab a cold beer from the refrigerator—that always helped him to think as well—when he heard the word *zombie* on the newscast.

He stopped in his tracks and watched as the pretty newscaster, a solemn look on her face, began describing an apparent attack by a man on drugs.

"...A Miami police spokesperson refused all questions about the man shot and killed on the MacArthur Causeway an hour ago, saying it was an ongoing investigation. Channel 4 News Miami has learned there is surveillance footage currently being reviewed thanks to the nearby Miami Herald building. Once Channel 4 News Miami obtains that video, we will review it. Stay tuned for more breaking news from this apparent zombie attack in Miami..."

"MacArthur Causeway? That's at least fifteen miles away from Opa Locka." Ozzie sat back down on the couch. "There's no way he walked fifteen miles without anyone noticing him. No way." *Maybe it was another, totally unrelated attack. Maybe a coincidence. Maybe none of this is happening, and I'm dreaming. But zombie does feel like the perfect way to describe the guy I shot and what he turned into.*

Ozzie knew damn well he had something to do with this,

and he needed that beer more than ever right now. Just as he popped the top off the aluminum can his cell phone rang in the living room again.

"Glad I didn't bother with a nap." He grabbed it and was confused. It was Krystelle again. She never called him back this quickly. "Hello, baby."

"Listen. Are you alone?"

"Yeah, why? Wanna have phone sex with your honey?"

"No, you idiot. Shut up and listen. There are three Russian guys here asking about you." Krystelle was whispering. "The bouncers said you came in all the time."

"Why would they sell me out like that?"

"Because, let's face it, everyone in here thinks you are a cheap bastard. But that's not the point."

Ozzie guzzled the beer in one fluid motion as he sat back down on his ratty couch.

"Are you in some kind of trouble? Fat Tony is here, and he knows I know you. Understand?"

Ozzie perked up. Fat Tony was one of the bosses who ran the smuggling in and out of the docks and the airport. But the problem was if Fat Tony knew Ozzie was helping the Russians and not cutting him in on the deal, Ozzie would end up as alligator bait in Biscayne Bay. Ozzie had never even been allowed near Fat Tony, but now . . . "I need you to let Tony know I have something important the Russians are looking for, but it has a huge price tag on it. Understand?"

"Enough to pay for a night at the Setai?"

Ozzie laughed. "Baby, enough to pay for a week there. Let him know that. Give him my number. I need to get rid of something ASAP. And stay away from the Russians. Are they still there?"

"Yes, but Fat Tony has his guy's escorting them out. I'm scared. They know me now. I can't go back to my place," Krystelle said, fear in her voice.

"Hole up in a seedy motel until I can come get you."

"Fuck you, Ozzie. You got me into this mess and you're going to take care of me. Book me a room at the Setai."

"I don't have that kind of money right now." Ozzie went back to the kitchen for a second beer.

"You just said you'd make enough for a week. Are you seeing someone else?" Krystelle asked. "Are you back with that bitch Jasmine?"

"Hell no, baby. I only want you."

"Then prove it. Make the call, and make this right or I will walk."

"I don't have the money yet."

"I'd hate for your home address to slip to the Russians. You know I don't want that. I just want to be safe."

Ozzie downed the second beer. "Fine. Tell Fat Tony we need to talk, and tell him it's about something in the news. That should pique his interest. We need to set up a meeting."

"When are you going to book the room?" Krystelle asked.

"As soon as I get off the phone with you. How does that . . . hello?"

≈

BORIS DRAGOV DIDN'T SEE OSVALDO RIVERA'S CAR PARKED OUTSIDE of his rundown apartment, but if he was smart he was either hiding it or he was halfway to Canada by now. No matter. Boris always tracked down and found what he was paid to find.

Sending men into the strip club to spook him was an easy way to smoke him out. Once he got the phone call from one of the skanks that he tossed money at, he would be on the move. If he wasn't already.

"I don't see any movement," Andre said in the driver's seat next to him, using the small binoculars. "Nothing."

"I hope he's already on the move," Boris said. Both men spoke perfect English, with thick Russian accents.

Andre put down the binoculars and stared sideways at his boss. "I don't understand, once again."

Boris laughed. "Are you a fan of music, Andre?"

"Yes, of course. All kinds."

"So am I. I was born in Russia but I grew up in Germany, as you know. When I was a child the other kids were listening to what is now termed classic rock. Have you ever heard of the band Deep Purple?"

"Yes, of course."

"Around 1985, when I was fifteen years old, I heard their *Perfect Strangers* album. It changed my life." Boris stared at Andre. "I was a small child, in a foreign country with a strange accent. The other children picked on the little Russian boy, calling me a Communist and the enemy. Ha! These German children, whose grandfathers had helped an evil dictator kill millions." Boris opened the car door and stepped out.

Andre followed suit, adjusting his tie in the side mirror before joining his boss at a brisk pace directly toward Osvaldo's apartment.

"The Deep Purple album got me through some very tough times. Six months later my family went back to Mother Russia. I didn't know it at the time, but my father was gathering information about a radical cell of Germans intent on world annihilation. My father did his job admirably, but at a price: he was gunned down three months after we returned to Moscow."

Andre nodded along silently and stood by as they got to the apartment door.

Boris had told Andre and many of his men this story, possibly several times, but he didn't care. It wasn't about them hearing it. It was about Boris cleansing himself one more time, about keeping the fire burning in his gut to exact revenge.

"Knock," Boris said.

Andre banged on the door.

"I blamed the Germans, and so did everyone else. My father had taken down over thirty men in one fell swoop, and he'd paid the price for serving his country. No matter. When it was my time I proudly joined the cause, but I always kept one line from the Deep Purple song "Knockin' At Your Back Door" in my head at all times."

Boris paused and stared at the door. "Kick it in."

Andre complied, smashing the door in with one strike of his boot.

"The line I kept in mind, the one I turned over and over and made it mine and the one that set the pace for everything I do in my life . . . *It's not the kill; it's the thrill of the chase.* No truer words have ever been spoken or sung. I savor this, you understand?"

They stepped inside to the cluttered and filthy apartment. Andre moved from room to room and Boris wasn't surprised when he came out and said Osvaldo wasn't there.

"I could have easily come here first, once we knew who this guy was. I could have sent Nicholai or Ivan to tail him. But where is the fun in that? I want to hunt this little man down like a hare. I want to sink my wolf teeth into his neck and watch as he vainly struggles." Boris pulled black leather gloves from his pocket and put them on. "Search this dump. I'm sure he didn't leave the item here, but no matter. We'll find his address book, see if he has a landline phone we can get contacts off of, and toss the place. I want him to know we were here."

Andre nodded but Boris could see he thought this was a waste of time. No matter. It wasn't about finding anything. It was about stalking the prey and getting to know the enemy. Boris flexed his arms as if he was stepping onto a wrestling mat, his muscles bulging under the dark suit. He patted his shaved head and went to work.

"It's not the kill . . ." Boris sang as he went to work, stomping on the coffee table and shattering it in half. He almost hoped a nosey neighbor would come over so he could break a human body. It had been too long since he'd been on the mat with someone that was a challenge.

When he was twenty he'd become something of a prodigy in a wrestling ring, twice the Russian National Wrestling champion. His dream was to become an Olympic gold medalist for Russia, and he toyed with the idea of a lucrative career in professional wrestling. He'd even defeated two American pro wrestlers when they'd toured Moscow in *shoot* matches, where the punches were real and there were no rules. And Boris had beaten them soundly.

But the SVR had other plans for Boris Dragov, noted son of one of their most revered agents before his untimely death. If Boris wanted to exact revenge against the Germans and the rest of the world that had conspired to snuff out his father's life, the SVR was now giving him the means to do so. On his relative terms.

"This man is a pig," Andre said as he came out of the bedroom.

"What do you expect? He is a filthy American." Boris shook his head. "Call Nicholai and Ivan and see if the stripper has moved, and if this man is with her. I'm growing bored already. I want to kill someone."

Andre dialed his cell phone as they walked back to their car.

Boris waved at an old man standing in his apartment doorway across the parking lot. The man slammed the door behind him as he rushed inside. Boris laughed, knowing his imposing six foot six inch frame, chiseled good looks and body, and the expensive Armani suit he wore threw people when they saw him. He was tanned after being in Florida the past three days, since he preferred natural sunlight to the confining spaces of hotel rooms and vehicles.

Plus, he spent three hours per day outside practicing Gracie Jiu-Jitsu and cleaning his mind of all negative thoughts. It didn't matter if it was raining, snowing, or there was a hurricane ripping across the lawn. Boris would be out there and getting in his workout.

As Andre drove the car out of the parking lot he connected with Nicholai on the phone. Boris didn't bother looking back at the decadent apartment complex and it was soon stripped from his mind. There was no room in his thoughts for anything other than the job ahead of him now. He pulled his lips back in a feral grin, and could imagine smelling his prey's fear. This weak man was running. Boris could feel it.

"The stripper went into an expensive hotel. They followed her in. It seems Osvaldo Rivera booked a room there for the two of them."

"How expensive?"

"Nicholai thinks it can charge over three thousand dollars for a single night."

Boris laughed. "Where does this little man get money for that? Unless he's sold the weapon already." Boris smiled again, sitting up in the passenger seat. "We might have a chase on our hands."

"If Osvaldo Rivera has already unloaded the weapon . . ."

Boris looked at Andre. "No matter. I never leave any part left open. Even if we see the weapon cross the street on the next corner, I need to pay Mr. Rivera a visit."

Andre smiled. "I will admit, boss, you are quite thorough when it comes to doing your job."

"This is not a job to me. This is a way of life." Boris was getting excited now, his adrenaline flowing. "We'll pay Osvaldo a visit in his hotel room. There I will extract the information from him and the woman."

Boris was glad he'd packed his Extraction Kit. This was going to be quite a workout for all involved.

≈

**JENNIFER LOVED THE MIAMARINA. THE DOCKS WERE SITUATED IN** the heart of downtown Miami, and right next to the American Airlines Arena. But it wasn't the basketball Jennifer came here to see. It was the hundred shops with such a diverse and eclectic array of international flavors and styles, and in the few hours a week she had to herself she could be found here, wandering in and out of places, a *cono de helado* melting in her hand.

"Funny how different this place looks in the daylight," Kostas said as he stepped out of the conversion van and stretched.

Jennifer nodded. A few hours ago they had been at the Port of Miami, at night and with this part of Miami sleeping, averting another Russian weapons threat. From their vantage point on the docks of the Miamarina she could see the port bustling with activity as docked ships were unloaded or loaded.

Mike Martin was leaning against a guard rail, Miami Herald folded in his hands. To the casual observer, he was just your average good-looking guy in his late twenties, wearing a subdued Hawaiian shirt and faded blue jeans. He was a typical tourist enjoying the clear Miami weather, with the beginnings of a tan. He looked out of place like everyone else who was roaming around, which was exactly the right way to do it.

Jennifer sat down on a bench next to him, with Kostas continuing to walk down the dock.

"Beautiful day," Jennifer said and raised her sunglass covered face to the rays of the sun. She looked like a local, with her gorgeous Costena skin complexion. "Nice day for a boat ride?"

Martin grinned and ruffled the newspaper in his hands. "How was your morning with Kostas?"

"Just as you can imagine. He spent the time staring down my top. Oh, and neglected to tell me we already had the keyword."

"Typical of him."

"What do we have here?"

Martin sat down next to her on the bench, an arm draped over it. "These aren't more Russians like we thought. Technically."

"Good." After last night's success, Jennifer didn't want to face more of them, or a cleanup squad intent on getting the weapons back right away.

"They're different Russians then we've seen previously."

"That's the technically, I assume."

Martin nodded. To anyone who noticed Jennifer walk up (and most guys in the area did), she was being hit on by this tourist in the gaudy Hawaiian shirt.

"We've already identified one of the three men on the boat: Ramzan Umarov, a Sunni Islamic and a key player in the radical Russian underbelly. Why he's here, ostensibly posing as a common boat owner, I have no idea. Yet."

"Where are Baker and Luciano?"

"The Russians are three boats down behind you, and they're two boats diagonal to them. They have been recording all morning but these guys are good. Even talking in Russian, they're acting like it is a beautiful day and they might go fishing or stroll the shops. Luciano has been translating, since he speaks both languages fluently."

"Did Baker loan you his shirt?" Jennifer asked with a laugh.

"Do you think I'd pay for this ugly thing?"

Jennifer smiled, enjoying this part of the job: being out in the open air of Miami, so like her native Cartagena. The smells, the sights and the people.

David Luciano was an operative that usually sat at a desk in Magic Productions and translated unencrypted material. Before joining ACES, he had been with the Agency for years. He looked more like an accountant, always wore a suit to work, and seemed to be in his thirties with a baby face despite being ten years older. He was a serious guy, even when he was joking, completely committed to his role on the team. He bumped heads with Kostas and his sloppy ways on an almost daily basis.

Tim Baker was almost his polar opposite. Edging over fifty, he had sharp eyes and a ponytail, always quick with a smile and a sarcastic retort, and wore outlandish Hawaiian shirts and sandals no matter where he was or what he was doing. He'd been CIA, and the ACES team used him from time to time for surveillance. He was one of the best Jennifer had ever seen. She knew she only had him for a limited time because he was involved in the case the FBI and DEA were conducting against the Black Death Motorcycle Club near Daytona Beach.

Jennifer casually watched as Kostas wandered the dock, ignoring the Russians and the other operatives as he went to the end of the pier and stared out onto the Port of Miami, just another Miami Dolphins fan with his Marino football jersey enjoying a stroll and checking out the expensive boats in their slips.

"I imagine we'll waste the rest of the day on this." Martin checked his watch. "I'm going to leave in fifteen minutes and get something to eat. I'll leave Luciano and Baker here. A guy in an ugly shirt standing around reading the paper and talking to pretty local girls might start to stand out after awhile."

"Why, thank you," Jennifer said with a laugh.

Martin looked away. "Sorry, boss. Habit."

They didn't speak for almost a minute, Jennifer trying to come up with something (anything!) to break the ice and get over the awkward silence.

When her phone rang she sighed. She pulled it from her pocket and answered on the second ring. "Sanchez."

"Get your team back ASAP." It was Kim L. from the seventh floor Langley Operations office. Never one to waste words, Jennifer knew before she heard the click the conversation was already over.

"What's the matter?" Martin asked.

"It was Kim L. She wants us to pull the team. I'm guessing something bigger is going on."

"Should I keep Luciano and Baker out here?"

"Yes. Let them know you've been pulled for now, but for them to keep in touch with you. I don't want to lose our eyes here in the event the Russians decide to do something other than fish or shop."

Martin pulled his cell phone from his pocket. "I'll let them know. Meet you back at Magic." He stood and walked away.

Jennifer texted Kostas to meet her back at the van in three minutes. She stood and walked away, breathing in the last of the beautiful air. Kim never pulled them away from a current case unless something major had happened.

Despite the beautiful weather, Jennifer suddenly felt very cold.

~

OZZIE SAW ONE OF FAT TONY'S MEN, ROCCO FIERI, SITTING IN THE lobby of the Setai. *Great. Krystelle told them where we'd be hiding out? What was she thinking?* About herself, obviously. He was beginning to think she only had her own best interest in mind.

He hid himself behind one of the pillars in the lobby and dialed her number.

"Hey," she answered on the first ring. She never answered on the first ring.

"Are you alone?"

Krystelle paused. "Yes."

Ozzie closed his eyes and leaned against the pillar. His head was throbbing. "Why did you tell Fat Tony where we would be?"

"You said you wanted to talk to him."

"On my terms, not his! I wanted to meet him in a neutral spot, not in a hotel room where he could kill me if he wanted to." Ozzie rubbed his eyes with his free hand. "Tell him I will call back in an hour and we'll set a rendezvous spot." He needed time to get away from here and hope he wasn't going to be followed. In truth, Ozzie had no idea what he was going to do now. He needed to dump this weapon and disappear.

"Osvaldo?" a deep male voice suddenly said on the other end of the phone.

"Hey, Mister, um, Tony . . ."

"Please, call me Antonio. I understand you want to talk to me."

"Yes, I have something you'll be interested in seeing."

Fat Tony laughed on the phone, a deep rumble. "Excellent. I'd rather chat with you in person, if it's all the same to you. I like to see who I'm dealing with."

"You know who I am," Ozzie blurted.

Fat Tony's voice lowered. "That's not what I mean. I don't like chatting with someone over a phone line. Come upstairs."

"What room?" Ozzie asked, but the phone disconnected. He was getting sick of being hung up on so many times in the last few days. Ozzie put the phone back in his pocket, hefted the backpack onto his shoulder, and decided to follow his gut instinct, which was telling him to run like hell and never look back.

As he turned to the front doors of the Setai, Rocco stepped in front of him with a smile. "Osvaldo." He took Ozzie roughly by the arm and led him to the bank of elevators.

When Rocco put a hand on the backpack Ozzie got pissed. He pushed Rocco away. "This isn't for a nobody like you to see. Back off or I walk."

"I don't think you have a choice," Rocco said with a smile.

Ozzie slid the backpack off his shoulder, feeling the weapon inside. "I think I do." He hefted the backpack just as the elevator doors opened. One quick glance told him it was empty. He stepped inside and slammed Rocco in the face with the backpack just as he stepped in.

Rocco went down, the gun shattering his nose.

"You'll pay for that," Rocco mumbled, blood spilling from between his hands as he covered his face. "You hear me?"

Ozzie didn't smile. He knew he was in way over his head with all this, and needed to come up with a plan that would keep him alive.

So far, he had nothing.

JENNIFER SQUIRMED IN HER CHAIR AT THE VARIOUS NEWSCASTS ON the split screen before them. Kostas, for once, was quiet as he watched. Martin glanced at her from time to time and shook his head.

Several reports about the zombie attack on the MacArthur Causeway, along with film footage, police spokespeople talking to the media, and even a supposed zombie expert on CNN filled the screens. When Kim explained about the weapons supposedly recovered last night and what the implications were, as well as what the media was already doing with this nightmare story, Jennifer thought she'd be sick.

"I need you to walk me through last night once more," Kim said over the speaker phone on the meeting room table. "Every last detail."

This didn't make sense. The weapons had been secured, the box taken from the Russians before they even had time to open it. There was no way one of them had been left behind or smuggled out once the van was secured and driven to a safe place.

Even though all three had written up reports for the night before, Jennifer began going over their step by step moves.

Until just now, she had no idea what the box they'd secured had in it, what it was capable of, or where it had come from. That was never her concern. Her only information she needed to know was where and what she needed to intercept. They'd done that.

*Obviously not,* she thought. "... then Osvaldo handed the box over ..."

"There it is," Martin said. He slapped his hands on the table. "Osvaldo Rivera stole one of these weapons."

"Would he be that stupid?" Kostas asked, sitting up. "Steal from the Russians?"

Kim cleared her throat on the line. "Before the tradeoff, did you have eyes on Rivera?"

Jennifer slumped her shoulders. "No."

"I wish to speak to Ms. Sanchez alone. The rest of you are dismissed," Kim said.

Kostas frowned as he stood and shook his head. Martin mouthed a *sorry* as he left.

"We're alone," Jennifer said when the door closed. She began pacing the room, circling the table. She knew what was coming.

"Do you have any idea what you might have done?"

"Ma'am, our focus was on the Russians. From our previous intel gathered, Osvaldo Rivera wasn't a person of interest other than the middle man between the Port of Miami and the Russians. If we had any reason to believe he was working on his own, we would have simply grabbed him beforehand, made the switch ourselves and taken down the Russians. The fact that he is involved, in hindsight, has dire consequences, but ACES had no reason to believe he was anything more than a delivery boy."

Jennifer stopped walking; knowing she'd babbled a bit too much and more than likely said a few things off the top of her head she should have left unsaid.

"Your new focus is to nip this in the bud with the press and keep it from reaching epidemic news media circulation. This is already a national story. You need to get to the coroner and do some spin control. Some scientists down the hall in S&T had an idea. I'm e-mailing you the material we've already distributed about bath salts."

"Bath salts?"

"Our angle right now is this man was high on bath salts, which is the street slang term for designer drugs sold as tablets or powder and purchased in convenience stores, head shops or gas stations. It is a stimulant that mimics the effects of cocaine, LSD or ecstasy."

"Will they buy that excuse?"

"They already have. Within the hour you'll be seeing it pop up on the news."

"It is also a good thing to spread the word that this drug is out there and easily accessible to the kids or users, too," Jennifer said.

Kim was silent for a moment. "Yes, of course. But we're not here to do public service announcements; we're here to stop someone from shooting normal citizens in Miami and turning them into raging monsters. If you don't put the spin on this then the city of Miami may try to evacuate or riot. Your ability to properly propagandize this incident could save thousands of lives. Do you understand?"

"Yes, ma'am. I'll get the team right on this. I'm sure Martin and Kostas are already downstairs with personnel gathering info."

"So far, there has only been the one attack. Ms. Sanchez . . . we cannot afford for there to be more attacks and a sense of panic down there. If I feel at any point you and your team are not controlling the situation, I will pull ACES and bring in another team. Is that understood?"

"Yes, of course. We will find Osvaldo and defuse the situation before there are more of these attacks."

"I hope you can. I'd hate to pull in Mr. Comstock and have him take care of business. And I don't think you and your team want that, either." Kim paused. "I'm sure Mr. Martin wouldn't be too happy to see him."

"Not a problem, ma'am." Jennifer had no idea who this Comstock was, but he was obviously someone held in high regard in Langley. And someone that Mike didn't want to deal with. Interesting.

～

**FAT TONY LOOKED AMUSED AS ROCCO RUSHED INTO THE BATHROOM** with his broken nose. "I underestimated you, Osvaldo."

"Please, call me Ozzie."

"Have a seat."

"That's all right, I'll stand." Ozzie watched Fat Tony, sitting on the bed of the suite. One of his men was behind Ozzie, blocking the doorway, and Krystelle was smiling, sprawled out on the bed and surfing through the TV channels with the volume off.

Ozzie was hit by a small wave of jealousy at the sight of his girlfriend so close and in a bed with the behemoth dealer. Bad thoughts raced through his head, but he needed to focus if he was going to survive the next ten minutes.

"Please, I insist," Fat Tony said and pointed at the chair next to the desk. Before Ozzie could respond, he was led roughly by the thug behind him and dropped into the chair.

"After all, this is your room, Osvaldo. You paid big bucks for it. Why not enjoy it?" Fat Tony said and patted Krystelle on her exposed leg.

When Krystelle grinned at Fat Tony and ignored Ozzie again, he almost pulled the weapon from his backpack and shot her with it. Or maybe he'd shoot Fat Tony and watch him attack her . . .

"Shall we get down to business?" Fat Tony asked and motioned his sausage fingers at Ozzie. "Krystelle said this had something to with that attack yesterday." Fat Tony squinted. "If you are lying I'll have my boys rip you apart, you do understand that, right?"

"I'm not lying." Ozzie pulled the gun from the backpack and held it before him, careful to keep his finger away from the trigger but close enough in case he needed to use it.

Rocco, toilet paper wadded and stuffed in his nostrils, came out of the bathroom and began laughing. "Did you buy that at the mall? I saw a kid playing with one of those for Halloween."

Fat Tony, smirking, waved his hand at Rocco. "Quiet. Osvaldo was just about to show us what it does."

"I can't really do that without, well, creating a major problem for everyone in the room."

Fat Tony stood. "Let me see if I have this straight. That

piece of crap science fiction gun in your hand is supposed to make people want to bite another person's face off?"

"It's on the news again," Krystelle said from the bed and turned up the volume.

The newscaster was talking about the various effects of bath salts and how this was purportedly found in the man's system, which caused him to be disoriented and aggressive and attack another person.

Rocco and the other henchman were laughing. Ozzie tried to keep his hand from shaking as he lowered the gun to his side to hide it.

"It seems we have a dilemma." Fat Tony glanced at the curtains. "Open the window."

"I swear, it works like I said it does," Ozzie stammered.

He watched as Rocco swept open the curtains and smiled. "Cool, we have a balcony. You get a lot with your money here, Osvaldo."

They were on the fourth floor. Fat Tony smiled and gripped Ozzie by his upper arm. "Let's get some fresh air."

They stepped onto the small balcony. Ozzie noticed the balconies were connected all the way in either direction, with only a partition separating them. The drop was about thirty feet or so, maybe more. Straight down to the sidewalk below and Ozzie had a vision of his body hitting the pavement like a pumpkin as the dozens of onlookers stared.

"I'm curious why you even bothered with that charade. Were you afraid the Russians would get to you? Do they think this is anything real?" Fat Tony crowded Ozzie and forced him against the rail. His two men got on either side and there was nowhere to move.

"Krystelle?" Ozzie called. If he was going to die he wanted to see her one last time.

"What?" Krystelle asked, clearly annoyed from the bed. "I'm watching this zombie dude eating the other dude's face. This is nuts."

"What if I can prove it?" Ozzie asked. He was putting a rough plan together in his head. Really rough.

"How?" Fat Tony asked with a look of curiosity on his face. He wiped his broad forehead with a meaty hand. In his dark suit and with his vast extra weight he was beginning to drip with sweat.

"I'll show you how it works." Ozzie lifted the barrel but Fat Tony put a hand on it and pushed it away. "Not on me, you idiot."

"No, of course not." Ozzie wanted to shoot Rocco with it but he'd also get attacked if he did. Two thoughts went through his head simultaneously. He glanced down at the street below. "If I demonstrate it, will you give me twenty grand for it?"

All three men laughed at Ozzie.

"This is serious. Once I point and pull that trigger, all bets are off. It will get really crazy down below. Fair warning."

"I'll believe it when I see it."

"Then we do this for twenty grand? Handshake deal?"

Fat Tony glanced at his two men and grinned. "I'll tell you what I'm going to do . . . if you can turn three, no wait, four people below into zombies, I will give you your twenty grand."

"Excellent." Ozzie knew there was no way this guy would pay him twenty cents after he started shooting, but his plan was forming in his head still. Just needed an answer to the second part. "Krystelle?"

"Jeez, what do you want, Osvaldo? I'm watching this."

Ozzie smiled. "Four people, huh? Watch, but stand back. It has a kick to it," he lied. "Anyone in particular?"

Rocco leaned over the rail. "How about the guy who just got out of the Hummer? He looks like a jerk."

"Sure." Ozzie didn't know how Rocco could tell the guy was a jerk from four stories up, especially since he himself was such a jerk. "Here goes everything."

Ozzie noticed they were all crowded to either side of him.

He casually moved around Rocco, who was alone to his right. "I need a better angle, watch out."

"Quit stalling," Fat Tony said. "It's too hot out here."

Ozzie aimed at the target, who was walking away from the valet and his Hummer. He pulled the trigger and the yellow light came on, barely seen in the sunlight.

"Fire already," Rocco said.

"I did."

"Toss him over," Fat Tony said.

"No, watch him!" Ozzie yelled just as the goons grabbed him.

The man below stopped in stride and bowed his head.

As another valet went to move past him, the man sprung and sunk his teeth into the exposed neck of the valet, drawing blood.

"Is this a joke? Is that guy in on this?" Fat Tony asked, but was still watching the scene below. "Shoot someone else. I said four people."

Ozzie knew this was going to get out of hand really soon.

He aimed and shot another man as he exited his red Porsche and the valet who was already running up.

"They're tearing people apart down there," Fat Tony said.

Ozzie was still too close to the men on the balcony. He turned his body and stared into the room at Krystelle, who was still watching television. He noticed her black thong on the floor on the side of the bed.

He'd been an idiot once again. He pointed and shot her without dwelling on it. He'd loved her, but she'd used him.

"Gotta run, boys," Ozzie said as he jumped over the rail onto the next balcony.

"Wait, we have a deal," Fat Tony said.

Ozzie pointed the gun at them just as they drew their own weapons. "If you don't put the guns down I will shoot. This is worse than getting hit with a bullet, and I think you are smart enough to get that now."

"I thought we had a deal?" Fat Tony asked, but before anyone could make another move, Krystelle was clawing and biting at Rocco and the balcony, packed with people, was a chaotic mess.

Ozzie began to hop from balcony to balcony until he found a sliding door open. He barged in, but not before a quick look at the utter chaos he'd wrought on the street below.

# EPISODE THREE
## Zombies at The Setai

**MELISSA LOCKHART, A MONTH FRESH FROM THE MIAMI POLICE**
Academy, swallowed the lump forcing its way up her throat. She planted her feet and pulled her service revolver, but her mind wouldn't translate what she saw before her.

Her partner and trainer, Joe McKinnon, stood on the opposite side of their police cruiser in the same stance. Missy (as they always called her) glanced over. "Joe, um, what's going on?"

Joe didn't move. "I'm not sure." He tapped his police radio hooked to his shoulder. "Dispatch, is there a movie being filmed on Collins Avenue? Some monster movie?" He remembered reading about a Hollywood, Florida company filming a low budget zombie movie near Miami, and knew of the many production companies in the area. His best friend had even been hired by Magic Productions near the airport for in-house security. Maybe they were out here shooting a scene.

"That is a negative," was the reply from dispatch. "Multiple calls about a riot in front of the Setai. More units responding."

This wasn't a riot. It was insane. He saw at least six bodies on the ground, and it looked like at least two had either jumped from above or been pushed. A BMW was spattered in blood, and a man, covered in gore, was biting another man's face.

*Biting another man's face . . .*

"What's the procedure on this?" Missy questioned.

"There is no procedure for this type of event. This isn't a movie set. This is like what happened on MacArthur Causeway yesterday, Missy. This guy is insane or on drugs or something."

Missy took a step back and now stared at Joe. "So what do we do?"

Before he could answer, another man covered in blood stepped out from the bushes in front of the hotel, dragging a body with him.

"How many are there?" Joe said with a hitch in his voice. He needed to remain calm and he needed to focus. This would be the ultimate training scenario for Missy, and he intended to use that idea to keep him grounded and from panicking. His knees wanted to buck but he sucked it up. "This is what we need to do, Officer Lockhart: we need to arrest these two men."

"You're joking, right? They look like something out of a Romero movie."

"Follow my lead." Joe wiped his hand on his pants, switched his pistol, and did the same with his other hand. He took two steps forward. "Sir, I need you to halt."

Joe was pointing his weapon at the oncoming man, who was shuffling his feet and staring blankly at him.

"I will not ask you again. You need to get down on your knees on the pavement or I will be forced to shoot you. Do you understand?" Joe felt a bead of sweat run down his cheek that had nothing to do with the Miami heat.

"I don't think he understands, Joe." Missy circled around the car and came up next to her trainer, gun still locked in her hands and pointing. "He's unarmed."

*I can't shoot him, but I can use my training to drop him to the ground and cuff him easily enough.* Twenty plus years on the job and Joe had thought he'd seen it all. Still training his

Glock 17 at the man's chest, he pulled his handcuffs from his belt.

"What are you doing?" Missy asked.

"Standard procedure, rookie. Watch and learn. When you run into these drugged out guys on the street, you don't want to panic or startle them. Your only goal is to get him on the ground and cuff him. In a few hours he'll wake from his stupor in a jail cell, and you'll be home eating a nice dinner."

"He bites," he heard Missy say quietly. "Maybe we should wait for backup."

"There's no time," Joe said but didn't know if that was really the case. "Cover me."

The bloody man, rage in his eyes as he mashed his teeth, ran at him.

Joe's intent was to sidestep him and trip him to the ground, diving on him before he could recover. As the man reached out, Joe did a perfect move to his left, and hooked the man's feet, smiling as he went down to the ground.

As Joe pinned the man's arms and locked the first handcuff to his wrist he smiled. It didn't matter if they were bloody, high on crack or heroin, or drunk off their ass, it was usually the same thing: get them on the ground and keep them on the ground.

"I got him," Joe said as the second cuff locked in place. The man kept struggling beneath him but there wasn't much he could actually do, with Joe's knee in his back. "Help me lift him," he said to Missy. "Watch his face."

Missy took two steps before she screamed.

Joe turned his body to see what she was looking at and was driven at an awkward angle onto the pavement. Another bloody mess, this time wearing a valet uniform, was gnashing its teeth at Joe's arm. Luckily, when they went down Joe had shielded his face and his forearm was now wedged under the valet's neck, but the strain was becoming too much with the valet on top of him. He locked eyes with the stunned rookie. "Missy, shoot him! Shoot him!"

Joe was bent over the other man, who was struggling to get his mouth around at Joe. He was now fighting them off at the same time. He didn't want to be bitten, he didn't want to die. The wild man's rancid breath hit him like a ton of bricks and he felt the bile rise in his throat.

He heard Missy yell to close his eyes and instinctively did, dropping his arm to shield his face. The gunshot was too close and brains and clumps of the man's face rained down on him, covering him in gore.

Joe gagged, rolling sideways and spitting the vile taste from his mouth.

"Here comes the other one," Missy said. "I can't just shoot him."

"You have to," Joe stuttered and tried to stand. If there were more than the three they were in serious trouble, and he wondered where the backup was. He rolled over onto his back again, spitting more blood out and wiping his face. He pushed the radio, glad to hear it wasn't damaged. His ears were ringing. "Dispatch, where is the backup?"

He watched the other man edging closer and Missy stepped past him, Glock 17 still leading her, two hands on it like she'd been trained.

"Shoot him," Joe said. Shoot all of them at this point. They needed to clear the area and get back to the squad car before more appeared. He wondered if this was really a zombie attack, some sort of apocalypse like in movies. Would he turn into one of them now that he had their cursed blood in his mouth? He didn't feel any different.

Joe, still thinking about zombie movies, turned just in time to see the handcuffed man as he dropped onto him and bit into his neck.

He heard Missy as she fired her weapon, but the man's head didn't explode. Joe felt a rush of heat down his neck as his blood spilled. She'd shot the other one.

He tried to call out to Missy but he had no voice.

Even through his ringing ears, Joe heard Missy as she continued to scream.

Joe raked his arm across the zombie's face, pulling off a chunk of cheek and letting blood drip down onto him.

*Great, there's even more blood in my mouth now,* Joe thought before he died.

━

MIKE MARTIN LEAPT FROM THE VAN AND SHOT THE ZOMBIE point-blank in the face using his trusted Tac-338 McMillan tactical rifle before he'd even set his feet.

"Get down," he yelled to the stunned female officer. "Now!"

She immediately dropped and stopped her screaming.

The cop was already dead, his carotid artery severed. Martin saw several bodies on the pavement.

Martin swept left, ready to shoot anyone that didn't look all there. As Martin reached the female officer he glanced down at her. "Holster your weapon and move back to the van, please."

"Who are you?" she asked as she got up onto one knee and put her Glock 17 away, staring at Martin.

She was beautiful, with dirty blonde hair pulled into a ponytail and cute little dark birthmarks on either side of her cheeks, a pale Irish complexion and a fit body under the police uniform.

And she was staring at Martin like he had two heads, asking him who he was again, and what was going on. "I'm the guy who just saved your life. Now move back to the van quickly. Just do what I tell you and you will live."

"Please get back to the van. The guy standing there is Kostas and he'll debrief you," Jennifer said as she stepped up to them, brandishing her AA-12 automatic shotgun.

Martin watched as the police officer hurried away, glancing back once and hesitantly smiling at him.

Jennifer smacked him on the shoulder. "Get over the puppy-love, soldier. We have things to do," but she was grinning when she said it. "You look quite smitten."

Martin turned and cleared his head. *Stupid*, he thought. *Get your head back in the mission.* "I'm on the left."

Martin and Jennifer swept through the area, checking the bodies as they moved with a quick push of their boot. The entire scene was unsettling, with broken bodies strewn about the front of the hotel.

"Clear," Jennifer yelled from her side.

"Clear," Martin followed.

Martin looked up as Jennifer joined him near the entrance. "There's a body on the balcony right there," he said and pointed. "Fourth floor. The sliding door is also open."

"Okay, but first we need to secure this area. We have to contain the situation. No one in and no one out." Jennifer sighed. "I'll put Kostas on the main road as well. The local cops will be here any minute and we'll have to keep a lot of mouths shut."

Three cars pulled into the parking lot.

"Looks like more of our team has arrived," Martin said. He nodded when the two panel vans drove up. Within minutes they'd both be filled with the dead. Before the news helicopters showed.

"What about the police officer?" Martin asked, trying to sound casual.

Jennifer shook her head. "We can't let her leave right away. But I'm sure at any moment Kostas will drive her so insanely crazy by hitting on her she'll have no choice but to shoot him."

"Amen to that," Martin said. He looked over to see her standing with Kostas.

"I promise before we cut her loose you can have a moment with her," Jennifer said.

"You're enjoying this, aren't you?"

Jennifer sighed. "Look, to be honest, I need something to distract me from the reality of the situation. Once we secure the area and round up all the hundreds of hotel guests and anyone else in this area, talk down the local 5-0 and tell them this is now a federal investigation, I'm going to call Kim. She can work her magic and have the FBI stand down long enough for us to contain and control the situation. After we're done, we'll let the Bureau come in, clean up the mess and look good for the cameras. I'm still going to have to tell her we are no closer to Osvaldo Rivera and this weapon, which he obviously used today. Again."

Martin nodded. Sometimes it was better to feel and act like the hired hand than to be the boss. He didn't envy her job right now.

"Pull in Baker and Luciano, get them in the mix ASAP. We need every member of the team out here right now."

"I'll call them," Martin said and let Jennifer walk away, lost in her thoughts.

Martin took a walk into the lobby of the hotel, scaring a few guests who were attempting to walk out with their luggage. A man carrying a machine gun will do that.

"I need everyone to go back to your rooms and stay there," he yelled as he moved to the front desk. He smiled at the shaking man behind the counter. "I need your management staff in this lobby in five minutes, and for you to call each and every room and explain to your guests they cannot leave their quarters until further notice."

"What's going on?"

"There is a situation." Martin knew he needed to tell this guy something, or it would elicit more questions and nosey guests trying to sneak outside to see what was going on.

The man picked up the phone and shook his head. "Sir? I need you to come up front right now. There's, um, a man with a gun that needs to speak to you."

Martin smiled again. "It's actually a Tac-338 McMillan." Martin decided he was going to loosen up a bit during this crisis and not get so wound up he would uncoil and explode. Besides, the police officer out there was still on his mind.

The man held the phone to his ear. "How do I keep hundreds of guests in their rooms?"

"Let them know we have a shooter in the area. Stay away from the windows, too." Martin knew it wasn't the smartest thing to say and Jennifer would be yelling at him when she found out, but it was the most economical way to keep them scared instead of curious.

When the manager, a balding pudgy man, came out with a frown on his face, Martin offered a hand. The manager kept his hands at his sides, eyes locked on the rifle. "What's the meaning of this?"

"Sir . . . Mister White," Martin said when he eyed the man's name badge, "We have a situation here that needs to be addressed."

"Who are you?" The man asked, noticing everything going on outside for the first time. He began walking toward the door.

Martin pointed at the desk clerk. "Keep calling."

"Who are all these people? Are those bodies in my parking lot?"

Martin gently steered Mr. White back to the desk. "Again, as I was telling your associate here, we need to keep the hotel guests in their rooms and away from the front windows. There's a madman in the area and we don't know if he's still at large. Can you help us out and call your guests and let them know to stay put for the time being?"

Mr. White squinted his eyes. "You aren't Miami PD."

"I'm with the government."

"Let me see your ID."

Martin wanted to tell this guy he was holding his ID and it

was loaded, but decided diplomacy was a better course of action right now. He didn't want Jennifer on his case for more than one or two things. Why had she given him this task? He disliked talking to the public and making these types of decisions. "This isn't a movie. I don't carry a shiny CIA shield around with me."

Mr. White glanced over when the ding for the elevator rang but then turned back to Martin. "I know my rights. You can't order me to do anything." He wagged a finger as he stepped closer to Martin. "You're violating my civil liberties and I have a pit-bull lawyer named Rosenblatt here in South Beach." Mr. White smiled. "By the time he's done with you the crossing guard job at the elementary school will be above you." Mr. White took another quick look as a guest was moving slowly toward him. "You won't get a job as a mall cop. You won't..."

Mr. White trailed off as the zombie from the elevator approached him. "Shoot him, shoot him!" he cried to Martin and tried to get behind him. Martin stepped off to the side and smiled. "What if he has the same lawyer as you? I'm sure Rosenblatt would be suing me over civil liberties violations."

Martin casually placed his rifle on his shoulder. "I don't believe I can carry a high-powered rifle as a crossing guard."

"Just do your job," Mr. White yelled as the zombie reached out and tried to grab him, blood dripping from its face.

Martin held out his rifle. "Here, you want to do it? After all, I like my job."

Mr. White was stopped from back-pedaling when he hit the counter, eyes locked on the zombie.

Martin, enjoying himself now and the man's fear, placed

the rifle in Mr. White's hands and manually placed his finger on the trigger. "It has some kick to it, so spread your feet."

"Huh? What?" Mr. White looked down at the Tac-338 McMillan tactical rifle and then back at the zombie.

"You need to shoot him. He's going to bite you," Martin said.

"This is a joke, right?"

Martin stood next to him but away from the oncoming zombie. "Seriously, he is going to rip your face clean off if you don't shoot him."

Mr. White raised the rifle with shaking hands.

"Aim for the face, like in the movies." Martin tried to be serious but grinned when he smelled Mr. White, who'd now obviously pissed himself.

"I can't."

"You must. I don't have a weapon," Martin said. "It's you or him."

Mr. White fired from only half a dozen feet, and the top of the zombie's skull blasted off. It turned and fell to the carpet.

"Lucky shot," Martin said and gently took the rifle from Mr. White's hands.

Mr. White, pants soaked, sighed.

"So now do I have your permission to continue with my mission or should we call you lawyer and ask him?"

"Whatever the CIA needs," Mr. White said softly.

Martin began walking away. "Oh, I'm not CIA. I'm ACES."

"What's ACES?"

"The team that just saved your life without violating your civil liberties."

⟿

**BORIS SMILED; DESPITE THE UNPLEASANT TWIST HE'D JUST** been given.

"What now?" Andre asked. They were parked at the far parking lot of The Setai, watching as the ACES team went about their cleanup business.

"We watch and learn. This must be the infamous ACES team here in Miami, sweeping the scene clean of anything unnecessary. I want to watch them in action so we can monitor their techniques, tactics and procedures. TTPs, very important." Boris turned to Andre. "And so should you, instead of getting impatient. Right before us is a veritable goldmine of information about our main adversary. You'd rather drive away."

"Sorry, boss." Andre put the binoculars to his eyes. "I see only three of them, and a female police officer."

"That would be Jennifer Sanchez, Mike Martin and Mark Kostas," Boris said with a smile. "If Martin is here, then Comstock must be close." He wasn't surprised when more cars pulled up and men and women began covering bodies. "The meat wagon should be arriving soon," he said with glee. Boris was impressed. Even the minor staff knew their roles and executed them with efficiency. He had no doubt the scene would be cleaned up and contained before the first news helicopter was in the air.

"Where are the police?" Andre asked. "I only see the one squad car."

"They will be here soon enough, but by then ACES will have cordoned off the area and spun a story to keep this out of the press." Boris grinned. "It also means their headquarters is close to here. Within five miles, I imagine." He turned to Andre again. "See? We've already added more information about them."

"Why don't we simply follow them back?"

"Do you think we'd be able to tail them that easily, while they drove us right back to their secret lair? Maybe we should drive around and look for a billboard with an arrow pointing to the ACES headquarters."

Boris watched as the cleanup vans approached and the crew began putting covered bodies into the cargo holds before they'd come to a complete stop. "Efficient. This is a worthy adversary."

"Do you think they have the weapon?"

Boris shook his head. "*Nyet.* I haven't seen anyone securing it, and I'm not even sure Osvaldo Rivera is now a corpse. More than likely, the man caused all this chaos and then slunk away. I think the gun is still out there, and we need to find it before the ACES team does."

Boris watched Mike Martin as he moved around the parking lot, steely eyes taking in everything. Martin was known to Boris only through the intel the SVR had acquired over the years, but the man's resume was quite impressive. He was someone who knew several mixed martial arts styles and had discipline and power.

"No match for me," Boris Dragov whispered. But the closest person Boris imagined would be a match for him, and even a small challenge. He wanted to be tested. He wanted to feel the slight twinge of fear again, the brief spiral out of control before he snapped another man's neck and righted himself.

Boris couldn't wait to get back to his hotel and dive into an extra hard training session with the Gracie Jiu-Jitsu before laps in the swimming pool to cool down. Now that he had a worthy adversary he could turn up the workouts and mentally prepare to crush Mike Martin.

"I will kill Martin first, then Comstock when he surfaces. I will prove to all the intelligence agencies that Alpha Spetnaz are superior to anything Delta has to offer," Boris spoke under his breath. "It's not the kill, it's the thrill of the chase," he said quietly, ignoring Andre's look.

Boris stared at the ACES team another minute and ran scenarios through his mind where he broke Mike Martin of body and spirit. He was going to enjoy this upcoming battle. "It's getting crowded here, we cannot be noticed. We must go. Now we find Osvaldo."

Andre pulled out of the far parking lot.

"It's not the kill, it's the thrill of the chase," Boris whispered and smiled.

≈

OZZIE WAS SLUMPED IN THE BATHROOM OF THE KUNG FU KITCHEN and Sushi restaurant, hands shaking. He jammed the backpack into the corner and sat as far away from it as he could, afraid the evil zombie gun would unzip the bag and fire at him.

"You are losing your mind. Get a grip." He stood on shaking legs and splashed cold water on his face. He looked away when the mirror caught his appearance. In less than two days he'd gained ten years and he looked like he hadn't slept in as long.

His girlfriend—the cheating liar that she ended up be-ing—was dead, Ozzie figured Fat Tony and his two thugs were ripped apart, and the cops would be after him. The room was in his name. Ozzie had the Russians looking for him. Could his life get any worse?

He cursed when his cell phone rang. Without even look-ing, he knew it was going to get much worse for him. "Hello?"

"Listen and listen good, you little piece of crap. You are a dead man."

*Damn.* "Fat Tony, is that you? How have you been?" Ozzie chided, trying to sound casual and relaxed, even though he wanted to throw up.

"You can't get far, do you understand? I've already put a price on your head. That weapon is mine, and when they find your body it will be unidentifiable, do you understand me? You'll be scattered to all four corners of the Bermuda Triangle."

"There are only three corners in a triangle, you stupid idiot." Ozzie was just about done with this conversation, this problem and this life. "Bring it on, Fat Tony. I'll be wait-ing for you. With my finger on the trigger. Do you under-stand me?"

When Fat Tony disconnected Ozzie slumped back to the floor. He needed a nap. His apartment was now off-limits. He was positive Krystelle had told them everything she could about him, and there would be someone waiting at his place.

Ozzie was only blocks away from The Setai and needed to get as far from here as possible. He needed to escape from

Miami, maybe even Florida. But where could he run to? He had no family, definitely no friends, and without any money or a vehicle he wasn't getting far.

His cell phone rang again and Ozzie contemplated ignoring it. More than likely Fat Tony had figured out another couple of threats to send his way. On the third ring he looked at the screen, but it was a private number. "Yeah?"

"I'm looking for Osvaldo. This is you?"

Ozzie sat up. The stranger on the other end of the line had a thick Russian accent. "Maybe." He knew as soon as he said it how stupid it sounded.

"Maybe you have something I'd like to purchase from you."

"I have no idea what you're talking about."

The man laughed harshly. "I think we can stop playing the games, friend. I have twenty-five thousand United States dollars I am ready to give you for it. Do we have a deal?"

"Do you know what it does?"

"Of course." The man paused. "Thirty-five thousand is my final offer. Cash."

Ozzie didn't want to meet another person who wanted to kill him and take the zombie gun. He was getting tired of running, and needed a safe haven. Standing in a restaurant bathroom wasn't going to do it. "I want fifty grand in unmarked bills placed in a backpack. I need a clean car." He was thinking as he was talking, pacing around the bathroom. "On 21st Street, near Collins Park, I want a car parked with the backpack in the passenger seat. I will hide the zombie gun in a location and tell you where it is once I am miles away."

"No, I will meet you face to face and we will make the exchange. For this much money I want to do it myself."

Ozzie shook his head even though he was on the phone. That would be a great way to get killed. "Then I will find another buyer." He hung up the phone, not knowing if it was the greatest or stupidest move of his life, or a combination of the two.

*And now you can't call them back, idiot. Even if you wanted to because they called on a private number*, he thought. Panic set in as the seconds ticked away. He stared at his cell phone and willed it to ring.

"Now what?" he whispered. He thought he heard police sirens outside, but it could have easily just been in his head. Ozzie was amazed no one had come into the bathroom of this busy restaurant yet to see the crazed man and his evil backpack. "You're losing it, man. Get a grip."

For the second time he splashed water on his face and looked away from the mirror. Ozzie was trying to figure out what Nebraska would be like and how he'd even get there, or where it was geographically in the country for that matter, when his phone rang again.

"Please be him, please be him . . . hello?"

"Fifty grand in a backpack will be placed in the trunk of a red 2002 Kia Spectra at the location you mentioned in one hour. Where will you be placing the item?"

Ozzie smiled. "I have already hidden the item at a distant location. Once I am several miles away I will call you back and tell you where it is."

There was a pause on the line. "You don't have my number."

"Give it to me."

"No. It doesn't work like that. I want to trust you, I really do. But in this line of business extending credit only goes so far. It would be foolish of me to think I could let you drive away with that much money and expect you to simply tell me where the item is. If you were in my shoes, Ozzie, what would you do?"

*He called me Ozzie. No one ever calls me Ozzie.* If there was a time he needed a good sign, it was now. "I understand your concern. How about in one hour and fifteen minutes you call me and I tell you? There has to be trust in this relationship." Ozzie grabbed the backpack and left the bathroom, just as a man and his son came into use the facilities. *Perfect timing,* Ozzie thought. Everything has to be done properly.

"And what if you simply drive off with my money and my item? That would make me very angry."

"I'm sure it would, but a face to face meeting isn't in the cards right now. We both need to be careful, but I have something worth far more than fifty grand and you know it. We can do it my way or I can find another buyer. It shouldn't be too hard, considering all the news coverage from today."

"From today?"

Ozzie walked outside into the hot Florida sun. "Never mind." He dramatically looked at his watch, even though he was on the phone. "You have fifty-four minutes to make this happen."

"The car will be in place right on schedule."

"Excellent," Ozzie said.

"Oh, and Osvaldo ... if there is one slip up, one wrong move on your part, I will personally hack you up into little pieces and feed you to my dogs. Do you understand?"

Ozzie swallowed hard but tried to remain cool. "Then we have nothing to worry about, because I always hold up my end of a deal. I hope you do as well."

≈

**"LET ME TALK TO HER. IT IS SO OBVIOUS SHE'S INTO ME,"** KOSTAS said and winked at Jennifer. The female officer had wandered back to her police car.

Jennifer pointed at the team van. "Go," she said like she was scolding a child, but Kostas got the hint and piled back into the 1999 Chevrolet Conversion Van Mark III and drove toward the main entrance to the hotel.

Jennifer approached the officer, who was leaning against the squad car and having trouble catching her breath. Their backup was already on Collins Avenue, keeping the traffic away from The Setai. Kostas would be able to coordinate, keep the police at bay, and stay out of trouble. She hoped.

Another car arrived and Tim Baker and David Luciano, who'd been watching the Miamarina boat, gave her a quick nod before running inside the hotel. They already knew to find anyone who had seen the battle in the street and try to squash it immediately. The last thing they wanted was the media to get a hold of this story and run with it, especially since the cannibal face biter story still had legs right now. Jennifer could only imagine if they now knew of three more zombie attacks so close to the other. There would be panic in all corners of Miami and beyond.

"What's going on? The other guy wouldn't tell me anything. He just kept staring at me," the officer said.

"I'm Jennifer Sanchez, and we have a situation at the moment."

"Missy Lockhart. I need to radio dispatch."

"I can't let you do that," Jennifer said and wasn't surprised to see the officer automatically put her hand on her holstered weapon. "This is now an investigation way above your clearance level. Your police chief and his commanding officers have already been apprised of the situation. We are asking for radio silence right now, and your fellow officers are on standby just down the road."

"And I'm supposed to just believe you?"

"Yes." Jennifer smiled as friendly as she could, but she was already exhausted. "You really have no choice, and that isn't a threat. It is just your reality right now. I need to debrief you, if you don't mind. Please come with me." Jennifer motioned to one of the team cars, which was out of the heat.

"Do I have a choice?"

"Not really. I think you understand that, though." They sat down in the front seat, grateful for the air conditioning. Jennifer grimaced when she saw the clutter in the car, with empty coffee cups and Dunkin Donuts wrappers on the floor. When she figured out whose car this was she would have to have a chat with them.

"Let's switch cars," she said and got back out, knowing Missy was going to be confused. *I'll just tell her I'm neurotic when it comes to clutter and things not in perfect order,* Jennifer thought sarcastically.

They walked over to another team car and Jennifer peeked inside. It was clean so she motioned for Missy to join her.

Jennifer had her attaché case with her, so she opened it and pulled her binder out, putting it carefully at a ninety degree angle in front of her on the dash. "I'll ask you a few questions."

"Then can I go?"

Jennifer ignored the question. She really did feel sorry for this woman, who probably still had a diploma from the Police Academy with drying ink.

"I need you to tell me everything that happened here, and leave no detail, no matter how small, out of it." Jennifer touched a button next to the radio in the car. "I'll be recording everything you say. You can start with your name and occupation."

"This can't be real," she said. When Jennifer gave her a stern but unkind look, she began talking. "My name is Missy, um, Melissa Lockhart. I am a patrol officer for the Miami Police Department. I'm twenty-four and I was born in Shirley, Massachusetts."

*Older than she looks. Mike will be happy*, Jennifer thought. She was only four years younger than Martin. Jennifer had never met anyone he dated, and knew nothing about his private life. That was the way they wanted the ACES team to interact. Casual.

She knew Martin and Kostas had gone to some baseball games and a football game or two, and there was nothing wrong with being out in a social setting. Jennifer always refrained, which was easy when it was Kostas simply trying to get her to accompany him to a seedy motel, as if he had a chance.

"I moved down here to Port Orange right after high school

with my parents, went to Daytona Beach Community College and then off to Orlando when I wanted to go into law enforcement."

Jennifer smiled. "I don't need your entire background, Missy. Let's skip to this morning." The girl was nervous, babbling as if she were in trouble. Jennifer supposed this was a bit unorthodox to Missy and her training, being the one questioned. Jennifer also knew she was always a bit imposing to other women, with her good looks (she could admit it) and her experience from being in her early forties and having been doing military or special forces jobs since this girl was still in diapers.

"Joe was . . . is my training officer. He's a really great guy, and he took a lot of crap from the guys for training me."

"Why?" Jennifer asked, already knowing the answer but trying to keep Missy calm, slow her down, interrupting with questions to break up her statement.

"The typical guy's locker-room talk. He's much older, most of the cops in the academy hit on me, and they called me his girlfriend when they thought I wasn't listening."

"Was he inappropriate?"

Missy laughed. "Joe? Heck no. He was . . . is an awesome partner, and he always told them to cut it out and treat me like a fellow officer instead of a chick in a Halloween costume. I was always respectful to him and he returned the favor. We have a great relationship and I wish I was going to be his partner for a long time, but Joe's already figuring out where he and his wife are going to spend his retirement. Fix up the boat and head to the Bahamas."

"Okay, so you get a call from dispatch."

"Typical 34, disturbance at The Setai. We were two blocks away, just patrolling while Joe went over some basic things with me. He always liked to use any situation for teaching. When we arrived I couldn't believe what was happening."

"What was the first thing you noticed?"

"The guy was biting another guy, just like we'd been warned might happen after yesterday on the MacArthur. Only you don't expect to see it yourself, you know? We'd all been briefed about the face biter this morning, but you don't expect to encounter it two hours later yourself. We assumed it was a unique event, some guy messed up on drugs."

Jennifer cut right to the chase. "Did you or Joe shoot the approaching one?"

Missy closed her eyes. "I did. I didn't want to. He was unarmed, but Joe was wrestling with the other two and I panicked. I should have gone to his aid. Maybe he'd still be alive."

"He had one in handcuffs already. It looked like he was doing what he was supposed to do," Jennifer said, trying to keep the woman from getting upset.

"I hesitated. If I'd shot the one right away I could have saved Joe. But the look in the guy's eyes was scary. Actually, that's wrong. The absence of a real look was scary, like he was looking right past me. He looked pissed, don't get me wrong." Missy looked off and seemed to be in thought. "No, he looked agitated, like he wanted to beat someone, like he was running into a fight. And he was running right at me. I should have pulled the trigger sooner."

"You can't blame yourself for making a split second decision like that."

Missy turned to Jennifer. "Have you ever shot an unarmed

person?"

Jennifer instinctively looked away. "Once, but it looked like they had a weapon."

"I knew he didn't have a weapon. But I shot him anyway. I graduated five weeks ago and already I'm involved in a shooting. Poor Joe went his entire career without having to use his piece."

"We'll sort this out for you," Jennifer said and felt bad for Missy. She didn't know if you could recover from something like that. Jennifer was still dealing with her own issues years later.

"I just shot an unarmed man and let my partner die. A month out of the Police Academy," Missy said and started to cry.

≈

THE RED 2002 KIA SPECTRA HAD A DENT ON THE DRIVER'S SIDE right above the front tire. Ozzie supposed it didn't really matter. His goal was to drive this hunk of crap as far north and west as he could before ditching it and finding a more suitable ride.

Fifty grand was a decent amount of money to start a new life, but he didn't know how he'd manage it. He had no real connections in other cities and wasn't involved in some nefarious network, where he could get a fake ID and a passport and be out of the country in an hour. That stuff didn't happen for Ozzie.

He hesitated when he put his hand on the door handle. What if it was wired? Ozzie dropped to his knees and glanced under the front end of the car, expecting a ticking bomb to greet him. Nothing.

He opened the door and when the car didn't explode he popped the hood and the trunk. Under the hood was just an engine, with nothing deadly attached. He kept looking around, expecting the Russians to show at any minute and gun him down.

The backpack was in the trunk. He opened it slowly, expecting to go boom. Instead he was happy to see banded twenties and fifties. He really wanted to count it but knew he had to leave. He closed the trunk and got into the car. The keys were in the ignition and he started it up.

Ozzie was excited but needed to stick to the speed limit. The last thing he needed now was to get pulled over with his freedom in the trunk and an escape plan formulating in his head.

Six cop cars, lights on, flew past him and obviously toward The Setai. He acted casual as he drove but his hands were shaking on the steering wheel. As Abe Resnick Boulevard turned into Venetian Way and South Beach was falling away in his rearview mirror and out of his life for good, Ozzie began to relax.

He wasn't being followed, although he wasn't exactly sure. There were no dark sedans with tinted windows three cars back or anything obvious like that. He wondered what the Russians could do if he never told them where the weapon was hidden, but decided against it. Besides, he was positive the cops were even now checking the hotel receipts and would be storming his apartment in the next hour.

And there was nothing in the apartment he needed anymore. His life would be a clean slate, a new beginning. Unlike in the movies, where you had an epiphany to get out of illegal activities, Ozzie decided to simply start over somewhere else, where they didn't know him. He'd blend in, get a job, and then start figuring out an angle to make some quick cash. Fifty grand was good money but it wasn't going to get him farther than a few months of living, no matter how frugal he was with it.

His cell phone rang and he hesitated answering it, looking around for a tail as he got back onto the mainland and turned right on Biscayne Boulevard. "Hello?"

"Are you satisfied with the vehicle?"

"It has a big dent on it."

"Haha. Do you know how hard it was to find a car and get the money together so quickly? I would think you'd be more impressed with me."

"I just want to be out of this, it's as simple as that. Once you get your item I expect to never hear from you again."

"I agree. Where is it?"

"I hid it."

"Obviously. We had a deal, no? I kept my end of the bargain and now it is your time, my friend. Like you say: tell me where it is and you walk away with the money and can wash your hands of this entire mess."

Ozzie was approaching the Route 195 exchange and decided he'd get on there and go west. He didn't see anyone suspicious following him. Would it be this easy? He supposed they didn't care about him, they only wanted the weapon.

"If you go ten paces straight into the tree line from where the car was parked you'll find the backpack under a bush."

"Excellent. It was a pleasure doing business with you."

Route 195 was packed at this hour but Ozzie was still moving and getting farther and farther away. Now that his adrenaline rush was over again, he was tired and hungry. But he didn't want to stop just yet. The more miles he could put between him and Miami the better.

But his eyes were drooping. He needed some coffee, and pulled off at the next exit before he got onto I-95 and north. He thought there was a Dunkin Donuts a couple of blocks down, and then he would run parallel to I-95 and catch it a few miles up. That sounded like the first part of his plan. *With my luck, I'll be driving and fall asleep at the wheel with fifty grand in the trunk,* he thought.

The light at the next intersection was just turning yellow when the dark blue sedan in front of him slammed on the brakes.

Ozzie swerved the car to the left, barely missing the bumper. "You idiot! You had a yellow light." He hated Florida drivers and was glad to be getting out of here. In the distance he could see a welcome sign: Dunkin Donuts. He'd be there within minutes. He decided to get a dozen donuts for the ride as well.

When the driver got out of the vehicle in front of him Ozzie sighed. What did this big goon want?

Ozzie rolled down his window as the man approached. "I didn't even hit your car, and you had a yellow light."

The man smiled, reached into the car with a snub-nosed pistol and shot Ozzie in the face before popping the trunk lock and retrieving the backpack and the fifty grand.

**THE NEWS CHOPPERS CIRCLED OVERHEAD, BUT THERE WAS NOTHING** to see. The team had cleaned up the area, gotten rid of the many blood stains, and loaded the bodies into the vans and were already driving away.

"The cops are getting pissed out here," Kostas said over the walkie-talkie. "I'm getting sick of these stupid questions."

"Kim has already spoken to Miami PD, so they know to stand down for now. Ignore them."

"And the worst part? The only hot cop in Miami is back there with you. I'm staring at a bunch of ugly dudes." Kostas sighed loudly. "Now I'm getting crap from the ones who are in earshot."

"Then you might need to be quiet and do your job without a running soliloquy," Jennifer said.

Kostas laughed. "You sure use fancy words, boss," he said in a fake Southern drawl.

"*Mantendrá a las palabras de una sílaba para usted,*" she said. I'll keep it to one syllable words for you.

"Now you said something dirty to me, I know it. Keep it in your pants, boss. We'll be doing the vertical Mambo soon enough, don't you worry."

Jennifer keyed the walkie-talkie several times so it squealed at him before turning it down. The last thing she needed was Kostas. But when did she ever need to take crap from him?

Her cell phone rang and she grimaced, not bothering to say a word when she saw it was Kim.

"Status report."

"Three down and six victims so far."

"So far?" Kim said irritably.

"There's another one on the balcony above."

"With news choppers flying overhead?"

Kim didn't miss anything. Jennifer almost looked around, imagining Kim staring at her with a scowl from the bushes.

"There is an overhang just above it. Unless they get low, they're unable to see it. Besides, they're focusing on the empty parking lot. I look like a hotel guest standing in the entryway with a cell phone."

"Where is the police officer?"

"I have her sitting in one of the cars right now. What do I do with her?"

"We keep her for now, until we know this is completely done. Did you find Osvaldo Rivera?"

Jennifer closed her eyes. "Negative. We know he rented the room and we're hoping he's the one dead on the balcony, to be honest."

"I don't care about him. I care about the weapon."

"I completely understand. I have men up there now, they should be calling me with information at any second," Jennifer said.

"Why aren't you up there?"

"I'm coordinating everything right now. There are a dozen police cars being held at bay by Kostas and they're getting angrier by the second."

"They've been told to stay in check until we give the clear. Their superiors have been briefed on the potential for a shooter to be in the area. Having the shooter's body would be great right about now, don't you think?"

"Yes, ma'am. I'm going upstairs right now."

"Where is Martin?"

"He's here, helping to coordinate. There are hundreds of guests and we didn't want anyone trying to leave out a back door."

"Ms. Sanchez, make sure we find the weapon. It's already walking the fine line between control and chaos. Do you understand me?"

"Loud and clear."

"Good. Did you mention Comstock to Martin?"

"No."

Kim actually laughed on the line. "I don't think Mike wants to hear the name. I'm sure he'll be quiet angry, in fact. Clean this mess up so I don't have to call in the big guns." She disconnected.

This was way out of hand, and Jennifer knew it. She stood and waited impatiently for the hotel elevator.

Jennifer's phone rang. "Ms. Sanchez, I think we have a problem up on the fourth floor," David Luciano said matter-of-factly.

*What now?* "You found something? Do you need me up there?"

She could hear banging in the background.

"What are you breaking?" she asked.

David sighed. "There's another one trapped in a hotel room. And it's trying to get out."

Jennifer closed her eyes and sighed. This was already out of control, and she had a feeling it was only going to get worse. She made sure her AA-12 automatic shotgun was still loaded as she waited for the elevator, knowing Kim in Langley was going to rip her another new one if this ever got cleaned up.

# EPISODE FOUR
## Losing Control

**"HELLO? ROOM SERVICE," TIM BAKER SAID WITH A LAUGH.**

David Luciano scowled at him. "Whoever is in there, be warned this is the police and we are going to ask you one more time to open this door and cease whatever it is you are doing."

The pounding continued as if someone was ramming their full body weight against the door on the other side.

Jennifer Sanchez came jogging down the hall from the elevator banks. "What's going on?"

"They won't step away from the door long enough for us to kick it in," Tim said.

Jennifer grinned. "Did you bother getting the key from the manager?"

Tim smiled sheepishly. "I want to kick it in."

Jennifer brushed past both men, moving them away from the door.

Bang ... bang ... bang ...

She quickly figured out the pace of the pounding and before the next one came she swung the AA-12 around and blasted the door open. Jennifer looked at Tim, "Don't be such a wimp, Baker."

"I wanted to kick it in," Tim said.

Jennifer held her AA-12 automatic shotgun in front of her. "Stop," she commanded when she saw the woman.

She barely recognized her as the stripper girlfriend of Osvaldo Rivera, covered in blood and her clothing ripped. She stood in the entryway to the hotel room, gnashing her teeth and staring with anger at Jennifer. She started moving forward.

"Stop, last time," Jennifer said but pulled the trigger before she got a second step. The shot, at such close range in the chest, pushed her back a foot before she fell to the ground.

"You kill them with a headshot," Tim said. When Jennifer and David looked at him he shrugged. "Don't you guys watch movies?"

While David carefully checked on Krystelle, Tim went to the balcony to see the body there.

"I need the last cleanup crew up to the fourth floor," Jennifer said into her walkie-talkie.

"Sending them up now. I'm coming up with them," Martin responded.

"What should I do?" Kostas asked, still blocking police traffic at the main entrance from Collins Avenue.

"Stay where you are. As soon as we cordon off this room we'll let the cavalry in. Until then, try not to antagonize too many of them. They have guns." Jennifer waited in the hallway until the team arrived, staying out of the crime scene. She was already spinning scenarios in her head about their cover story.

"I have an ID for the guy on the balcony," Tim said. "Rocco Fieri."

"Any idea how he ties into this?"

Tim smiled. "I've been watching his boss for months. Ever hear of Fat Tony? Antonio Tozzi is a major player in south Florida, whether it's guns, drugs or stolen property. The bureau has had this guy on their radar for years, but can never seem to get him." Tim frowned. "Do we have positive ID on the victims outside?"

Jennifer nodded. "I'll get those names in a second."

"I guarantee Fat Tony isn't one of them. You'd know if the

big boy was down there, and it didn't look like it. My guess is one or more of his other boys were caught up in this."

"That would be consistent with what we saw out there. It looks like at least one man fell from above. I'm still trying to piece together how there were three people affected below." Jennifer stepped past the team already bagging Krystelle and joined David on the balcony, careful to avoid the body there. She turned to David. "What do you see?"

"I see a struggle on the balcony. Notice the chairs are moved and the planter is tilted. I think Osvaldo or someone shot the woman, who in turn bit Rocco and at least another person up here, who fell to their death." David leaned on the rail and looked down. "Maybe Osvaldo then shot the people below? It looks to me like two customers coming, with their cars still below, and a valet. This would have been a great spot to shoot from. Then there was chaos below and chaos in the room."

"So, where is Osvaldo?"

"Once again he creates a mess and leaves. This guy is pretty slippery. Are we giving him enough credit? He seems to be more than a bumbling middle man to me."

Jennifer shook her head. "Did you see his file? There's nothing in it to lead me to believe he's anything but lucky at this point."

"Then eventually the luck is going to run out," David said.

"Jennifer, I have some intel for you, and you'll want to hear this," Martin said as he stuck his head out to the balcony. "Come with me."

He led her a few doors down in the hallway to an open door.

"Mister Hart, this is Jennifer Sanchez. Let her know what you just told me."

The man was slumped on a chair at the hotel room desk, tapping his fingers on the wooden top. He smiled faintly when Jennifer said hello, but is eyes darted around the room. "I was taking a nap when a shadow passed over me from the sliding glass doors." He pointed at them. "I opened my eyes and this deranged lunatic with a gun was in my room. Before I could speak he pointed it at me and told me to close my eyes, count to a hundred, and if I so much as moved he would shoot me dead. I thought he was going to kill me, but then I heard the door slam. He didn't even take my wallet. Isn't that strange?"

Jennifer looked at Martin. "Have we pulled the surveillance tapes yet?"

"Working on it. There are just too many variables here right now; we're wasting time playing catch up. We don't have the manpower, either. I've called back the two teams once they secure the bodies to make sure it isn't an infection or contagious, but that could take awhile."

Jennifer sighed. She kept hearing Kim's voice in her head. *"Ms. Sanchez, make sure we find the weapon. It's already walking the fine line between control and chaos. Do you understand me?"* She thanked Mister Hart and went back out into the hallway with Martin following.

"As soon as these last bodies are cleared, can we let the cops in? Kostas is really needed with us right now," Martin said.

"Yes." Jennifer sighed. "We'll have him circle the parking lot and make sure no one is trying to skip out. I'm amazed there haven't been indignant vacationers attempting an escape at this point."

"Yes, it could be much worse than it is. Still, there's too much to do."

"Take Missy with you and go through the surveillance tapes."

"Who?" Martin asked, but Jennifer could see the excited look in his face.

"She's in the car. Have her work with you, and be professional."

"You think I'm Kostas?"

"No. But I'm just suggesting you be professional," Jennifer said.

"I'm never anything but," Martin said. "How does my hair look?"

"Too funny." Jennifer watched as the team carried the bodies and bagged evidence down the hall to the elevators.

Jennifer went back to the open door of the hotel room and sighed. There was still a large stain on the carpet, but one of the techs was already cutting the piece out of it. Within minutes all evidence would be gone, the balcony would be power-washed and there would be nothing left for the police or anyone else to see or find. This was just the way ACES needed it.

A media press release detailing the shooter would be forthcoming within a few hours, but it would help if Osvaldo Rivera was apprehended. Then they could point their finger at Osvaldo as the 'crazed shooter on a rampage' and be done with it. Unless, of course, he was still out there on an actual shooting rampage with the zombie gun.

Jennifer remembered Kim's laughing about whoever Comstock was. She still didn't get it, but knew it was yet another obstacle in her way. If this didn't wrap up quickly, she was in trouble of losing more than face; she was going to lose her job. All they needed was another major catastrophe she couldn't control and she'd be the scapegoat.

～

MARTIN WAS TONGUE-TIED. HE SAT NEXT TO MISSY, ARMS TOUCHING whenever he moved even slightly. They were staring at the bank of monitors before them, taking in several hotel camera angles at once. He'd figured out the controls pretty quickly, much to the consternation of the hotel security guards who now stood in the doorway, looking useless.

"What are we looking for exactly?" Missy asked, her eyes on the screens before her.

Martin glanced at her and then went back to the controls, rewinding the footage back several hours on each camera. "A guy who would have left the fourth floor and then left through an exit without checking out."

"That should narrow it down to five dozen people today," she said with a chuckle. "This is a big hotel."

Martin smiled and pointed to a screen to her right, away from him. He casually leaned close to her. "You have the fourth floor elevator and stairway cameras in front of you."

"There he is," she said almost immediately.

Martin was disappointed. He was hoping this would take awhile and he could get to know her. Instead, their work looked to be done already.

"He's carrying a backpack. Moving fast, taking the stairs. Give me a shot of the lobby at this time," she said to him.

"You got it, boss," he said with a grin but she was too busy staring at the screens to respond to his playful remark. He quickly found the footage of Osvaldo slipping out a side entrance into the parking lot, and another outside camera angle of him running away toward the south and Collins Avenue.

"We know he's on foot. He's only been gone about two hours," Missy said as she checked her watch. "Unless he stashed a vehicle, this guy is still pretty close." She turned to Martin. "What does he have to do with what happened in the parking lot?"

Martin had the incredible urge to kiss her, which was so unprofessional even thinking it he felt like he should be fired. Never in his storied career had he succumbed to such teenage lust. "I can't tell you," he managed to say.

"Whatever." She looked pissed. "Is there any chance I can leave?"

"Um, sorry, not yet."

"Can I go to the bathroom at least, or is that a federal offense?"

"You can go to the bathroom." Martin stood when she did and followed her into the hallway and past the idling security guards.

She stopped suddenly and glared at him. "I'm a big girl. I think I can pee without you coming into the bathroom with me. Unless you're some kind of perv?"

"No, not at all." Martin stopped short. "I'm sure you'll be cut loose very soon."

"I hope so." She walked down the hall and into the bathroom at the other end. Martin watched her walk away, and couldn't help but stare at her butt. Wow, she was breathtaking.

"Martin, anything yet?" Jennifer came over the walkie-talkie.

"Yes, I was just going to contact you. I have a visual on our subject leaving on foot and heading south on Collins Avenue approximately two hours ago."

"Then he didn't get too far. I'm going to cut the female cop loose, and we're wrapping this up here and going on our search."

"Roger that." Martin was disappointed he would have to say goodbye to Missy.

"Kostas, we'll need a ride," Martin heard Jennifer say over the radio.

"You might want to hold up for a second. I have some breaking news," Kostas said.

"I'm listening," Jennifer said.

"Give me a minute."

Martin paced up the hallway, holding his Tac-338 McMillan tactical rifle in one hand and the walkie-talkie in the other. Just as he got to the woman's bathroom the door swung open and he was nearly knocked over by Missy.

"Wow, you really are a perv," she said.

"No, I was just walking. I'm waiting for something," Martin stuttered. *This is not going well at all. By the time this day is over with, she'll be filing sexual harassment charges against me.*

"Waiting to get a peek at me on the toilet? What is wrong with you?"

*I am so screwed. Just walk away. Let her know she can leave.*

"There's nothing wrong with me. I was, uh, waiting for a radio call."

"I don't believe that for a second."

Martin held the walkie-talkie and clicked the send button a couple of times; hoping Jennifer or Kostas would say something and bail him out.

"Can I leave yet?" Missy asked, hands on her hips.

"I'm waiting for the official word. Just give it a second," Martin said and didn't know why he'd just lied. The sensible move would be to cut her loose and never look back. Life seemed simpler a couple of hours ago. Point the Tac-338 McMillan and shoot the bad guys.

"Jennifer, you copy?" Kostas asked.

*Thank you*, Martin thought. He smiled and held up the walkie-talkie, as if the motion made any sense.

Missy still looked pissed. "So what?"

"Jennifer here."

"Do you want to hear the good news of the bad news first?"

"Spit it out, Kostas."

"The Miami Police Department has just located Osvaldo Rivera."

"That's the guy on the surveillance?" Missy asked Martin quietly. He nodded and smiled. Excellent, they had him in custody. Now they needed the zombie gun and this mess would be over.

"Is that the good or bad news?" Jennifer asked.

"Oh, that is definitely the good news. The bad news is the hole shot through his face and the missing weapon."

"Damn. Kostas, pick us up right now. Martin?"

"I'm here."

"Did you let Missy go like I asked you to?"

Missy pushed his arm. "What?"

Martin started walking away as Missy rained light punches on him. "Uh, yeah, now that you say to let her go I will do it."

"What? I told you ten minutes ago to cut her loose," Jennifer said.

"You aren't just a perv; you're a jerk, too. Were you planning on kidnapping me?" Missy asked.

Kostas added his own two cents with a chuckle. "Nice move, Mikey. I hope you got her number already. You do know there are Florida stalking laws? Penalties for lying to people? False imprisonment issues?"

Martin groaned. "I'll meet everyone in the parking lot." He looked at Missy. "I was actually going to tell you, but then you started yelling at me."

"Have you ever killed someone?" she asked suddenly.

"Um, yes. Why?"

"You seem like a super tough dude, like you can take care of yourself and never crack under pressure. I imagine you being shot at and never flinching during a firefight. Am I right?" Missy asked.

"Very much so." *What was she getting at?*

Missy smiled. "Then why are you letting me tease you so much and acting like a wounded child about it?"

"Huh?"

"I think you're a good-looking man. Heck, you're a cutie. I killed someone an hour or so ago, but I'm holding up pretty well. If I give you my phone number, promise you'll call me?"

Martin had no idea what was happening but he nodded his head and tried not to jump around like a teenager after his first kiss.

~

**THE FINANCIAL DISTRICT WAS PACKED THIS TIME OF DAY, WITH** people hustling to and fro. Men and women in business suits, carrying briefcases and attaché cases, went in and out of the buildings. It was just a typical gorgeous Miami day and the working class was busy doing the nine to five before getting home to the family for dinner. Tomorrow it would start all over again.

The dark blue sedan drove slowly up SE 14th Street. No one paid it any attention, just another vehicle passing through the area like hundreds the suits would see each and every day of their life.

"Here is as good as any. Pull to the curb, but make sure you can pull out quickly. When the traffic is light enough behind you, let me know."

The rear window to the sedan, closest to the curb, rolled down.

There were at least fifteen people on the sidewalk, within twenty feet of the sedan, going about their business, as well as tourists with bored children in tow. A bell was constantly ringing nearby, the bell attached to the top of the door to a coffee shop, patrons in and out before the door could fully shut.

"We have a window with the traffic," the driver said simply in his thick Russian accent.

The zombie gun was placed on the car door, just jutting out from the open window. The trigger was pulled, the yellow glow appearing.

A middle-aged man, wearing a cheap suit and dirty sneakers, suddenly stopped in the doorway of the coffee shop.

"Excuse me," a balding man carrying a full coffee cup carrier said behind him.

At the sound of the voice, the man in the cheap suit turned and lunged at the balding man, hot coffee spilling and covering the open door of the coffee shop.

The two men stumbled backward and into the coffee shop.

As a woman inside screamed, the zombie gun was pointed down the block at another man. Again, the trigger was pulled. Again, another attack ensued.

"We have traffic coming up quickly," the driver said.

"Two more and then we should be done in this location." Even as the backseat passenger spoke, the zombie gun was aimed in the other direction down the sidewalk and another man was shot. A man ran out of the coffee shop, fear in his eyes, and was next.

"We're good."

The driver pulled away from the curb and blended into traffic.

"Let us head to a bad section of town next. I think we need another scene as well."

They drove away with the mass chaos playing out behind them.

≈

***THIS IS NOT HAPPENING, JENNIFER THOUGHT AS SHE SAT IN TRAFFIC,*** knowing what was up ahead. She could picture Osvaldo, sitting in the car, lifeless and unable to tell them who took the weapon, with cops and gawkers surrounding him. *Why are we wasting time going to see his dead body, when we need to be regrouping and finding out who took it and where?*

When Jennifer did a K-turn on the street and headed away, neither Kostas nor Martin said a word. She supposed they felt the same way, but with no clues and no closer to the zombie gun and with Kim breathing down her neck, they didn't want to go off or start nailing her with questions. She'd figure this out. She always did.

She hoped this time was no exception.

"I only spent a few minutes with the cop, but let me ask you a serious question: are those babies real? I'm thinking she's a B cup, Mikey," Kostas said from his desk in the rear of the van.

Martin shook his head slowly and glanced at Jennifer.

"I know you definitely noticed the great ass on her, too. Wow, right? I wonder if she was wearing a thong. There is nothing sexier than women in uniform with something naughty underneath."

"Shut up," Martin mumbled.

"That was the wrong thing to say. You just egged him on," Jennifer said quietly but laughed. Kostas had hit a nerve with the Mighty Martin. She was glad for the distraction and genuinely wanted to see how far Kostas could push him about Missy before he snapped.

Kostas laughed. "The good thing about her, besides the great ass, is that she doesn't have a criminal record. Not even a speeding ticket. Wow, she's my age. Coincidence, I think not. She probably isn't into older guys, though. Sorry, Mikey."

"I'm twenty-eight," Martin said with more than hint of annoyance in his voice. He continued to look straight ahead in the passenger seat next to Jennifer.

"Much too old for Missy Lockhart."

"Stop illegally looking into her life," Martin said.

"Now you're suddenly her dad? Unless she needs a father figure, I think you're too old for her. You might be twenty-eight but you act like you're twice that age, my man. You need to lighten up. Give me a second to see if her dad is still alive for you."

"Enough," Martin said.

Jennifer glanced in her rearview mirror and winked at Kostas, who was absolutely giddy behind them, bouncing around in his seat. "Hey, she lives in nearby Hollywood, too. Don't you live out there?"

"Last warning," Martin said.

"I hope we wrap this job up soon, because I'll probably hang out in her neighborhood, talk to her neighbors and get to know her. Find out where she drops off her dry cleaning for her uniforms. She rents an apartment. I hope they have community washers and dryers in the basement."

"Stop," Martin mumbled.

"I can watch her while she's doing her laundry and then steal a pair of her thongs. Want me to grab a pair for you, Mikey?"

Martin turned in his seat and put a hand menacingly on the assault rifle behind him. "I will use this on you."

Kostas grinned. "When I'm with Missy, I'm going to grab

my crotch and say the same thing to her."

"Pull over," Martin said.

"Why?" Jennifer asked, stifling a laugh.

"Because I'm going to pound this little weasel into the dirt."

"Fine, fine!" Kostas said loudly. "I won't say another thing about her. I didn't realize it was such a touchy subject for you. Like you two were soul mates after a ten minute meeting."

"Pull over."

"I'm done. Remember, I'm a lover, not a fighter."

"You are fraying my last nerves," Martin said.

Jennifer was glad it was someone besides herself being relentlessly annoyed for a change. Kostas normally was pretty grating and once he thought he was bothering you he'd turn it up ten notches. Now that he knew he'd finally found a taboo subject to bust on Martin about, he would keep going. Even after Martin threatened him with serious violence, which was going to eventually come.

She admired Kostas, in a strange way, because he was much smaller than Martin, but he had balls. He wasn't intimidated by anyone no matter how big or bad they were, and she supposed it was the reason the guy had survived this long in his career.

"I wonder what the weather is like in Shirley, Massachusetts this time of year," Kostas cracked.

Martin looked confused.

"I didn't detect one of those Bahston accents on her, but in all fairness I was trying to imagine her naked."

Martin understood and put a hand on Jennifer's arm. "Please pull over so I can choke him out."

"Mikey, didn't you give some kind of oath to your sensei you would never use that karate stuff for evil?" Kostas asked.

"You are the epitome of evil, Kostas. Pull over so I can at least crush his larynx."

Jennifer could actually see Martin was serious and fuming. The Mighty Martin had finally been bested, and all it took was the hot button of a female he really liked at first sight.

Jennifer's phone rang and when she looked at it she sighed. "It's Kim."

She answered it on the third ring, after pulling into a strip mall parking lot. Kostas and Martin ended their bickering immediately.

"This is getting out of hand," Kim said without preamble. Jennifer had her on speaker phone. "And I'm realizing this is way too big for just Miami ACES, to be honest. Nothing personal."

*How is that* not *personal,* Jennifer wondered, but wisely kept her mouth shut.

"I'm sending in another team to deal with the latest problem."

"We have this under control, I assure you. Osvaldo Rivera is no longer in the picture, but we are gathering leads on the weapon as we speak." Jennifer rubbed her temples.

Kostas snapped his finger and turned one of the computer screens so she and Martin could see it.

A news cast was showing live shots of another attack, this time in the Financial District. It was happening again and happening right now.

"We are en route to the latest event right now," Jennifer

said.

"This feels like it is getting much worse before it will get better. At this point you are moving from location to location and putting out the fires, but with the news choppers already in the air and this one so close in geography and time since The Setai, we can't sweep this under the rug."

"Who are you sending in?" Jennifer asked.

"I'm flying in some other ACES teams to assist. I think the situation calls for someone to get rid of these messes while your team concentrates on getting the weapon back. There will be many more attacks and we can't afford the constant media attention. Deal with this new threat right now."

Jennifer was already pulling back onto the main road and off to the latest ordeal.

Martin leaned forward. "What cleanup crew are we talking about?"

"Some old friends, Mister Martin. You know them well, having served with them before ACES," Kim said.

Martin put both hands on the dashboard in front of him, his knuckles white. "Dale?"

Jennifer could imagine Kim with a huge smile on her face right now, leaning back in her office chair, hands behind her head and feet kicking in pure joy.

"Yes. Mister Comstock will be meeting you at Magic Productions within four hours. Now go and fix this." Kim disconnected as per the usual.

"Who is Dale Comstock?" Kostas asked.

Martin shook his head. "He's the guy who trained me in combat and in Gracie Jiu-Jitsu. He's also the most intense man you will ever meet. And he's the best at what he does."

"I always thought you were the best, Mikey," Kostas said with a laugh.

"I am when it comes to humans. Dale Comstock is . . . damn, he's like a machine or something. Unreal. If the guy ever bled it would come out as motor oil."

"He doesn't sound so scary to me," Kostas said.

Martin turned around in his seat. "Trust me: this is one man you do not want to mess with. He has a sense of humor but would just as soon break you in half than share a laugh with you. He is all business, and nothing personal, Kostas, but he will look at you as a weak tech guy who brings nothing to the table."

Kostas waved his hand. "Still not impressed. What about Jennifer? What do you think he'd say about her?"

Jennifer saw Martin's face go white as well when she looked over at him.

"He'll like Jennifer." Martin looked out the window. "He likes Latinas."

≈

**THE FINANCIAL DISTRICT WAS A WAR ZONE. AS JENNIFER PARKED** the van at the end of the road between two police cars, she could see people on the ground, people running, and people attacking.

Martin was out and already moving.

Jennifer stepped outside and tried to see who was in charge, but it was utter chaos. She counted at least ten Miami police officers, weapons drawn, moving in the street. The hum of news helicopters overhead added to the insanity.

"I've got three different live newscasts on this right now," Kostas said. "The cops have been told we are here, but they aren't too happy about it, especially after The Setai. The ETA for the vans is about three minutes for cleanup."

"Stay in the van and monitor this. Keep me in the loop." Jennifer watched as Martin, his Tac-338 McMillan tactical rifle leading him, suddenly found himself surrounded by four Miami officers with guns aimed at his head.

"Stand down," one of the cops was yelling, and Martin complied.

Jennifer ran over, AA-12 pointing to the ground. "Who's in charge here?"

One of the officers put up a hand. "This is a secure area. I don't know who you people are, but you need to turn around and leave."

A cop next to him spit on the ground. "These are the same ones from South Beach. Damn. What's going on?"

"Right now we need to secure the area," Jennifer said. She really didn't want to explain herself to these men. Who knew how many people had been turned into monsters?

There was a single gunshot down the street, and two police officers walked out of a coffee shop and gave a thumbs up. All the while the scene was being filmed from above and broadcast in everyone's living room. So much for keeping control of the situation.

"Status," the officer said into his radio.

Several clear messages came back.

"Set up a perimeter in a two block radius. We need to empty these buildings and make sure there aren't any more of them." He turned back to Jennifer. "I think we got them all. Mind telling me what you know?"

Jennifer shook her head. "I wish I could, but your superiors have been told everything already."

"That's crap," the spitting cop said. "This is the third crazy attack in a couple of days, and all we can do is shoot people that are acting like zombies. Another government cover-up. And people wonder why there are so many conspiracy websites."

The first cop told the other officer to go make himself useful somewhere else.

Jennifer could see the frustration in all their faces, but there wasn't much she could do or say to make this any better. "Let your men know my partner here is going to sweep the area as well, and I want them to leave him alone."

"On what authority?"

"On a higher authority than you can even comprehend. Let your chief know we're here, and he'll tell you to back off." Jennifer didn't want to be a hard ass but they were wasting time. If there were more roaming around, biting innocent people, they needed to be found and dealt with.

Martin gave a nod before moving off down the street.

Jennifer moved past the cops, who gave her a wide berth, and inspected the first body on the ground. The man had been mangled, the right side of his face shredded and the ear missing. His expensive suit was in rags, his white dress shirt underneath covered in blood, his tie undone and streaked with gore. This was an innocent working man who probably took a walk for lunch to get a cup of coffee or stop by a food truck.

She kept moving, telling an officer to get away from a

woman bent and broken in the middle of the street. "Don't touch anything or anyone," she said.

"Is this contagious?" one of the cops asked.

She knew it wasn't and didn't know what her hang-up was. These people were dead, gone, just more victims. But Jennifer's anger welled up inside of her. These weren't military fighters, warriors who knew the cost of battle. They weren't even civilians living in war-torn Bosnia, thinking at any moment they could be shot down and killed for no reason. In the Middle East, stray bullets could kill.

This was Miami. Sure, there was violence, but not of this ridiculous caliber. This was . . . *uncalled for*, Jennifer thought.

She met the officer's eyes and saw his fear. But it wasn't the fear she was used to in combat, the calm right before the storm when enemy fire was zipping overhead, the noise alone enough to wet yourself. There was a certain expectation when you engaged the enemy that not everyone would come back alive and none of you would return unchanged.

This cop had the fear of the unknown. He was no military veteran, just your average guy who probably grew up watching cop shows or came from a long line of police officers in his family, and all he wanted to do was serve and protect. He was probably calm under pressure from drug raids, gangbangers, stakeouts and traffic stops. Then, there was the assumption that the guy before you might be carrying a .357 but he wasn't likely to bite you until you were dead.

"It isn't contagious, no," she finally said to him. "I'm sorry."

"What is going on here?"

Jennifer shrugged and walked away, shotgun pointing at the ground. She wanted to be done with this day forever.

She'd been in fire-fights; she'd killed her fair share of the ene-my. But today the enemy seemed to be regular people, Amer-ican civilians, who couldn't help but attack their friends and family. It was more than she could take.

Martin ran back to her. "I think we're secure. The Miami PD is beginning to bag and tag. Of course, all of this will be featured on every local newscast." He pointed to the news choppers hovering above the street. "What else is there for us to do?"

"I don't know." Jennifer composed herself. She was the team lead and there was no point in questioning too much. *Relajarse. Consígalo juntos.* Relax. Get it together.

Martin looked at her funny but didn't open his mouth. In-stead, he turned away from her and tapped the walkie-talkie.

"Yep?" Kostas asked.

"Where are we right now?"

"In a world of YouTube videos and Facebook comments, my friend. This thing is going viral at an alarming rate. Un-less Kim can figure out how to shut down Twitter, we are screwed."

Jennifer clicked in. "Any good news?"

"Of course. I still want to sleep with you," Kostas said.

Martin held up a finger to Jennifer. "One minute in the back of the van with him, that's all I need."

"It is very tempting right now," Jennifer said and grinned. Leave it to Kostas and Martin to lighten her mood, even in such a dark hour.

"Thirty seconds. Hell, one good punch should do the trick."

"Let's get back, pull everyone off of what they're working on, and get every contact we have in Miami up to speed on what we are looking for. I think the cat is out of the bag on this one. If we take heat for too much information, so be it. I'd rather be dressed down by Kim with this weapon safe and secure, than tiptoeing around town while more of these hotspots flare up."

Martin nodded. "I think we're in for a rough couple of days ahead."

"I just hope whoever is pulling that trigger takes a break, because if they really wanted to they could create mass panic in South Florida."

"Do you think that's what's on the agenda?" Martin asked as they went back to the team van.

Jennifer got in and started the engine. "I'm not sure. The normal M.O. for the Russians is to stockpile these weapons for later use. Maybe because it was stolen they're pissed and using it on Miami civilians."

"As a warning?" Kostas asked.

"It could be the answer. Who knows at this point."

"But with Osvaldo dead and the weapon recovered, wouldn't simply hiding it and going about their business be a much better plan?" Martin asked.

"Who knows what their motives are at this point. Their contingency plan could have been to use it if recovered." Jennifer shook her head. There was too much they didn't know at this point and it was too late in the game to play catch-up. "I just don't know."

"There's also something else you two are forgetting," Kostas said. "You are assuming the Russians recovered it. What if it was another Osvaldo? Some low level thug, or Fat Tony himself? Maybe he's pissed and wants to hurt some people, or maybe this is a distraction for something else."

Jennifer sighed. There were too many variables.

Kostas was excited now. "What if Fat Tony was planning a big score and needed every cop in the city occupied?" He laughed. "This is like a Bruce Willis movie. I love his movies."

Jennifer hoped this wasn't some far reaching Hollywood production, with more innocent people killed, explosions, and the bad guys almost getting away.

≈

OPA-LOCKA WAS A SHELL OF ITS FORMER GLORY, A FOUR SQUARE mile collection of apartment buildings, businesses and home to various illegal activities set in the northeast corner of Miami-Dade County. It was also home to a strong and rough working class.

None of that would help the citizens of Opa-Locka on the street today. As is usually the case, they were simply at the wrong place at the wrong time. In the middle of the day, with the sun beating down on them, people went about their business.

The radio reports were coming in fast and furious about the attacks in the Financial District, with each station having a conflicting report about terrorists, a madman with a rifle, zombies and a gang or drug war erupting.

One part of the report was always the same: there were dead people in the street, and the area was swarming with Miami's Finest.

"Time to stretch the police of Miami even farther. Pick a

busy parking lot, please."

The driver circled the block twice before pulling into a fast food restaurant. The drive-thru line was ten cars deep and there were at least a dozen customers coming or going from the establishment.

"Don't bother stopping, just drive as slow as you can."

Once again the rear window was rolled down and the zombie gun was pointed out. The first person selected was a woman walking back to her car balancing two large drinks and a bag of food.

As they drove past her she dropped the items and turned, anger in her eyes.

They drove around to the back and the window behind the driver was opened, just in time to shoot a passenger in a Honda Civic. Two cars later, at the front of the drive-thru line, another man in the passenger seat with his window down was chosen.

"Slow down when we get to the takeout window."

The young girl, smiling as she handed a bag of burgers and fries out, suddenly tensed when the ray was directed at her.

"That should keep them amused inside for a bit."

They pulled back onto the main street.

"Where to now?"

"Find another business in this town. I think if we hit the four corners and create more spots, this town will be quarantined as a hot zone. I can't wait to see what the Miami news will be saying about it. Imagine an entire city shuttered and closed because of some strange, unknown virus or disease? Something strange creating zombies of harmless citizens? This will make the news worldwide."

"The American fast food restaurants seem busy. Should I pull into another one?"

"Yes, but farther away from this spot. I want to spread this out in all parts of town. You've given me a great idea, though. We need to find symbols of the United States influence, like these eateries to get the children fat, or government and police buildings. The Financial District was the perfect strike."

Over the next two hours they drove around Opa-Locka, targeting the gas stations, restaurant parking lots, banks and the police setup at a convenience store, shooting two police officers standing next to their bicycles.

"They won't be able to contain this." He laughed. "There, across the street. A grocery store, a perfect place to create havoc."

The sedan pulled slowly into the parking lot and the zombie gun was placed on the door and aimed. The light didn't go on.

"We seem to have a problem."

"What?"

"The gun . . . it's empty. Maybe. I don't know."

"Now what?"

"We go back, and try to figure out how to recharge the batteries on this weapon."

"Do you know how?"

"I don't have a clue."

The sedan pulled out of the parking lot and sped away.

≈

**"THIS IS NOT HAPPENING,"** **JENNIFER WHISPERED AS SHE PARKED** **THE** van and pulled her AA-12 from its storage behind her seat.

The sun was about an hour away from dropping below the horizon, and blazing right in their faces. She shielded her eyes, not surprised to see Martin already moving down the street with his rifle drawn.

Four bodies were on the ground, three torn apart and the fourth with a bullet hole through its forehead. Police sirens filled the air, and no one bothered to stop her as Jennifer walked, sweeping from side to side with the AA-12. "Talk to me, Kostas."

"It's all coming in too fast. We have at least three—no, wait, five—hotspots within driving distance. There might be dozens of people turned into monsters, and it is all over the news. This is bad."

"You think?" she asked sarcastically. "What do you see, Martin?"

"I see a cluster . . . a mess up here on the next block. Those infected by the weapon are just ripping into people, and the police don't seem to be able to organize through this chaos. Plus, I see too many officers trying to tackle or stun them instead of just shooting."

"Head shots," Kostas chimed in. "I've seen the movies."

"Didn't you already use that lame joke?" Jennifer asked. She kept moving, tallying the dead and wounded around her in her head. She also wondered whether or not she agreed with the police who were hesitating before killing innocent victims. This wasn't a cheesy film like Kostas was joking about. The people made into monsters looked just like your friends and neighbors, although they looked pissed. They didn't shuffle around with arms held before them and moan, they just . . . attacked. And didn't stop attacking until the person was ripped apart.

"I've figured out a route the Russians took with the weapon, and it extends several blocks through Opa-Locka. As more reports come in I'll update it, but it doesn't look good. The Miami PD is out in full force, but they are spread out so much I don't think they will be able to contain this before a lot of people die," Kostas said.

Can we contain this? Jennifer came to an intersection where there had been a car accident, bodies strewn on the street. She heard a series of gunshots and knew it was Martin methodically going about his business.

"Kostas, come pick me up. We need to get to the end of this trail and see if we can get behind them as more spots flare. I'm only a block away." Jennifer began heading back.

"I'm going to keep moving. The Miami PD are playing footsie with them now, and we need this cleared and cleaned ASAP. I'm handling it. I will meet you somewhere," Martin said over the walkie-talkie.

"Roger that," Jennifer said.

Kostas pulled up and let her take the wheel while he slid into the passenger seat, setting the GPS. "Just follow the destruction to the end, or where I think it is."

Jennifer drove away slowly, avoiding the stalled cars and multitude of police cars parked at odd angles everywhere.

"This is like a maze," Kostas said. "I hear more sirens up ahead."

Jennifer came to a stop just as six police cruisers shot through the intersection.

"Follow the rabbit," Kostas said.

*"Puede usted por favor, dejen de hablar?"*

Kostas grinned. "Something about me not talking enough?"

"I know damn well you can speak Spanish, so stop playing dumb when I talk about you."

"Take Ali Baba Avenue," Kostas said, even though Jennifer could see it on the GPS. "Right on Perviz Avenue."

"I can see that."

"Just trying to change the subject and lighten the mood." Kostas glanced at her and smiled. "You know, all this death and devastation gives you a new perspective on life, doesn't it?"

"I will never sleep with you, not in a million years."

"Only a million? Last time you said billion." Kostas laughed. "I'm wearing you down slowly."

"At a glacial pace."

"I can wait."

Martin suddenly broke in. "Jennifer, where are you?"

Before he clicked off she thought she'd heard rapid gunfire in the background.

"Just pulling onto Perviz Avenue. What's up?"

"I need you back at the corner of Northwest 25th and Ali Baba. We have a problem. A big one."

"He sounds pissed," Kostas said.

"I'm on my way. What is all the background noise?" Jennifer asked.

"That would be an HK416 set on full automatic."

Jennifer was confused. "The police are shooting an HK416?"

"No." Martin held the send button on the walkie-talkie and Jennifer and Kostas could hear what sounded like a one-sided fire fight. "He's here."

"Who?"

Martin audibly sighed. "My old teammate and mentor. Dale Comstock is marching down Ali Baba killing them with a smile on his face. He's leading a small ACES unit of four."

Jennifer sped up. "We'll be there in a few minutes."

"Take your time. He'll probably be cleaning his HK416 by the time you get here."

Kostas laughed, clapping his hands. "This is going to be so much fun."

# EPISODE FIVE
Dale Comstock

**MARTIN AIMED HIS TAC-338 MCMILLAN TACTICAL RIFLE AND WAS** about to caress the trigger when the target's head exploded. Martin swung the rifle around in search of a new target, but he could already see another head burst as a .223 round entered through the forehead.

"There are other people here who want a turn," Martin yelled in frustration.

Dale Comstock laughed. He fired twice more from his HK416 and two more bodies hit the pavement. "Clear," he called out.

Martin wanted to scream. *This is such crap*, he thought. *I can do this job. Who needs this guy?*

Dale Comstock walked slowly to Martin with a smile on his face. He was even bigger than Martin remembered him. Back in the day they called him the American Badass Dale 'The Force' Comstock. He had to be pushing fifty, but he was still in top shape. He wore a ripped camouflage muscle shirt with his head shaved and his goatee cut close. It was always the intense eyes that Martin watched. Dale could be smiling one minute and breaking your neck in the next one and his eyes would never give away his intent. He was like a machine.

"This dude is like a cartoon," Kostas said as he watched Dale strut over.

Martin closed his eyes. This was going to be a long day, especially with Kostas making comments. Although, it would be nice to see Comstock put Kostas in his place . . .

"He's the real deal." Martin returned the smile when Dale stopped in front of him and moved the HK416 to the side.

"What, no hug for your old mentor?" Comstock asked.

"Nice try," Martin said.

"Were you two lovers or something?" Kostas asked with a laugh.

Comstock turned to Kostas without his smile fading. "Ever have a rifle shoved up your ass sideways, little man?"

"Can't say I have."

"Do you want a hug from me?"

"Not really. You look like you could bear hug me to death. You're like the love child of pro wrestlers Tony Atlas and Superstar Billy Graham." Kostas took a step away and toward Martin.

Comstock glanced at Martin and winked. "I'd love to stand here and reminisce but we have heads to shoot. What say we do this for old time's sake, Martin?"

"Just don't cheat this time. Shot for shot."

"This isn't a game," Jennifer chimed in. She'd been silent, standing off to the side and watching the exchange.

Comstock approached her. "No, this is real life. But this is what we do when we're fighting the enemy. These aren't people anymore, and to think they are means you'll be bitten. Look at half the bodies on the street, ma'am." Comstock pointed with his HK416. "These cops and civilians hesitated." Comstock walked away and checked his magazine. "And when you hesitate in battle, you die. I do not hesitate. There is a job to do."

"They were people. Husbands, wives . . ." Jennifer said.

Comstock stopped smiling. "But they aren't anymore. Right now they are cold blooded killers who will bite the face off of a baby. Do you understand that? There isn't going to be a miracle cure flown in from some secret research laboratory. There won't be some magical antidote to save them.

No, I am here to save the people that are in the way of these killing machines. I'm here to make the streets of Miami safe. Do we understand each other?"

"Loud and clear, Mister Comstock," Jennifer said.

He smiled. "You can call me Dale."

"What kind of name is Dale?" Kostas asked.

Comstock turned to the tech. "You can call me Mister Comstock."

"We're wasting time," Martin finally said. He wanted to get this over with, and he also wanted to see if he could still keep up with his former mentor. It had been several years since they'd been in combat together and even though Martin was feeling like his manliness had been usurped by Comstock and he was looking pretty weak in the eyes of his ACES team, he still owed the man his life.

Quite literally.

～

**THEY'D BEEN ON ONE OF THOSE MISSIONS THAT WAS SO SECRET THEY** never knew exactly where they'd been dropped off. Martin just remembered the stinging sand making his night vision goggles useless until they entered the cave system.

There were three two-man teams but no one knew names or cared. They had twenty-four hours to complete their assignment before they would go their separate ways and onto the next kill no capture mission. And that's exactly what they were heading into, taking out an enemy cell secreted under the desert floor.

Since Comstock was the lead based on his status and the

pull he had on these missions, those two went first. Martin remembered how suffocating it was, the dust and the trapped heat in the natural caverns, with some walls chiseled and sculpted by man, while others still had marks of animals and the settling of time.

But this wasn't a geography or history expedition. This was about getting in, eliminating everything in sight, gathering intel, and getting out.

What they never show on TV programs and movies is the reality of shooting a weapon in close quarters, when the heavy shooting starts. As Martin and Comstock rounded the next corner they were set upon by a man with a knife, who was no match for their Heckler & Koch MP5SD4's with sound suppressors. He was quickly dispatched and they moved on, but the smoke from the two spent cartridges was already lingering in the air as they moved.

Even with the sound suppression, the MP5 was like a cannon in such close and oppressive quarters, and an alarm was raised deeper in the caverns.

"Move it double time!" Comstock yelled to his unit, and they skirted into the next chamber and Comstock shot two men as they stood.

They moved single-file down a tight hallway, Comstock shooting and moving. The next room was carved out of the mountain with a high vaulted ceiling and it was a rudimentary command post, with outdated equipment, old computers and so many power lines running across the floor and up into cracks in the ceiling that you could barely move.

Martin shot the closest man as he stepped to the side and let the rest of the team in. Within seconds the room was filled with weapons firing, spent rounds bouncing on the floor of wires, and a smoky haze before them, the few light sources in the room extinguished during the assault.

Comstock pointed at Martin and another man and then forward, while the other half of the team began dismantling the equipment and searching for anything of importance. Even though it was a kill no capture mission, it was always a bonus to find unencrypted messages or maps.

Martin tried to get past Comstock but he was quicker. Always faster than any man, even at nearly twice his age. His MP5SD4 began lighting up the hallway before him, and Martin could only follow along as Comstock cleared a path.

Three bodies were stepped over, and another two were tangled together where they tried to run from the onslaught.

"Leave some for me," Martin said over his headset.

Comstock either ignored the request or didn't hear it, since his MP5SD4 was buzzing again, filling the area with gun smoke.

But it was too thick, smoke billowing from behind Martin.

Then he smelled the fire. Later, after they'd successfully cleared the cave system, accounted for thirty-two of the enemy defeated, and recovered several key documents, would Martin learn the fire began after the hot rounds had dropped to the wiring below their feet and sparked.

He was trying to keep pace with Comstock, gun still blazing ahead, when a darker figure appeared from above and dropped onto him.

Martin, a great student of Gracie Jiu-Jitsu (which he trained with his mentor, Dale Comstock), immediately went into defense mode, one of the main ingredients to the style. However, in such close quarters, with smoke at his back and now surrounding him, and with an opponent he could barely see, he slipped and fell against the right wall.

The knife was all too visible as it plunged into his left shoulder, slicing through his jacket. Martin swept his leg but didn't encounter the enemy.

But he felt the knife as it jabbed him in his left thigh. Martin couldn't see through the smoke and his goggles had slipped. He wasn't panicking, but his eyes were stinging through the haze and he was cut in two places and bleeding.

When the man rose up in front of him, Martin threw a strike that connected with the man's chest, but from his awkward position it only knocked the man back instead of dropping him. That's when Martin saw the muzzle of the Browning M1911 pistol through the thick fog, aimed at his head.

The next moment the man gave a strangled cry and his weapon arm was twisted behind him. Martin tried to stand but his thigh was on fire and his legs gave out.

Comstock pushed the enemy away after snapping his neck and lifted Martin with his free hand. "Can you move?"

"I'm fine. Let's keep going," Martin said, trying to fight through the pain.

Comstock shook his head. "Back out and give me another two from the unit. We need to finish this."

Martin was going to protest but his eyes were watering so much he could barely see. He used the wall for support and retreated. By the time he made it back to the main chamber, the fire had been put out and one of the men was fanning the smoke with a stack of papers. "Lead needs two guns."

There was a chair in the corner, which Martin sat on and surveyed the damage to his shoulder and thigh. Both weren't anything more than flesh wounds, but he was bleeding. Over the next fifteen minutes he managed to dress the wounds and stop the blood flow, and he could stand gingerly on his hurt leg.

That's when he heard and felt the explosion, a deep rumble from somewhere inside the bowels of the mountain. He stumbled on his feet but it wasn't strong enough to throw him or the remaining men in the room, who were busy dressing down the equipment.

Martin felt helpless. He wanted to be side by side with Comstock and clearing each room and hallway. Like he'd been trained. And like Comstock had further trained him.

It seemed like an hour passed before Comstock and one man came back, dirty and sweaty. Comstock motioned silently to wrap up, and the team did.

Martin refused help as he was able to walk on the hurt leg. He knew there wasn't any permanent damage, although he'd have a nice scar to add to the collection.

Once they were standing outside, two men wired the entrance with explosives.

"We're missing a man," Martin said quietly to Comstock.

"He didn't make it." Comstock turned to Martin. "He was right behind me when he triggered the wire. It took out ten square feet of solid rock with it. There wasn't much left of him."

Martin looked away. "That would've been me."

Comstock shrugged. "Probably. I saved your sorry ass twice today, I guess. You owe me big time. You can start by buying the first two rounds when we get back to civilization."

"Sounds like a deal."

But that was the last time they'd run into one another. While Martin went to a military hospital to heal, Comstock was like the wind, off to another mission and a new partner.

Martin was grilled once he was back to normal, and it was decided he'd be better off in a completely new assignment: the ACES team and a spot in the United States. He'd fought it, but in the end he knew it was useless.

He also didn't know what the official story about the raid was and knew he'd never find out the truth. Or what they offered as the real story, but he did know a man had died. Someone Martin had never spoken two real words to, and didn't even know his name. Martin had been demoted in his eyes, taken out of a situation he could control.

And he wasn't sure if Dale Comstock had anything to do with his leaving the unit and going to ACES.

≈

**JENNIFER ANSWERED HER PHONE ON THE THIRD RING, KNOWING** exactly who was calling her again, for the third time today.

"Update," Kim said without a hello.

"Between the Miami PD and your killing machine, we should be done in this area in the next twenty minutes," Jennifer said.

Kim actually chuckled. "I hope everyone is getting along down there."

"So far, so good. Kostas is monitoring police bands as well as the news to see if there are anymore hotspots."

"As am I. It seems to be contained to that Opa-Locka area for now."

"My fear is they're on the move with the weapon and another infected area will present itself very soon," Jennifer said.

"Your team needs to find a pattern, a method to this madness, and get ahead of them."

"I'm well aware of that, ma'am," Jennifer said, trying to keep the edge off her words. She was frustrated at lack of real information and the seeming randomness of these latest attacks. They needed to regroup but with Martin and Comstock now in a macho shootout and Kostas trapped in the van, searching for the next attack, Jennifer felt like they were reacting instead of acting. Always a dangerous move in her line of work.

"I'll check back in the next thirty minutes to hear about your progress." Kim disconnected.

Jennifer walked back to the van just as four police cruisers from neighboring Hollywood and Fort Lauderdale pulled up. She could only imagine the manpower being brought into this, and what a mess it was creating. She was sure by the time she got home and took a hot shower and dropped onto her couch (which was a few days off, she knew), this story would be going international. If it hadn't already, with the internet and aggressive local news outlets.

"What have you got for me?" she asked Kostas, trying to sound happy and positive and failing miserably.

"Not much. So far I haven't heard a peep about new attacks anywhere within a hundred miles. Of course, if they wanted to really screw us, they would be driving up to St.

Augustine or out to Orlando or Tampa and wreaking havoc. You just don't know where this is going to happen next."

Jennifer dropped heavily into the chair next to him and rubbed her eyes. "We need something, anything. Have any of the agents checked in with new information?"

"Nothing that really pertains to this case."

"I need everyone to stay focused." Jennifer needed to practice what she was preaching, because right now she was starting to feel overwhelmed. And it was so unlike her. She needed to get a grip.

"Baker and Luciano just called. They want to know if they need to head back to the Miamarina, or if you want them in another position?"

"Have them do a quick pass of the Russians and then return to base. Tell them to get ready to move, because if we get another attack we need them there as well. Our goal right now is to contain these outbreaks before more and more civilians die."

"And before the living, breathing G.I. Joe action figures that are Martin and Comstock end up on the Channel 6 news taking turns shooting people in the head. Both with kung fu grip, too." Kostas smiled at Jennifer. "That Dale guy is something, right?"

"Yes, I suppose," she said and looked at her feet.

Kostas laughed. "Wow, someone has a crush."

"What? Give me a break. I'm a grown woman."

"Right now you sound like a teenage girl, and your body language doesn't help," Kostas said. "I'm not as stupid as you think."

"I think you are quite intelligent," Jennifer said, trying to change the subject.

"Whatever. I saw the way you looked at him when he came over, and I honestly saw the way he looked at you."

"What do you mean?" she asked and then grimaced. Damn. She was acting like a school girl with a bad case of puppy love.

"Do you want me to pass him a note in homeroom for you?"

"*Quiero que usted cierre su boca,*" she said.

"I won't shut my mouth, it's too damn cute," Kostas said.

"I knew you understood Spanish."

Kostas grinned. "Just a few things, and you've actually been teaching me some good phrases. I recognized that one because you've said it often enough to me."

"I'm switching to Japanese from now on," Jennifer said.

"Cool. I need to learn some disparaging remarks in Japanese as well."

"I know quite a few. I'm fluent in several languages, you know," Jennifer said.

"Stop trying to change the subject. I am fluent in code, which is the only language you need these days. Are you going to ask him out before he takes off, hanging off of a helicopter skid and flying off into the sunset?"

Jennifer laughed at the visual of Comstock swinging with one bulging arm as he waved with the other, his big smile and bold eyes focused on her . . . *damn,* chica, *get a hold of yourself,* she thought. Kostas was right. She'd been so focused on the mission and all the horrible twists and turns she'd ignored the simple fact: Comstock was hot. *El fuego.*

"I'm still not seeing or hearing anything about another attack. This doesn't add up. We need to go pick up our two natural born killers before they run out of shiny things to shoot at and turn on each other." Kostas laughed. "And I haven't forgotten about you and your new future boyfriend. My goal now is to get you two together, because when he starts hitting that fine ass of yours I want him to give me all the details."

Jennifer laughed as she started the van. "Even if he got that lucky, do you really think he'd tell you, of all people?"

"Why not? We're bonding over this mission. I totally think Comstock and I will be heading out for a beer after all this blows over."

"I hope you're joking," she said.

"You'll see. Three beers into the conversation he'll be detailing every last birthmark and freckle on your body for me."

Jennifer pulled the van from the curb and laughed. She was almost positive Dale Comstock was going to break Kostas in half.

〜

**"IS THAT ALL OF THEM?" MARTIN ASKED IN FRUSTRATION.**

Comstock only laughed and made sure the HK416 was cleared. "It looks like it. Four for me and two for you."

Martin glanced at the bodies on the ground. "I think one of yours was someone bitten and not a monster."

Comstock made an exaggerated shrug. "Fine. Then I still win three to two."

"Whatever."

"Why are you so mad? Would you rather half of Miami

was trying to kill us so you could get your kill count up? Really?"

Martin began walking away, frustrated with himself.

"Soldier, what is your problem?"

Martin spun on his heels. "I'm not a soldier anymore, I'm a member of the ACES team."

"Once a soldier always a soldier, and you of all people should know that."

"I haven't been a soldier since they stripped me of my rank out in the desert."

Comstock's eyes narrowed. "They stripped you of nothing. In fact, they placed you in a much safer environment, I guarantee gave you a bigger paycheck, and a nice place to sleep with actual running water and no real threat of bombs going off 24/7. Am I right?"

"It's not about that stuff."

"Then tell me what this is about? Ever since I touched down you've had a chip on your shoulder. Is it because I didn't send you postcards from Basra or Khost? A stuffed animal from Al Jahra? Where do you think I've been for the last eighteen months while you've been playing Don Johnson on Miami Vice?"

Martin felt like an ass. "I was mad."

"You're still mad, and it looks like it is eating you up inside, bro."

"Don't call me bro," Martin said and couldn't help but laugh.

"I'm wondering why the hostility toward me since I got here?"

"I'm not sure," Martin lied.

Comstock put his face near Martin's and locked eyes. "Bullshit."

"I thought I was reprimanded back there and you didn't have my back. If you were really my partner and my mentor, you would have fought for me to stay with you. Instead, you disappeared and I was shipped back like a wounded veteran . . . here's your papers, here's your medal, go away. It was nice knowing you before we strike your record and replace you."

"Do you hear yourself?" Comstock growled. "Did you join the Unit for the glory? Did you want to go on CNN or Jon Stewart and talk about all the terrorists you killed or the job we did in South America? How about Austria or Oslo? Come on, you can't be serious. You know as well as I do that this job takes from you and never gives back."

"I feel like I was snubbed. By you."

"By me?" Comstock said with a humorless laugh. He stomped away, circling Martin before coming back to stand before him. "Are you accusing me of something, bro?" This time *bro* was said without affection.

"You let them reassign me without even standing up and making them keep me with the Unit, and you didn't even say good-bye." Martin knew he was sounding weak and like a whining baby, but he also knew he had to get this out now before it kept eating him up inside. He could keep going and make pretend it didn't bother him, but he also knew he might never get another chance to be alone with Comstock and clear the air. Even if it meant Dale walking away, or punching him out.

"Let me address the last part of your statement first, okay?

I never said good-bye because they took you and made sure your wounds weren't infected. You went one way and I went another. Within six hours I was in another cave system and doing what I do best: point and shoot. You got the luxury treatment, am I right? Clean sheets, three squares and all the pretty nurses in white you could ask for."

"I wasn't dying. I had a stab wound. I fought through worse than that and you know it. Something smelled fishy then and it still does."

"Don't interrupt." Comstock got in his face again but he was calm. *At his deadliest, when he has the emotions in check,* Martin thought.

"Sorry, sir," Martin said immediately.

"I saved your ass in that cave not once, but twice. And a darn third time once we got back to safety."

Martin didn't understand but he knew better than to interrupt again.

Comstock continued, backing up a foot. "They wanted you, Mike. They wanted you really bad, but I refused to let you go until I was sure you were ready."

"Huh?"

"You think you got sent to ACES to be punished? Heck no. I let them transfer you because I did you a favor. You earned that promotion. And that's all it ever was. A chance to shine for you instead of always being my second, always being the guy that had my back and nothing more. I'm pushing fifty but I'm in better shape than most men half my age. And I intend to die with this HK416 in one hand and my Colt .45 pistol in the other. There is nothing more for me, and I can accept it. But you . . . Martin, you have what I had in my mid-twenties, and you don't want to waste it by just pointing and shooting. It gets old really fast."

"What are you saying?"

"I'm saying the morning before the mission I spoke to our boss and told him you were ready to move out and up. You had learned everything you were ever going to learn from me in combat, Gracie Jiu-Jitsu or common sense. It was time for you to show ACES what you had."

"But why didn't you tell me?"

"I was going to, but not before a mission. How many guys do we both know who get their walking papers or word of a new command, and look past their here and now, and get themselves killed? I didn't want to do it to you. I couldn't. My intention was to tell you in front of everyone after we'd secured and gotten back to base that night. I knew I was moving out again, but you were shipping back to the States. I knew the fight was coming to America. I knew the battleground was going to be Florida and Texas and California. We need the best here."

"I don't know what to say."

"You can start by apologizing," Comstock said with a laugh.

"Next time we walk into combat together, I'll beat you."

Comstock shook his head. "It will never happen. I taught you well, but not every one of my tricks."

≈

JENNIFER WATCHED FROM A RESPECTFUL DISTANCE AS MARTIN AND Comstock had a heated discussion. She knew there was obviously a long history between the two men, but decided unless it came to a physical altercation, she wouldn't interfere. How could she? Both men were strong. She knew if she took an accidental blow from either of them, she'd be in trouble. It was best to let them work this out and have their moment.

Martin would talk to her in private in the next few days, once this mission was finished and Comstock was gone. He'd share some of the information and she wouldn't try to pry the rest from him. In the short time she'd worked with Mike Martin, he was quiet about his past and his present life. She knew where he lived but it was just an address to her. She'd never been there and she had no intention of ever seeing his place. Jennifer imagined camouflage painted walls and an obstacle course set up from his bed to the front door to keep him in shape.

Jennifer glanced back at Kostas, who was now seated in the driver's seat for some reason. While he loved to tell stories about the waitresses and models he was out with last night, he was also tight-lipped about his past. She knew he'd gotten in trouble and that's why he was in ACES and her problem. She could easily guess it was sexual harassment. Heck, she could have written him up half a dozen times a day for the comments he made to her.

Kostas was relatively harmless, but around other women in the field he probably seemed like a menace. But Jennifer had to admit he was great when he got down to business. Even with the jokes and constant sexual innuendo, he was good at what he did. But no matter how good Kostas was at his computer work, the stigma of being a jerk would always follow him in his career. And he'd earned most of it, if Jennifer was being honest.

Martin and Comstock broke off, Comstock walking in the opposite direction.

"Where is he going?" Jennifer asked as Martin approached her.

"He said he had to make a few calls and check in. We have his number and he is ready for the next hotspot. He'll be there in minutes," Martin said.

"Some day."

"Just another day at the office," Martin said and opened the passenger door of the team van. "Why are you driving?" he said to Kostas.

"Just get in. We need to hurry," Kostas said.

Jennifer sighed. *Would this menace ever end?* "Are you sure you need to be driving?"

"What are you trying to say?"

"She's being subtle. I'll come out and say it: you're a horrible driver," Martin said.

"Me? I'm an excellent driver."

"You drive like you're starring in a cheesy action movie. You drive like a lunatic," Jennifer said. "Slide over."

"Nope. I need to drive, I know where we're going. Get in, you're wasting way too much time. Lives are at stake here."

"You want the front?" Martin asked Jennifer.

"What a gentleman," Kostas said with a snicker.

"I just don't want to go through the windshield," Martin said.

"Neither do I." Jennifer took a seat at the desk in the back.

"I'm fine back here in Kostas World."

"Don't touch anything," Martin said with a laugh, but it was half-hearted.

Jennifer turned her attention to the bank of radios and computers. There was chatter on the Miami PD channels but nothing more than usual. She watched as a reporter from Channel 6, blazer freshly pressed, stood behind a blockade of police cars where they'd previously been and smiled as he talked about this new 'zombie attack'. Jennifer kept the sound off. "Where are we headed? I don't hear or see anything new back here."

"We have a meeting to attend to," Kostas said.

"With who?" she asked.

"You'll see."

"I need to check in with Langley."

Kostas smiled at her via the rearview mirror. "I already talked to Kim. You can update her in two hours, unless something else happens beforehand."

Jennifer sat up in the chair. "What do you have up your sleeve, Kostas?"

"I procured some alone time for the three of us. Oh, and food."

"We don't have time for this," Martin said.

"Just relax, Mikey, and go with the flow."

They drove in silence for nearly twenty minutes until Kostas pulled into the parking lot of an unassuming budget motel and pulled the team van into the farthest spot from the office. "Here we are."

"I don't know about Sanchez, but I'm not going into a seedy motel room with you," Martin said.

"Not again?" Jennifer asked with a laugh. "Seriously, what are we doing here?"

Kostas jumped out of the van and knocked on room 14. An older man and woman greeted him at the door and ushered the three ACES members inside.

"Let's eat," Kostas said. He turned to the man. "Thank you for helping on such short notice, sir." Kostas pulled five twenty dollar bills from his pocket and handed them to the man. "We'll be gone within ninety minutes. Did you remember the hot sauce?"

"But of course, Mister Shula," the man said.

There were two twin beds in the room, and the TV was showing the news with the sound off. On the desk was a spread of ham, salami, bologna, turkey and roast beef slices as well as three different kinds of cheese, a pile of hard rolls, various condiments and pickles, and an ice bucket with soda cans.

"Mister Shula?" Jennifer had to ask.

Kostas winked. "Every great undercover agent needs a secret alias."

The man and woman went to the door, both smiling. "Do you need anything else, Mister Shula?" the man asked.

Kostas waved at him. "No, this is perfect. I cannot thank you enough."

"I also took the liberty of taking the garbage out in your room this morning. It was getting out of control again, sir," the man said.

Kostas looked annoyed. "Thank you."

Martin grabbed a hard roll from the table. "You live here?"

Kostas shrugged. "I have to live somewhere."

"I'm guessing you make enough to afford a nice condo," Jennifer said. She was famished, and despite the odd situation they were currently in, the sight and smell of all this food made her stomach growl. They'd been going nonstop for so long she couldn't remember her last real meal. She resisted the incredible urge to straighten out each slice of meat so they were all equidistant and all the silverware was lined up perfectly.

"I can afford a great place, but what would be the point? I'm sure this is another temporary career move for me."

"You can't mean that," Martin said as he stuffed roast beef into the roll. "We've been a team for over a year."

"Yet we know almost nothing about one another. I've been to a couple of Miami Dolphins games with you, but never done a thing with Jennifer. And I don't mean that in a sexual way, I just mean we don't hang out."

"You know they frown on us forming too tight a personal bond," Jennifer said simply.

"I get it. Tomorrow one of us could be shipped to the Dallas or Chicago ACES team. Or we could add a fourth member, someone transferred from San Diego or Hawaii. Understood." Kostas made a sandwich and sat down on one of the beds. "I've been all around the world for the government since high school, and in the few years of my life that mattered, I haven't worked with two people I cared more about."

Martin sat down on the other bed. "What's the punch line?"

"No joke." Kostas smiled. "I mean, let's be honest, Jennifer here is a hot cougar and I'd love to nail her. I won't lie. But I consider her a great team lead first, then a friend, and then a sweet piece of ass."

"Thanks, I think," Jennifer said as she sat down next to Kostas. "Hey, you finally got me in the same bed as you."

All three laughed.

"So, why are we here?" Martin asked between bites. "And what's with the food?"

"I thought we needed a little break. We needed to get our heads out of this case, recharge with some food and light conversation, and then dive back in refreshed."

"That does sound good right now," Jennifer admitted. "What should we talk about? The weather? Sports?"

Kostas stood. "We're going to talk about your feelings, and your current problems, and maybe gain some closure on some childhood issues."

"Huh?" Martin said with a grimace and looked at Jennifer.

~

HE SAT AT THE SMALL TABLE AND TAPPED THE SIDE OF THE VODKA bottle. It was empty and made a high ringing noise when he used his nails. He didn't drink it. He never drank, didn't smoke and didn't get caught up with women and their games. Those things were for the weak.

"I have located someone."

He tapped the bottle one last time, loving the sound it made. So crisp, so clear. So clean. "And?"

The other man stood a respectful distance. "I didn't know if you wanted him to come here or if you wanted to drop the item off with him."

The man looked up. "I want neither of those options. We

will meet him in the morning at a location outside of Miami. If he can help with recharging the item, I will be greatly in debt to him."

"Yes, sir."

"Instead of torturing him or using the weapon on him, I will end his life quickly once he is done being useful. Understood?"

"Of course."

"Make the necessary arrangements." He went back to his focus on the empty bottle. They were wasting too much time. His goal was to keep moving in and around Miami, creating havoc and making this too big for the United States government, locally and nationally, to be able to handle. He wanted mass hysteria and people rioting in the streets. He wanted to see fear in their eyes and bloodshed.

He envisioned the American government going on the offensive against the enemy who brought this reign of terror to idyllic South Florida and beyond, who attacked on U.S. soil, the enemy who had the gall to kill innocent civilians and turn them against one another.

The Russians, the eternal enemy of the Americans.

And Ramzan Umarov, Sunni Islamic from Russia, would watch as World War Three was begun over his actions.

He went back to tapping on the empty vodka bottle.

≈

DAVID LUCIANO HAD AN EIDETIC MEMORY, WHICH WAS VERY USEFUL in this line of work. Especially now, when he was standing in line at Dunkin Donuts and about to order coffee and sandwiches for six people.

The Russian boat was no longer at the docks, so they'd made their way back to Magic Productions to await further instructions. It seemed the ACES team was involved in some big hush-hush meeting right now and was unavailable.

When everyone said to him the usual, they knew without a shadow of a doubt he was going to get the orders right. David didn't mind being the gopher at times like these, because it got him out of the office. Most of his days were spent doing paperwork, internet research and wrapping up the boring details.

And he liked everyone he worked with, event the temporary personnel in and out like Tim Baker. On paper, they were completely different in both looks and philosophy. But they got along because under the laid-back attitude of Tim was a consummate professional who took his job seriously, the same as David.

David placed his order and stood off to the side, adjusting his tie idly as he waited. His mind was always racing when he was this much a part of an actual mission, instead of just being a paper pusher. He'd been searching the database for Russians of interest currently thought to be in Florida and especially the Miami area. Unfortunately, there were dozens and dozens of suspects currently unaccounted for. Any one of them could be using the weapon.

He was ready to go, and balanced two drink trays and two bags of sandwiches, bagels and donuts in his arms as he left and walked back to his car. Placing everything carefully on the roof of his Ford Focus, David pulled his car keys out of his pocket.

That's when he noticed the dark sedan two spots over, and the man stepping out from the passenger side. The man glanced over at David before putting his sunglasses on and walking into Dunkin Donuts.

*Boris Dragov is in town,* David thought. He tried to act casual and went to follow Boris into the business when he noticed the driver staring at him. David looked down, feeling his cheeks burning. He'd been had. He took his time getting the coffees and bags into the car, trying to appear as if he wasn't stalling. The driver was still watching him.

David got into his Focus and slowly pulled away, rounding the Dunkin Donuts and immediately pulling onto the street and into the parking lot of the gas station next door. He kept an eye on the street as he pulled out his cell phone. "Baker?"

"Don't tell me you forgot my order."

"No, I have it. Listen, I just ran into Boris Dragov."

"Is he an old school chum?" Tim Baker asked with a laugh.

"He's Russian and I didn't think he was even in the country. That can't be good, and I don't believe in coincidences."

"I'll pass it along. Sanchez isn't back yet, but a team will be out. Are you following them?"

"Of course. I mean, I'm going to try. I've never done it before, but I'm sure I can keep them in sight. Gotta go, they just passed my hiding spot."

"I'll get a lock on your phone from here. Just back off and don't be a hero, buddy. We'll let the real ones handle this. And don't let my coffee get cold."

"Roger." David hung up the phone and eased into traffic, trying to stay within sight of the sedan but far enough back they wouldn't spot him.

Three blocks up, the sedan turned into a busy strip mall. David sped up to keep pace, and barely caught sight of them as they parked in front of a Publix supermarket.

*Backup is on the way, all I have to do is keep visual contact with them,* he thought. *Just do my job.* He parked a few cars away from them and watched as the two men walked into the store. David tried to be casual, picking up a hand basket and wandering over to the fruits and vegetables. He did need some onions for dinner tonight, and he thought he was out of milk.

"Really? This isn't shopping time," he whispered and felt his face grow red when an elderly woman close to him turned with a quizzical look. "Sorry," he mumbled.

He put onions in the hand basket, since he had to look the part of a casual shopper, and began wandering the store in search of the two men.

David's goal was to stay an aisle or two behind them, keep them in sight, and then when the backup arrived he could simply walk out, after paying for his onions.

Boris Dragov was standing in the corner, near the doors leading to the stockroom, eyeing the egg cartons. David watched as he opened a carton, tapped on each egg in turn, closed the carton, and put it back in place. Each subsequent carton was done the same exact way, and it was mesmerizing to David.

"What is the point of that?" David said softly.

The barrel of the pistol jammed suddenly into David's back.

"The point of it is simple: to distract you long enough so I could get behind you, stick a gun in your ribcage and ask you to nicely walk to the stockroom without incident," the voice said in David's ear in a heavy Russian accent.

"You're making a big mistake."

The driver pushed him with the pistol. "I have no qualms shooting you right here. It really is up to you how this is going to play out."

"Fine. But I don't know who you think I am." David lifted the hand basket, hoping to distract the driver with it or use it as a makeshift weapon, but Boris was already next to him and gripping the handle.

"I will count to three, and then he will shoot you. Is that really what you want?" Boris asked. "I just want to talk to you. I'm not here to buy eggs, I'm here to gather information. Do you understand? I will not ask again. I am sure you have men on their way to take over for you, people who do this for a living. I don't feel like you do. Am I right?"

"I don't know who you think I am . . ." David said but Boris suddenly jabbed David in the neck, the strike choking him and forcing him to take a step back.

The driver and Boris grabbed him by the arms and dragged him through the stockroom doors and straight past the open bay doors and onto a landing dock.

"Bring him over there," Boris said, and they lifted David, still holding his throat and trying to breath, and propped him against the side of the building.

"Why are you following us?" Boris asked.

The driver searched David's body and pulled David's revolver out of its holster and stuck it in his waistband, tossing his cell phone into the weeds. "He's clean now."

David saw stars and he wanted to vomit. He'd never felt

such intense pain in his life, but knew he needed to recover in order to get out of this alive.

The gun was jabbed back into his ribs by the driver.

"We're going to do this quickly, my friend." Boris smiled. "I have to be honest, it doesn't look too good for you right now. You don't seem to be very cooperative, and I really can't have that. I'm going to ask why you are trailing us, and I had better get the real answer."

David needed to stall, but he wasn't sure how. "I'm trying to buy onions for dinner."

Boris almost looked pained. "That's not the right answer."

The driver punched David in the stomach, but David was able to turn and take the shot in his side. His training kicked in, and he head butted the driver and dropped him to the pavement, reaching out to grab him before he fell so David could get a weapon.

The driver rolled over and tried to rise on one knee, exposing David's gun.

David gripped it and pulled it. His goal was to point it at the man's head and keep Boris from striking or shooting him until the cavalry arrived.

When the driver swung around and put a hand on the barrel David's reflexes took over and he pulled the gun back, finger squeezing the trigger. It happened so fast with two quick gunshots.

David watched as the driver fell back to the ground, a pinpoint of crimson on his shirt getting larger and larger. He was still breathing but it was coming in wet-sounding gasps. David watched, fascinated, as the driver stopped breathing and seemed to sigh.

It was getting dark, and David felt clammy. The gun slipped from his hands and he heard it bounce on the ground as if it was in the far distance.

*Two shots?*

David felt something sticky running down his side, coating his hand. He'd been shot. He'd been hit.

Boris Dragov aimed the gun at David's head but only watched as David lost control of his legs and fell to the ground, his face slamming into the pavement.

Davis Luciano thought about the onions he needed for dinner tonight, before his world went black.

# EPISODE SIX
## Alpha Male

# ARMAND ROSAMILIA | A.K. WATERS

RAMZAN UMAROV WISHED THERE WERE MORE OPEN ZOOS IN HIS native land. Even as a small child, an annual highlight was the Moscow Circus traveling through nearby cities. His parents would take him and he would marvel at the elephants, great cats and monkeys. It was this handful of warm memories that got him through some deep pits in his life, and to this day seeing a monkey, dancing from tree branches and going about its business, brought a grin to his face.

The ones before him were squirrel monkeys and Ramzan knew he could sit here for hours and watch them. He wanted to see how they interacted with one another, and what their small society structure was like. Ramzan immediately focused on the largest male, the alpha in the cage. He was standing above the rest, surveying his prison kingdom. Ramzan's eyes gleamed when the alpha male squawked, driving the rest as far away from him as they could get.

"That is the power of dominating with a simple command," Ramzan whispered. "Just the simple fear of your actions, and the reaction of those around you. Wonderful."

"Sir, it is done."

Ramzan kept himself from turning back and slapping the man. "I take it everything went as planned?"

"Of course."

Of course. If it had not, the man would have run. He would have hidden and waited for the inevitable hammer to be dropped upon him by Ramzan. He would have begged for death. Because Ramzan was the alpha male, and all he needed to do was squawk and everyone around him would flee in fear.

"The weapon is once again fully functional?"

"Yes. I was also able to procure a backup battery for it, and he showed me the proper installation." The man stepped up to the rail next to Ramzan. "I also found out where the original parts came from, and if need be I can order them directly."

"Excellent." Ramzan waved his hand. "I will meet you at the car in one hour. Then we can begin our drive around Miami."

"I took the liberty of filling the gas tank as well, sir."

Ramzan laughed. "Even better. In fact, go find the nearest American fast food restaurant. I am in the mood to try something different today. The Americans brag about their culinary skills. I want to see what the average person in Miami eats. I want to experience what they are shoving down their throats, before I destroy their precious city."

"Do you want ketchup for your French fries?"

Ramzan nodded. "Find out how they eat these items and what condiments they use. I want the full experience." Ramzan went back to staring at the alpha male monkey, who was dominating one of the smaller females. He noted the manner and ease at which the male worked, and the arrogance of the monkey in front of the others. He was showing off his power, and daring another, lesser, male to step up and take what was his.

Ramzan knew it would never happen. The alpha male was the true king of the jungle.

"HOW IS HE?" JENNIFER SANCHEZ ASKED TIM BAKER AS SHE approached the hospital room. Tim looked tired, and she was sure he hadn't slept all night. Despite Luciano and Baker only working together sporadically, she knew a bond had formed between the two men and they loved working together whenever possible.

"They don't know if he's going to make it. The bullet is still lodged inside of him and it nicked some organs. That's all they'll tell me. He's been in surgery for the last twenty minutes." Tim sat back down on the chair in the hall and sighed.

"You need to get some coffee," Jennifer said. "You look like shit."

"Thanks for noticing. These nurses have been feeding me coffee all night."

"Maybe you need to go home and get in a power nap." Jennifer leaned against the wall. She was pretty tired herself but she'd gotten three hours of sleep at Magic Productions before the sun came up. "Or at least get some real food. I hear the cafeteria downstairs makes a killer filet mignon."

Tim laughed. "I don't doubt it. Whenever I have a hot date I take her here. Who needs fancy South Beach restaurants when you can come to University of Miami Hospital, right? I could use something light to eat and something besides burnt coffee to drink." He stood and closed his eyes. For a second Jennifer thought he was sleeping in the standing position. "I think I'm going to crash in the backseat of my car for a couple of hours. If he comes out of surgery, I want you to wake me up. Even if he comes out in the next five minutes."

"Tim, you can go home. I'll take over from here. Get some

sleep because this is far from over. We still have so much work to do, and I need you now more than ever. I already called in the favor and you'll be staying on with us until this is resolved."

Tim was staring at Jennifer like he wanted to say something.

"Go get some sleep, Baker. Your little buddy will need you at full strength."

Tim laughed. "I'll let him know you called him that. I'm sure Dave will appreciate it." His smile faded. "I told him to stay put and not be the hero. He isn't the type. If I'd known he was going to keep following, I would have . . ."

"Would have what? Magically teleported there and took the bullet for him? Damn, you know more than most how this game is played. You understand the risks we all take on the job. And Luciano sure knew the risks."

"He was a desk jockey. He's not cut out for the field."

"Luciano wanted the experience, and that's why I paired him with you. I knew he'd learn what it was like out in the real world. You aren't a risk-taker, you might mess around with the jokes but you're a great agent. I'd love to have you full time on this team, except you're too valuable to other agencies. I knew if anyone could show Luciano the ropes it would be you."

"But I wasn't there when he needed the best advice I could offer: back off and let the experts take over."

"So it was your fault he went for donuts? Don't beat yourself up over this. Go get some sleep. I have a bad feeling about how today is going to play out."

Tim nodded. "Me, too."

# ARMAND ROSAMILIA | A.K. WATERS

~

**BORIS DRAGOV KNEW BETTER THAN TO GO BACK TO THE SAFE HOUSE.**
With Andre dead and the ACES member either in the hospital or already gone, he knew there would be a price to pay from both the Americans and his bosses back in Moscow. He was amazed he was able to get Andre hidden near a dumpster and retrieve the body, even with four police cars and an unmarked ACES vehicle swarming the shopping center.

But he wasn't going back until he retrieved the weapon. To do so would be foolish. At this juncture, it was either finishing the mission or die trying. Boris had been in the room or been the executioner when agents came back empty-handed, and the answer was always the same: you failed, and you will never do so again.

Of course, driving around in the sedan with a dead body in the trunk was nerve-wracking until he'd checked into the seedy by the hour hotel just west of Fort Lauderdale, far enough away from the action but close enough to still monitor what was going on.

Sleep had eluded him so far, and a cold shower wasn't enough to take the edge off. He decided to take a walk in the morning air of Florida, collect his thoughts, and get some coffee and something to eat.

*Why did you let the ACES man live?* He asked himself over and over, but an answer wouldn't come. If the man died in surgery or was D.O.A. by the time they rushed him to the hospital, he wouldn't have to dwell on it. But until he knew what ultimately happened to him, he knew it would gnaw at his thoughts.

Boris walked to a Dunkin Donuts a block away, running the confrontation over in his mind, from all different angles and speeds. He could see the struggle between Andre and the man, and the gun appearing and the shot going off. Boris had legendary reactions, so when the pistol appeared in his hand like an extra finger it was no big deal. The trigger was pulled like it had been fifty times in his life, without a hesitation or a thought. In movies they talked about a weapon becoming an extension of your shoulder, arm and hand. It was true.

Yet . . . the man was on the ground, eyes rolling in his head, blood leaking from the gunshot wound. But he was alive, and he'd seen the two of them. Boris was confident the man had at some point during the tail called it in. He obviously recognized Boris, enough to break from typical protocol and follow. He'd made the mistake of getting too close. Obviously a rookie. Most likely not even a field agent, but a gopher out getting coffee.

Boris ordered a large black coffee and a cinnamon raisin bagel with tuna, one of the best combinations he'd found in America. When the young girl behind the counter scrunched her nose at his order and asked him to repeat it, he wanted to reach into his jacket and extend his pistol in one fluid motion and snub out her pitiful life.

He ignored her, repeated his order slowly and sarcastically, purposely allowing his Russian accent to confuse her. But in the end he switched the coffee to decaf. He didn't feel like shooting up the place and killing every man, woman and child just now. And he thought he might. He needed sleep.

The walk back to the hotel was longer than he remembered, with his thoughts racing and his mind a jumbled mix. This wasn't like him. Normally he was in total control, and looked for things in each mission to keep him amused and involved because most jobs were pretty cut and dry: find the target, eliminate the target, move on to next target.

*It's not the kill, it's the thrill of the chase,* he thought. But this time the iconic line from Deep Purple didn't feel fun anymore. It felt like a constriction, as if he'd placed a time limit to himself, and it no longer made sense. He needed to finish this work as soon as possible and forget about it. There were plenty of people to be killed out there, and time was wasting.

He sat down on the lumpy bed of his hotel room and sighed. The usual safe houses for him were exotic places, million dollar homes in classy neighborhoods with a view of the women on the beach. Boris turned the small television to a news channel, excited when he saw the news footage of the attack, but then realized it was just looped footage since no new ones had occurred. Yet.

The cinnamon raisin bagel with tuna went down quickly, and he didn't even savor the taste. He was too busy thinking. Osvaldo Rivera was dead, a bullet through his head, and there weren't many people around that could kill a man in broad daylight with such ease.

Boris sipped his hot coffee. Who could do such damage, such concentrated destruction? The shootings seemed random enough, but there was a definite game plan to create as much chaos as they could. Yet, it had stopped suddenly. If Boris had the weapon, and the goal was to turn Miami into a war zone, he would follow the same basic course and the idea would be the same. He'd been trained to do just this move if the time came to attack . . .

Boris nearly spilled his coffee. Was it really so obvious he'd immediately dismissed it? There was only one person he trusted right now, but it was still risky. If Moscow had already figured out this mission was spinning out of control, they might have already decided to pull the plug on it, call him back to Moscow and put another agent on it. And Boris would end up in an unmarked grave in a field somewhere.

Boris dialed the number from his burner cell phone and held his breath. There were certain keywords and phrases he'd put together with his contact over the years, and if there was any problem it would go into effect.

"Da?" the voice at the other end said. "Can I help you?" in Russian.

"You might be able to, but I'm not sure."

There was a pause and Boris was about to hang up. "What are you doing over there? The Complex is going wild with rumors, saying it is you shooting those people and creating a huge problem."

The line was safe. "Yuri, it isn't me."

"It looks like your handiwork on a crazier scale." Yuri dropped his voice on the phone. "They think you've gone mad with power suddenly, and are going to plunge us into a war we are not yet ready for."

"Why would I do that?"

"Does that ever really matter? You are going to become the scapegoat unless you fix this. Can you fix this?"

"I can, but I need some information quickly. I want to know what other operatives are currently working in Florida, and move the search farther out if need be."

"You think it is a rogue?"

"I think it is someone making it look like Russia is interested in creating this havoc. This isn't the work of local thugs or gangbangers. The pattern is pretty easy to figure out when you look at it. Someone has taken the same courses and training as the rest of us. The problem becomes there are possibly a score of agents who could be behind it."

"I'm working on it as we speak."

"Thank you, old friend." Yuri was a scientist and a loyal man. It also helped he was married to the younger sister of Boris, and he was extremely afraid of the power Boris held both in the svr and in the family.

"Call me back every two hours, on the hour, and update me. If you cannot, send a K text." They called it a K text because it was actually just the letter K you would text, which meant you were disposed or busy but you weren't in any danger or trouble. You never wanted a Q text. And definitely not a P text.

After hanging up, Boris was hungry again. He suddenly felt better about his chances of finding whoever was behind the attacks. Now it wasn't just a question of completing a mission and retrieving the weapon, it was also about life and death. His own. To come back empty-handed was akin to suicide.

He decided another walk to Dunkin Donuts was in order, and another cinnamon raisin bagel with tuna. He hoped the girl behind the counter wouldn't ruin his sudden good mood by rolling her eyes. There was only so much Boris Dragov would take before he started shooting.

**"HOW MANY PEOPLE YOU THINK YOU'VE KILLED?" KOSTAS ASKED** Dale Comstock as they sat in one of the meeting rooms of Magic Productions.

Dale grinned without looking up, cleaning his multiple weapons before him on the table. "How many have you killed, tech?"

"Thirty-seven," Kostas said with a nervous laugh. The real number was three.

"Then I have more confirmed kills," Dale said and picked his head up for a second, locking eyes with Kostas. "By a lot. And mine are actually real."

Kostas turned away and was pissed he'd done so, not able to trade stares with this cartoon action hero of a man. He closed his eyes and folded his hands behind his head, leaning back and ignoring the snicker from Dale.

*I've had the same basic training as you, pal,* Kostas thought. *I was one of the top graduates in my class. Especially when I hacked into the system and put myself at the top, but I could've done the work.* He was also a pretty good shot, but his main forte was the technical aspects of the ACES team. Anyone could learn to hold a pistol steady and shoot someone (in his estimation), but it took actual skill to hack into a university halfway across the country and give himself a doctorate in a subject he had no idea about. Or when he methodically got back at everyone in his troubled youth with new warrants and deletion of certain public and private records.

"Ever kill a man with your bare hands?" Kostas asked.

"Yes. And I shot a man in Reno." Dale didn't look up from

his cleaning. "Just to watch him die."

"Seriously?" Kostas asked.

Dale laughed again. "That's actually a line from *Folsom Prison Blues*."

Kostas stood up and walked to the side counter, looking to get a cup of coffee and try to relax. *This dude is way too intimidating.*

"I could use a cup of black coffee, if you don't mind."

"Not a problem." Kostas pulled two Styrofoam cups from the cabinet. "I just assumed they hooked you up to a battery or poured oil and gasoline down your throat to keep you going."

"They only do that right before I go back into the warehouse, until the next mission."

"Good to know," Kostas said.

"So tell me about Jennifer Sanchez."

Kostas stiffened as he poured the coffee. He cleared his throat, taking his time. "What do you want to know?"

"She's quite the boss."

Kostas didn't know if Dale was messing with him. "What do you mean by that?" He handed him a cup of coffee

"No need to get defensive." Dale grinned. "You two aren't romantically linked, are you?"

"No."

"I didn't think so. Jennifer Sanchez seems like the kind of boss that plays by the rules. No flirting or dating the ACES members around her."

"I'm sure she wouldn't date any ACES members no matter where they were," Kostas said quickly.

"Something tells me I'm glad I don't work for ACES."

Kostas sat down in his chair and sipped his coffee, trying to ignore the obvious attempt to get a rise out of him. He glanced at Dale and watched the man down the cup of coffee in one gulp, even though it was scorching hot. *Damn.*

"Mind if I get another cup?" Dale asked.

Kostas shrugged and watched the man move like a panther across the room. "How long have you and Martin known one another?"

Dale poured another cup and looked at Kostas. "That's classified knowledge."

"I'm sure I can look it up."

"I'm sure you already have. I'm not in the mood for small talk, if it's all the same to you. I need to finish cleaning my weapons and getting ready for the next attack."

"Suit yourself. I'm just trying to kill time." Kostas was getting annoyed.

"There isn't time to waste. You need to focus on the day or days ahead and nothing more."

"Huh? You asked me about Jennifer. Does that have to do with the mission?"

Dale smiled. "I never said your mission and my mission were exactly the same thing. Did I?"

Kostas had had enough. "I'm going to my office. If I hear anything I'll let you know. Keep playing with your guns."

"If I hear anything I'll let you know," Dale said before going back to cleaning.

Kostas walked out; completely frustrated the man had gotten the best of him.

≈

RAMZAN WAS STILL STARING AT THE MONKEYS WHEN DMITRY returned with his food, wrapped cheeseburgers and French fries in small red cardboard boxes, grease soaking through the paper bag.

"I had an idea when you were gone," Ramzan said quietly, ignoring the offered bag of food. He looked around and pointed at the many couples, children and workers moving around the Miami Zoo. "Get the weapon."

"Sir?"

Ramzan felt his cheeks get red. "Did you question me?"

"Of course not." Dmitry looked nervous. "I just don't want to get caught in the zoo when the people turn."

"Neither do I." Ramzan smiled and took the fast food bag from his driver's hand. "Start in the far corner of the park and casually walk to the entrance, turning people as you go."

Dmitry nodded. "Whatever you wish."

"I wish for the park to be turned into a combat zone." Ramzan pointed at the alpha male squirrel monkey. "I want him turned, and only him. He will show his absolute dominance in his kingdom. Do you understand?"

"Yes." Dmitry smiled. "Can the weapon turn the animals?"

"We're going to find out, but I don't see why not. I'm not completely sure of the technology but it seems like it will bring out their aggressive nature. Let me know what happens when he is hit."

"I will."

"Walk me back to the car, but don't use the weapon until you get to the farthest point away from the exits. I want mass hysteria when it begins."

"What about the animals? Besides the squirrel monkey?"

"If the opportunity presents itself, but don't go out of your way. If you think you can get the cages opened then do it."

"I don't want to get attacked."

Ramzan smiled. "Use your best judgment."

They got back to the car, which was parked two lots over. People were coming and going, oblivious to the terror about to be unleashed. Ramzan sat in the passenger seat and put the food bag down. "Which soft drink is mine?"

"Either one. I haven't taken a sip yet," Dmitry said. Ramzan shoved two French fries in his mouth as his driver went to the trunk, procuring the zombie gun.

"Hurry back, we have a full day ahead of us," Ramzan called to him. "And it is hot in this car."

"Yes, sir." Dmitry gave him the car keys. "Feel free to move the car to the exit, and keep it running with the air conditioner on."

Ramzan opened a wrapped cheeseburger and took a bite. It was tasty. Dmitry disappeared through the lines of cars and happy people who were just looking for a fun day at the zoo. He imagined the local news tonight, interviewing some of these same families, as they talked about being bitten by husbands and wives, children sinking their teeth into one another. If Miami thought they were out of the woods yet . . . Ramzan was suddenly quite happy with the way things had turned out. It was like he'd planned this dramatic pause before the attacks started anew, this time with even more force.

No one would be spared. No area of Miami would be safe. No part of America would feel secure after this monumental day.

Ramzan took another bite of the burger and smiled. He

hoped before the structure of the United States came crumbling down around him, he'd get a chance to taste another of these delicious treats.

He finished his food and drink and slid into the driver's side. He needed a better look at the chaos. People were still in line and entering the zoo. It was another beautiful Florida day. If he didn't dislike this country so much he could get used to the life of excess and ignorance. Ramzan envisioned a perfect world where his radical Russia took control of the entire world, destroying the weak ideology of Mother Russia and shaping it back into a global power, controlling all aspects of the world's resources and power.

The phone ringing startled him. He frowned when he saw the number. "What?"

"You have a problem."

Ramzan snorted. "I doubt it."

"Boris Dragov knows you are in Miami."

"Impossible. We sailed in. No airports, no reason they would know we're here. In fact, only a handful of our superiors know we aren't where we are supposed to be. This is not good."

"No one else has put it together yet."

"It doesn't matter. Boris knowing is the worst possible scenario. I've seen what he's capable of." Ramzan shuddered despite the air conditioning from the car set to high. "When did he find out?"

"His contact alerted him moments ago. Luckily, we monitor everything in and out. It was simple enough to intercept it."

"Who is his contact?"

"I cannot tell."

Ramzan knew but thought he'd try anyway. Someday Yuri, his contact in the Yasenevo District, would slip up and give away the contact's name. And then Ramzan would eliminate them. "How much do you think he knows?"

"He knows you are there and has most likely guessed you are behind the attacks. I didn't have enough time to throw them off onto another agent."

Ramzan glanced in his rearview mirror. He wouldn't have been surprised to see Boris, grinning maniacally, seated behind him with a garrote in his hands. The man was that deadly. "I can't stop now. The second phase of our plan is already in motion, and in order to keep this going I need to do what I have to do. Regardless of my own well-being or safety. This is all for Mother Russia, after all."

"Where are you with the second phase?"

"I'm putting it in motion as we speak."

"Should I let you go?"

"No. I have someone else doing the dirty work, of course."

"Dmitry?"

Ramzan laughed. "Exactly."

"You do know he is married to a cousin of Boris Dragov, no?"

"Of course I know. But he is a loyal man to me, and I have no doubt he would kill Boris if I asked him to."

"He could try," Yuri said quietly.

Before Ramzan could respond he heard the first scream from inside the park, even with the car running and the air conditioner on. "I need to go. It has begun again."

"Good luck. And be careful."

Two women came running from the exit, fear in their eyes. They pushed through the masses attempting to enter to see the animal displays, enjoy the educational and fun of a working zoo, oblivious to the horror awaiting them inside.

≈

**"I'M LOOKING FOR CHIEF ALVAREZ," MARTIN SAID TO THE WOMAN** behind the desk. The Miami Police Department was buzzing with activity, but he didn't know if it was always like this or if the attacks yesterday had worked them into a frenzy. There were so many uniform and plainclothes officers moving in and out of the lobby it was startling.

"The chief is tied up at the moment," the woman said. She eyed Martin suspiciously. "What is this in reference to?"

"I need to speak to him. It is of utmost importance."

"He's busy. Take a seat and someone will get right to you."

Martin knew exactly what that meant: he'd sit in the lobby until he grew bored or impatient and left, or Chief Alvarez would simply wander by and he'd miss him completely. "I don't want to announce my credentials, but let's just say I have precedent over anything he currently has in front of him."

"Are you the Governor of Florida?"

Martin shook his head. "No, I'm not, but . . ."

"Then have a seat and someone will get right to you."

"I'm with the ACES team."

The woman shrugged. "And I'm on the PTA." She pointed to the chairs in the lobby. "Have a seat."

Martin didn't know what Chief Alvarez looked like, but

he decided to wait this woman out. She was simply doing her job, but he figured anyone of high rank walking through the lobby could get him an audience. He'd give it twenty minutes before he pulled rank and had Jennifer call Kim in Langley.

"Mike?"

Martin turned to see a gorgeous woman standing and smiling near the main doors. She was resplendent in a pant suit, dirty blonde hair cascading down her shoulders, and the cutest birthmarks on her cheeks. "Missy?"

She smiled. "What are you doing here? Stalking me? I can easily get a restraining order, you know." Missy winked. "I have connections in this place."

"I hope you do." Martin went up to her and resisted the urge to hug her. She looked beautiful out of uniform. "I need to see Chief Alvarez."

"I'm heading to his office now, actually."

"Mind if I tag along?"

Missy chuckled. "He might. But it would take the sting out of the tongue-lashing I'm sure is headed my way."

"What do you mean?"

Missy stopped smiling. "Joe is dead, the only partner I've had in my short career. There are attacks going on in Miami, but protocol means I have to be pulled from active duty for a few days while they sort it out. Meanwhile, we are so short on patrol officers, and I keep getting a million questions from the brass upstairs over what I did or didn't see. This will be my fourth interview, but first with the chief. He isn't exactly a pleasant man to chat with, if you know what I mean. It's like being called to the principal's office when you're caught smoking in the girl's room."

"Then let me do all the talking," Martin said. He glanced at the officer seated at the desk and staring at him. "You just need to get me past your guard dog."

Missy laughed. "Jenny isn't so bad. A little crazy, but she's actually my best friend in the entire world. Trust me, you'll love her."

"I doubt it."

Missy went up to the desk. "Are you giving this guy a hard time?"

Jenny looked up, eyes twinkling and her mouth spread in a grin. "Maybe he was bothering me."

"I'd like you to meet Mike Martin. Mike, this is Jenny Adams. My bestest friend and big toe."

Martin smiled and nodded. "It's a pleasure to meet you, Jenny."

Jenny laughed. "The pleasure is all mine." She glanced at Missy. "I've heard so much about you."

"All good, I hope."

Jenny winked at Missy. "Mostly. Where are you kids heading to, lunch? Sex in a broom closet?"

"Jenny!"

"Really? You can feel the sexual tension between you two. You could cut it with a knife, or a glowing orange—"

"Stop!" Missy yelled. "Please don't go there." She took Martin's hand in hers. "Let's get away from her before she tells all my secrets."

"What's orange?" Martin asked, squeezing her soft hand.

"Nothing." Missy shot Jenny a dirty look.

"It takes three AA batteries," Jenny offered with another grin. "You kids have a great time."

They walked up to the bank of elevators.

"You kids have a great time?" Martin asked.

Missy laughed. "She's in her late thirties, although at times she acts like she's much younger than you and I. I love her to death."

"I take it you told her about me."

"Of course. I told her about all your fumbling around and lame attempts to get me to go out with you."

"You gave me your phone number."

"It's a fake one. It rings at the arena."

"I had Kostas check it. Nice try," Martin said. The elevator doors opened.

They rode the elevator in awkward silence, Martin trying to think of something witty or interesting to say before the doors opened. He stared at her profile next to him, loving the way her smile lit up her face, and the way she slowly rocked back and forth, purposely looking anywhere but at him.

The doors opened and Martin motioned for her to exit first like a gentleman.

"I see you're still smitten with me," Missy said.

"No idea what you're talking about."

Missy got ahead of him. "Then why are you checking out my ass?"

Martin, who was indeed checking out her ass, looked at the awards and posters lining the hallway. "No idea what you're talking about," he repeated.

Chief Alvarez was an imposing man, with a weathered complexion and fixed beady eyes. He was watching as the two approached, arms folded across his wide chest.

"Chief, I'd like to introduce Mike Martin from the ACES

team," Missy said.

Martin offered his hand but Alvarez didn't take it. *This is going to be fun*, Martin thought.

"I know who you are and why you're here." He walked into his office without inviting them to follow. "Your boss made it abundantly clear you and your people were in charge of this situation." Alvarez sat down and put his hands on his desk. "Of course, I see it differently. Especially when the mass hysteria gripping *my* Miami is so prevalent. I don't care what the ACES team *thinks* they are going to do, I want answers and I want a solution before the next attack."

Martin didn't want to get into a pissing match with Chief Alvarez, especially in his office. He completely understood the frustration the situation and sudden loss of control the department suddenly had. Martin had been in this spot many times in the last year, although usually not on such a grand scale.

"I'm sure my boss, Kim, apprised you of the current situation."

"She told me everything I already knew. Nothing about the cause of this virus."

"It's not a virus," Martin answered quickly.

Chief Alvarez smiled. "You've just given me more information than she did in forty-five minutes of her prepared bullshit. Have a seat." He eyed Missy. "You can wait outside."

"In all due respect, I'd like Officer Lockhart to stay. She was witness to part of this mess, and I'd like some insight from her as well." *Plus, she is damn cute and I want to spend more time with her.*

"Fine. I need to address some of the moves she made,

anyway. Since you were there, perhaps you can give some of your own insight. Officer Lockhart, do you object to this guy being in the room while we talk?"

Missy glanced at Martin. "No, Chief."

"Excellent." Chief Alvarez leaned back in his chair. "I'm suspending you with pay for the next thirty days and taking you off of the active roster."

"You can't be serious," Missy said, lunging forward and planting her hands on the chief's desk. "I did nothing wrong."

"Chief Alvarez, in all due respect, sir, Missy did nothing wrong."

The chief grinned. "Missy?" he looked at her. "So we're on first name basis already? You made quite an impression on this guy, it seems."

Missy stood up, anger clearly in her eyes. "You can't suspend me. I did nothing wrong. I want to see my union rep. Don't I get a hearing? Due process?"

Now Chief Alvarez leaned back in his chair farther and cupped his hands on his head. He was blatantly smiling. "If we were in normal times, you'd be getting a hearing. The board would find you did nothing wrong, and you'd be back on the street within a week. But these are trying times. Zombies, Mayan calendars, a recession . . . and ACES showing up on my doorstep and commandeering my hotshot rookie for their own purposes."

"What?" Martin asked.

"She's all yours. Langley has decided I need to loan her to ACES for the next thirty days, effective immediately."

Martin smiled. *Kim didn't miss a beat, and you could get nothing past that woman.* "Excellent."

Missy turned to Martin. "Excellent? What did you do?"

"I didn't do anything."

Missy jabbed his chest with a finger. "Am I some sort of conquest to you, some chick you're looking to impress so you can bang me? Seriously?"

"Not at all."

Missy turned back to the chief. "I refuse the assignment. I'm a Miami Police Officer, and damn good at my job in the short time I've been on the force. You can't do this to me."

"It's out of my hands," Chief Alvarez said. He turned to Martin. "I hope you realize what you asked for."

"I didn't ask for this," Martin said. But had he? When he'd talked to Kim and Jennifer in their quick conference call before Jennifer left for the hospital, he had brought her up again. And his formal paperwork from The Setai incident was heaping with praise for her. Kim had asked him about her, point-blank asking if it was a romantic thing. Of course, he'd denied it. How could it be if they had never dated or spent more than a few minutes together doing work-related things? If Kim had asked Martin if he was attracted to her or interested, he would have answered in the affirmative. Now Martin knew why she hadn't prodded or asked.

Now Missy turned back to Martin. "I'm going to fight this. As far as I'm concerned, you are dead to me. Get it, you arrogant prick? You will never get in my pants. I don't care if you're the last man alive. You blew it."

"I had nothing to do with this," Martin said. "I swear."

"To think I was going to ask you to lunch, flirt with you, and see where it got me." Missy threw up her hands. "It got me in this mess."

Chief Alvarez stopped smiling. "In all seriousness, Missy, this is a career-making opportunity. I can name a dozen guys right now who are going to be quite envious of the position you gained today. And I want you to know you deserve it, wherever it takes you."

"I want it to take me out on the streets of Miami, in my patrol car, serving and protecting this community."

"It just might, and in bigger ways than you can through the department. Keep an open mind, Lockhart. You might be doing some real good."

Martin felt very awkward standing there, and once again he was tongue-tied.

"I need your badge and your weapon. From what I understand, ACES will be giving you temporary identification and a weapon of your choice."

Missy put her shield and holster on the desk and sighed. "This isn't right."

"I think long-term you'll disagree." Chief Alvarez extended a hand to Missy. "Good luck, and make Miami PD proud of you."

Missy reluctantly took his hand and shook it, but Martin could see she was deflated.

"I'm done here. I want to be kept in the loop when it comes to further attacks, is that clear?"

Martin nodded. "As soon as we get anything, we'll try to coordinate with your staff so we can defuse them as they come."

"I've pulled in neighboring municipalities as well as the Sheriff's Office to assist. Everyone is on high alert. We just need to know what we're looking for."

"Kim will tell me when it's time," Martin said.

"I hope it isn't too late by then. Dismissed."

Missy shot out of the office and nearly ran down the hall to the elevator.

"Look, I had nothing to do with this," Martin said.

"It sure looks like you were very instrumental in ruining my career."

"This will be a good thing for you."

Missy didn't even look at him. "Doubtful. I've only been on the police force for months and now I'm getting special treatment and joining a secret government team. I'll be a pariah around these halls when I return. All because of you."

"I'm sorry," Martin replied weakly.

The elevator doors opened and Missy stepped inside. She put up her hand to stop Martin from joining her. "You can take the next one. I'm mad at you."

Martin nodded. He wasn't going to push her. He'd give her some space and let her cool off. Maybe a ride alone would help her.

"You know what the worst part is?" she asked as the doors began to close. "I'm wearing a red thong because I thought there was even a small chance of seeing you today. Now you'll never see it."

≈

DMITRY WAS HAVING THE TIME OF HIS LIFE. HE'D STARTED IN THE farthest southern corner of the Miami Zoo, casually walking up to a family of four as they stepped off the monorail and approached the Rhea enclosure.

The zombie gun's yellow light barely registered in the direct sunlight, but Dmitry could see the change immediately come over the father when he was shot. Dmitry heard the wife scream but was already jogging to the west and down the path, looking for the next people to turn into monsters.

He stopped at a huge enclosure and read what the animals were: Thompson's gazelle. He aimed the weapon and one of the herd immediately started to slam itself into those around it.

A couple, previously at the other end of the display, stopped kissing as they watched the gazelle attacking the others. The man pointed a finger at Dmitry. "What did you do?"

Dmitry smiled and lifted the gun to eye level. "I'll give you until three to run."

The man only seemed irritated now. "Are you threatening me with a toy gun? Really?"

"This isn't a toy." Dmitry pulled the trigger. "You'll see."

The man's demeanor didn't change too much, but Dmitry knew it had worked. He took another step in Dmitry's direction before gaining speed.

*Uh oh.* Dmitry hadn't thought it through, and the man was heading right for him. He turned and began running. *I should have shot his ugly wife and let her bite him.*

"Hey, watch it!" a young lady yelled as Dmitry barreled past her and almost knocked her over. Her scream stopped Dmitry, and he slowed to a fast walk and turned, happy to see the man attacking her.

Around the next bend was a large group of children and adults, all wearing matching bright yellow T-shirts. Dmitry opened fire, hitting only three of them and watching the chaos as the others were attacked. A woman ran past him and he hesitated, not daring to shoot her and risk being attacked. Using the zombie gun was an odd experience, since he was used to pointing and killing as enemies approached. Instead, he had to keep in mind a fearful running person would be biting him if he wasn't careful in choosing his victims.

He walked fifty yards around the bend and shot three more random people, giving them wide berths as they attacked those around them. The zoo was packed today, and Dmitry decided to keep moving and shoot people in the distance, not knowing how far a range he actually had with the zombie gun. It was worth testing it out and seeing what damage he could do, and at what range.

Dmitry didn't discriminate. He shot men, women, children, animals and anything in his path. By only shooting one out of every four or five people, he kept those shot occupied with fresh screaming people. He would aim, shoot, and then watch the person change and attack. Most times the potential victim would run away, but the zombie would find an innocent bystander in the area and drop on them.

Already, there were patches of blood on the pathways and screams all around him. His only concern was getting lost in the maze of the Miami Zoo and being unable to escape, or worse, running right into a monster as he circled around to a spot he'd been in previously.

A woman ran past him, followed by two children. Dmitry shot the last kid and kept moving. So far, no one was putting two and two together and seeing what he was up to, and he hoped his luck wouldn't run out. He had so much work to do today before the authorities were going to show and crash his party.

Dmitry came to the squirrel monkey enclosure and saw the alpha male Boris was so fond of still standing at the top of the cage. It was a funny scene, with the other squirrel monkeys going about their business of eating, swinging and huddling below him.

He paused, knowing Boris well enough to know he would want a description of this shot and scene. He wouldn't bother asking about anything else.

"Good luck, my friend." Dmitry aimed and pulled the trigger. The alpha male slipped off the topmost branch and landed on the ground, where he moved silently to the nearest male and sunk his teeth into the neck.

"Amazing," Dmitry whispered.

The alpha male squirrel monkey began chasing his panicking cell mates around, but they had nowhere to run and nowhere to hide from the slaughter.

# EPISODE SEVEN
The Miami Zoo

**DMITRY, RAMZAN'S DRIVER, SHOT THE MAN AT POINT-BLANK RANGE** in the face, still expecting his head to explode. Instead, he just looked angrier than he'd been a second ago, when he noticed Dmitry aiming the zombie gun at people.

The man grasped Dmitry by the shirt sleeve and sunk his teeth into his shoulder. Dmitry gasped and slammed the gun across the man's head over and over, but he wouldn't let go. He was holding on with a death grip, and Dmitry could feel the man's teeth penetrating into flesh through his shirt.

Dmitry tried to focus and remember his training. He swung his frame back, allowing the man to move with him, before sliding to his right and hip-tossing the monster to the ground. He felt a chunk of his skin rip as the teeth were pulled away. Dmitry kicked him, but the zombie was still trying to attack.

Two people came running by and Dmitry tripped one of the women, circling her prone body and forcing the man to attack her. It was an easy solution to the problem, but it was getting out of hand. Dmitry figured he'd already turned at least fifty people into raging lunatics, but had only managed to get halfway out of the Miami Zoo.

He needed to pick up the pace. It had only been about thirty minutes since he'd started and he'd already done some real damage. But the police and military would be upon him in no time.

Dmitry kept his long-range shooting plan, hitting another couple of stray people as they tried to escape. There was a large crowd ahead, bottlenecking the path to the exits.

He stopped and shot the two men at the rear of the pack and smiled when they began biting those before them, creating a stampede.

The left side of the crowd was the perfect target, and he turned another five into zombies and watched the fear roll through the crowd. Strong men knocked down old ladies and children; women abandoned strollers and carried kids like footballs as they sprinted to the exit. But there were scores of panic-stricken people between them and freedom.

There was nothing else to do but steer clear of those he'd shot and make his way slowly forward, keeping away from the crowds. Dmitry didn't want to get trapped, swallowed up by slow movers and unable to run away. In the movies the undead were slow, shambling creatures, moaning and groaning, arms raised and their pupils glazed over and unseeing.

These monsters *ran*, and their burning eyes were filled with anger and hatred. Dmitry thought they were much scarier, and definitely more deadly. The only saving grace was the fact they would latch onto the closest person around and bite them. All Dmitry needed to do was keep living, normal people between him and a monster. But he knew his luck would run out at some point, especially with so many of them now loose in the zoo, and so many others bitten and/ or dead. The odds of survival were steadily getting away from him he.

Dmitry was also smart enough to know Ramzan wouldn't be too heartbroken if he died, but upset to no end if the zombie gun fell into the wrong hands. They had to protect the weapon at all costs, and the more innocent folks they could turn and run interference the better. He didn't know what the ultimate plan was and he didn't care. He was here in Miami to do whatever it took to make Ramzan happy and create conflict in America.

Plus, he was blatantly pointing a gun at people and pulling the trigger and doing real damage. Heck, each shot was killing several people. He felt invincible, although the throbbing in his shoulder was telling him differently.

The line was moving too slow and the mass of people too great. Dmitry was still way too far from the park exit, and he knew soon enough the monsters would finish with those trapped in the park behind him and rush this line in a great force.

His phone rang in his pocket.

"Hello?"

It was Ramzan. "Where are you? Six Miami police units just pulled up, and I hear another couple of sirens in the distance. It's time to get out of there."

"I can't. The people are pressing to escape. I'm trapped back here."

"They are streaming out, but there are too many people alive. You need to get out here and contain them. You are failing me and Mother Russia."

"What do you want me to do?"

"Shoot your way out if you have to."

"If I turn people into zombies in front of me, they will bite me. I've already been bitten once. My shoulder is throbbing."

Ramzan audibly sighed on the line. "Use your real weapon, you idiot."

Dmitry wanted to face-palm himself. Of course. He pulled out his Gsh-18 from his inner holster, making sure it was loaded. "Good idea. I'll see you on the other side."

"Three more police just pulled up. You'd better shoot your

way to the front and then act like a scared zoo tourist."

"Will do." Dmitry turned his cell phone off.

He heard screams coming up behind him and turned to see a bloodied teenager chasing after what was probably his mother. They ran into the crowd, the teen jumping onto the back of another woman and driving her to the ground.

"Time to get out of this mess," Dmitry said and shot into the crowd, the round striking a man in the back. Blood began to bloom and Dmitry smiled. This he could understand. Pointing and shooting meant blood and pain and power.

The crowd heard the shot and seemed to scream louder, but they still had nowhere to go. Dmitry decided on a new game plan. He pulled the zombie gun out and shot three people.

They immediately tore into others, and the lines parted to escape, some people running back into the park. Dmitry moved another fifty feet toward freedom. When one of the monsters spotted him and charged, Dmitry shot him in the head with a Gsh-18 round.

He used the zombie gun again, turning another man into a monster to take his place. The plan seemed to be working, because people were scattering now. He could see the front gates and the flashing lights from the police.

All he needed to do was to walk out, and make his way to wherever Ramzan was waiting with the car. The police were already trying to move against the crowd, guns drawn and held high. Dmitry decided to holster his Gsh-18 so he didn't get shot. Besides, he was just another scared tourist unlucky enough to be wandering around in the Miami Zoo during another strange outbreak.

The surge of bodies suddenly shifted right at him, and he was bumped about ten feet backward. He spun to get around everyone, but one of the monsters he'd recently created was on the other side. His new turn took him farther away from the gates but at least away from imminent danger.

Then he was pushed-shoved-carried by a mass of bodies down the path and away from the exit, his arms pinned as the crowd moved. He was being led away from freedom and directly into the path of a swarm of zombies searching for blood.

≈

JENNIFER SANCHEZ TRIED HER BEST TO IGNORE DALE COMSTOCK as he sat at the meeting room table and smiled. She went about her business, looking over reports her staff had recently completed and needed signed off. She sipped from her coffee mug, and made sure her pens were lined up properly before her on the table.

"If we don't get any more action here soon, I'll have to leave."

Jennifer didn't look up. "I understand."

"That would be a shame."

"Why?" She couldn't help picking her head up and immediately regretted it. His eyes were so expressive and so . . . "You itching to kill someone, soldier?"

Dale smiled. "I need to keep busy. If I don't kill someone here, it will be overseas, or in another city. Maybe even my own backyard. Who can say?"

"Where is home for you?"

"Right now I'm based in Florida, although I hardly ever get home. Panama City, in fact. It's a long way from Miami, but worth it if I had a reason to come back and visit."

Jennifer put her head back down and felt the stinging blush on her cheeks. *What are you, fifteen again?* "Panama City is a nice place. I'm sure your girlfriend likes it."

"We'll see," Dale said smoothly.

Jennifer shuffled more papers, the words and numbers blending together. *Damn, he's good. Sigue actuando como estoy quince. I set him up for that one.*

The door opened and Kostas stuck his head inside. "We have a situation you might want to squash, boss." He smiled at Comstock. "How's it going in here, G.I. Joe Action Figure Dale Comstock Limited Edition Model?"

Jennifer sighed. On one hand, she wanted to spend a few more minutes alone with Comstock, but she knew it was the wrong thing to do. She couldn't date him. Or could she? He wasn't technically ACES, and wasn't even close to working with her. Well, he was temporarily, but there shouldn't be too much of a problem once this was over and he'd gone. Of course, then he would be a half a world away, in the Middle East or Europe, doing his thing, while she was still here in Miami . . .

"Why are you smiling and ignoring me?" Kostas asked her.

Jennifer came out of her daydream embarrassed. She looked at the grinning Dale Comstock. "Lead the way to this trouble."

"Step outside into the hallway and follow the yelling," Kostas said.

Jennifer could hear a female voice screaming inside Martin's office, even with the heavy door closed. "Who is that?"

Kostas smirked. "The hot police chick. She's ripping Mikey a new one. She curses like a sailor, too. I'm glad I dodged that bullet and didn't date her."

Jennifer went to the door and held her fist up to knock. They didn't need this right now, especially with all hell about to break loose again. Jennifer could feel it in her bones. Something bad was about to happen somewhere in Miami, and the team didn't need to be fractured and bickering in the meantime.

She knocked. "We have a team meeting in two minutes."

The door suddenly burst open and Missy Lockhart nearly lunged at Jennifer. "Did you do this?"

"Do what?"

"Add me to ACES without my permission."

Kostas moved behind Dale in the hallway. "She doesn't need permission to do anything in ACES."

Jennifer put up her hands defensively. "First of all, shut up, Kostas. Secondly, I had nothing to do with you being loaned to us and neither did Martin. It was a call from above."

"This is unfair," Missy said with anger in her eyes.

Jennifer had had enough already with all the pettiness of late. "I don't remember asking you if it was fair or not."

That shut everyone up.

"You can cry all you want once you're out of my hair. You think I want some rookie cop on my team? You think you're really going to help me? I don't think so. In fact, I guarantee you'll only get in the way. But it is what it is, got it? Now shut your mouth, stop bitching like a rookie, and get some proper gear. Or should I send you back to your chief with your tail between your legs?"

Missy stared at Jennifer, her face softening. Jennifer felt bad for talking to her so rudely, but they were wasting too much time. Yet again.

"I want everyone in the meeting room right now," Jennifer said and snapped her finger for emphasis.

Missy, Martin and Kostas moved down the hall, but Comstock stayed where he was, leaning against the wall.

"That means you, too, soldier," Jennifer said. She started walking past him and didn't look into his eyes.

He casually moved to block her way.

"I would move unless you want me to move you," she said.

Comstock put his arms out, flexing his muscles as his fingers touched the walls on either side. "Do you think you can really move me?"

Jennifer charged him, putting her head down and driving like she was going for a head-butt to his crotch. At the last moment, just as Comstock sidestepped her, Jennifer came to a complete stop and planted both feet. She gripped his steel-cable bicep and pivoted, tossing him over her hip.

Comstock went down to the ground, flat on his back, with a smile on his face. "I think I'm in love," he said.

Jennifer turned away so he didn't see her blush yet again. *This is getting ridiculous,* she thought.

"Can I get a hand up, ma'am?"

Jennifer kept walking to the meeting room. "You're wasting time, soldier. Let's go."

Comstock let go a deep laugh behind her.

She knew without a doubt he'd helped her hip-toss him to

the floor, but she didn't care. If this was the game he wanted to play she thought she would play it. She walked into the meeting room. Everyone was in place.

Jennifer ignored the image and remembered the feel of Dale's gorgeous arm when she'd grabbed him. It was time to focus.

She sat down and eyed everyone in turn except Comstock when he walked in, his smile gone and looking like he meant business.

"Let's figure a few things out," Jennifer said.

Everyone's phone went off at about the same time, including the meeting room phone. That could only be Kim in Langley.

"Uh oh," Kostas said.

≈

RAMZAN WISELY DROVE THE SEDAN TO THE FAR SIDE OF THE LOT, parking between two other cars but still able to get a clear view of the Miami Zoo main exit.

The Miami P.D. was swarming the area, sirens blazing and lights flashing. They'd set up a wall of their cars about a hundred feet from the gates, stretching in both directions. As the mass of people came out, the cops stopped them to check for those infected. It wasn't working too well, as panicked people began flooding out in droves and knocking the police down in order to escape what was coming behind them.

Ramzan laughed as an officer was shoulder-blocked by a large man, and tossed to the ground. Before the officer could recover, a crazed woman was leaping onto his back and taking a large bloody chunk out of his neck.

People screamed, trying to climb over the wall of cars to safety. Ramzan wished he had a zombie gun out here, because too many people were escaping. The utter chaos was impressive, but he wanted to see more dead bodies. He wanted the death toll to me massive, and put this part of the country into a panic. Then it would spread like wildfire, and they could drive to other cities and do the same thing.

It was a win/win for Ramzan and his supporters. The attacks would throw America and Russia into World War III, and a new pecking order would rise from the ashes of nuclear war. Ramzan would take the reins and become the leader of this new world.

But first he needed Dmitry to escape so they could move on to another area of town. He hoped the alpha male squirrel monkey had already destroyed his playmates. Ramzan now wished he'd thought to have Dmitry stop and take video footage with his camera, but maybe it would have been too risky.

The first news helicopter began circling overhead and Ramzan smiled. It wouldn't be long before more joined this one, sending live coverage to all the media outlets showing the extent of this newest attack. And while the entire police force and ACES were busy trying to contain it here, another war zone would be popping up miles away.

A woman carrying her infant managed to slide across the hood of a police car with a monster in pursuit. The man behind her (probably her husband) wasn't so lucky and he was pulled down by two of the raging beasts.

Ramzan watched her run across the parking lot and past

more units driving up. She'd escaped, but there weren't many so far. The police were crowding them into one area, but it was working against them. The zombies were in their midst, biting everyone around them like a flesh buffet.

"Stupid police," Ramzan whispered. "You are helping to kill innocent people." He smiled when a second and third news helicopter joined the sky above. With any luck, the incompetence of the police force would be going live any moment. It would be a bonus feature in this wonderful reality television show, a concept these bloated Americans seemed to feed on.

Three unmarked cars and an aging custom van pulled into the parking lot and parked away from the cluster of police cars. Ramzan wasn't surprised to see it was someone important, either CIA or FBI or maybe ACES. They moved quickly and calmly, barking orders for the police to back up and let the people free of the cars.

Immediately, two squad cars were pulled back and a steady stream of people fled the scene, with the government team spread out, weapons drawn, and searching for zombies.

One of them caught Ramzan's eye. He was a huge hulk of a man, dark-skinned and carrying an HK416. The man kept one arm stiff before him, parting the crowd. A zombie ran at him and he dispatched him with a shot to the face. Now people were giving him a wide berth, but his teammates were to either side and sporadic gunfire played out as they separated the living from the infected with ease.

"Dale Comstock," Ramzan said. He'd only seen the man in video, and was quite impressed with the way he carried himself. But he was confused. He was now sure this was the

Miami ACES team, but Dale Comstock wasn't part of the equation.

Ramzan smiled. "They've called in the big guns. This is better than I thought." He just hoped Dmitry could get out without being spotted. If ACES was here, they would find him soon enough and this mission would be over. While the bosses back home would consider it a minor success, Ramzan wanted this to be a rousing one, with a nation in peril. He knew enough about Americans to know it would only take a sporting event or a celebrity scandal or sex tape to change the focus away from this tragedy.

The helicopters suddenly veered off and away from the Miami Zoo. At the same time, two news vans parked near the entrance sped off. Ramzan didn't understand what was happening, especially with so much great footage right in front of them. Even a handheld camera crew was now running back to their van and leaving.

Ramzan pulled his cell phone out to call Dmitry again. The window for getting out safely was closing. His phone had no bars. He tried to dial but couldn't get a signal. At all.

Frustrated, he tossed the phone onto the passenger seat. Something was going on but he couldn't figure it out just yet. Ramzan had a bad feeling suddenly, and wanted to drive away, but he couldn't leave the zombie gun. He needed to retrieve it.

He checked his weapons before exiting the sedan, confident he could hop a side fence and get inside the compound before anyone was the wiser. The police wouldn't walk straight into the zoo, preferring to get everyone out first. That might buy him enough time to get in and out. It was worth a shot. If he could save Dmitry it would be even better.

Ramzan's intent was to calmly walk to the far corner of the lot and scale the six foot fence and then find Dmitry. He'd simply shoot anything in his way.

Movement caught his eye and he stopped three steps from the car.

Boris Dragov, resplendent in a black leather jacket, stood with one hand on the fence in the exact spot Ramzan was going to walk to. Boris was smiling and moving his free hand.

The bullet slammed into the sedan a few inches from Ramzan. It was a warning shot, because Boris Dragov never missed.

Ramzan, shaken, put his hands up and climbed slowly back into the car, watching as his former friend and now enemy scaled the fence without a look back.

Suddenly the game had changed, and for the worst. Ramzan lifted the cell phone with an unsteady hand, but there was no signal.

≈

KOSTAS, SEATED IN THE TEAM VAN, GRINNED WHEN HE HEARD THE news choppers overhead flying off. He figured by the time they knew what hit them this mess would be over with and cleaned up. Any communication within a six block radius was now technologically thrown back into the Stone Age.

The exterior cameras on the van, still functional like everything else Kostas had before him, picked up the news vans driving away. Every cell phone, land-line phone, camera or recorder was now dead. There were no signals and most of the memory and battery life was also erased.

If the helicopter pilots had been stubborn, a quick pulse to get their onboard computers to temporarily shut down would have gotten them moving. Kostas didn't want to do that. He wanted to simply get prying eyes away from this mess. So far, so good.

Now, he could sit back and watch the rest of the ACES team shoot things while he sat in air conditioning and relaxed.

"Great job, Kostas," Jennifer said over his headset, one of the few electronic devices not affected. "Think you can get a drone in the air?"

"It's already been placed in the takeoff position. I was just waiting for my sexy *senorita* to give me the word."

"I need to see how many more people are currently trapped inside, and if there is another exit currently blocked."

"You got it." Kostas was in his element now, sitting up and preparing the drone, which was really just a foot long remote controlled helicopter that looked like a child's toy, although it had four mounted cameras and cost more than some countries. "It will be zooming over your position in the next thirty seconds."

With a range of three miles, this high-tech toy was one of his favorites, although he rarely got to use it. The irony of the TX-72d model was the fact Kostas had hacked into and taken control of the TX-72a version when he was still a teenager, fresh out of high school. That was the first major SWAT team bust-in at his parent's house. Kostas smiled when he remembered the look on his mother's face: not of surprise or shock, but of anger that her son had yet again forced the government to kick down her front door.

Kostas figured the fourth broken front door had done the trick for his parents and the government, because they 'recruited' him during the interview/interrogation that followed.

The drone was in the air, and all four cameras were operational and feeding a three-second delayed image back to the bank of screens in the van. Unlike cheesy TV shows or cheap convenience store security cameras, Kostas could tighten the shot and count freckles on an Irish stripper's ass. "Which I haven't done yet," he said out loud. "But this coming weekend . . . Boss, there is another one at ten o'clock, feeding behind the red mini-van. G.I. Dale, you have two at one o'clock, where the sign says Parking Lot B. Martin and your new girlfriend, your way is clear to the gates. You just have a press of people coming at you. Wait, another one just ran out to the right of the ticket booth."

There was too much going on at once, with the Miami P.D. herding people away from the zoo, the panicked running in all directions and knocking others over, and the ACES team moving through the chaos and trying to restore order.

"There's another one due east of you, Martin." Kostas kept the drone moving, cameras taking in the sea of humanity underneath it. "How many tourists visit this place? I've never been there. I might need to go."

"I'll tell you how it is once we get inside," Martin said.

"Ask your girlfriend if she knows any hot chicks. We can double date."

"I can hear you," Missy said over her headset. "And I don't dislike anyone enough to set you up with them."

Kostas laughed. "You have one about twenty feet straight

ahead, Killer Comstock." He moved the drone higher in the air to get a better view of the crowd. "Are we working the outside first?"

"The police don't seem to have a clue how to contain this. So yes," Comstock said. "Once we're clear we'll make the move inside."

"Are civilians still filing out?" Jennifer asked.

"Affirmative. I don't see an end to them from this vantage point. Luckily, it seems there are many survivors."

"But that number is shrinking fast. At this point we need to assume by the time we get inside everyone is either dead or infected," Comstock said.

"That's not very positive," Kostas said. "Maybe everyone is inside right now, singing songs and feeding the animals."

"Feeding them what?" Comstock snapped. "You talk too much. Help me to see."

Kostas let the drone glide for a few seconds, moving it slowly and letting the cameras pick up the crowd. "There are only a few left. I think you have a clear shot through bodies to the front gate. Jennifer, keep moving to your left. The cops there aren't doing too well. They let one run right past them."

"I'm on it," she said.

"How're we looking?" Martin said. A gunshot was clearly heard over the headset. "I'm in a clearing right now."

"I see you. And Missy as well. She has a nice ass, buddy. Good luck trying to tap that."

"Seriously?" Missy asked. "I can hear you."

"And that's the fun of this, Sweet Cheeks. You two are clear. I'd start heading to rendezvous with Comstock at the front gate."

"Gather up as many officers as you can along the way," Jennifer said. "If this weapon has been used nonstop since this started, we might be dealing with dozens of them."

Kostas glided the drone over the front gates and frowned. "I have good news and bad news."

"Good news?" Jennifer asked.

"I don't think there'll be many more survivors impeding your way. They seem to mostly be outside the zoo now."

"Bad news?" Martin asked.

"I hope you're carrying extra mags, because there could be as many as fifty of them swarming in your general direction. Good luck out there."

≈

THE MAKAROV PMM WAS IN HIS HAND AGAIN AS SOON AS HE GOT over the fence, and Boris went in search of the zombie gun. It was obvious after watching Ramzan sitting idly in his car he didn't currently possess the weapon. *Leave it to Ramzan to make someone else do his dirty work*, he thought.

The only person left was Dmitry, who Yuri had filled Boris in about his exact association with Ramzan and his cause. Boris didn't really care one way or another about why Ramzan was trying to create such havoc and force the world into another war, and he didn't care. Boris knew he was a small cog in the wheel of Mother Russia, and his goal was simply to do what needed to be done. It was in his best interest right now to follow the orders before him and get this part done quickly and cleanly. There was no longer room to linger, play with the mouse like the cat he was, and savor the kill. Now was the time for action. The fact that Dmitry was technically family (married to his cousin Yelena) didn't matter, either. If he got in the way he would be taken care of. Erased from the equation. Another death on the long list of Boris Dragov.

The Miami Zoo was quiet in this section. With the birds squawking and the warm breeze blowing, this was probably a fun destination for tourists. Boris could imagine the kids begging for money to buy cheap shirts and knick-knacks with Miami Zoo stamps on them, and the parents shuffling along like zombies as they spent their hard-earned money for this vacation, before going back to their boring middle class lives of excess, wasteful spending and reality television programming.

And what would Boris go back to after getting the zombie gun? Yet another mission to some exotic locale, with a new challenge in life and another man or woman to eliminate. Someone else to stalk like weak prey, someone that wouldn't even know they'd been killed, because he was that good. Boris actually hoped he would be staying in the United States because there were parts of the country he'd yet to see. Before the world ended (either because of nuclear war, the Mayan prophecy or just bad timing), his intent was to see as much of the world as he could. And all the while killing everyone he was contracted to kill.

"See the world, meet new and exotic people, and put a bullet through their head," he whispered with a harsh laugh. One of these days he would settle down in a bungalow near a deserted beach and watch the dolphins frolic in the waves as he opened a cold imported beer and sipped it, listening to the surf.

But today was not that day. He rounded the pathway bend and saw the first signs that everything wasn't exactly still fun-loving in the zoo: three dead bodies, mangled and bitten, strewn across the path. At first he thought a wild animal had escaped its cage, but a closer look and he knew it was human bites. Not that it mattered. Man or beast . . . if it got in his way, he would dispatch it without care.

The light rustle of a bush to the right of the path brought his quick reactions into play, and he'd turned and shot before he even saw the zombie coming at him. The bullet took it square in the left eye socket, putting it down for good. Boris didn't want to keep using his Makarov PMM if he could help it, since gunshots would attract the zombies and the Miami PD. And scare away Dmitry.

There were more bodies as he moved. He saw a young man moaning and covering his ravaged face as the blood pooled around him. Boris didn't want to waste a bullet putting him out of his misery, so he simply walked past. It wasn't his problem.

He heard a woman scream somewhere ahead, but there were dull gunshots coming from the front of the zoo, and another scream echoed through the trees from somewhere else. It was hard to pinpoint, and Boris didn't know how he could find the zombie gun before the police found it.

Three men, crying and sobbing, ran past him. Boris assumed they were running from a zombie and set his feet. If he had to waste another bullet, he would. He didn't have time to hide or fight hand to hand with these mindless people. He needed to find Dmitry.

Boris laughed when he saw the lion cub rounding the

bend.

But the look in its eyes told Boris something wasn't right with it. Sure, it was a wild animal that had been caged its entire life. But it was still genetically a ruthless killer. King of the Jungle and all that.

And this lion cub, despite its size, looked enraged to kill. The lion cub had been shot with the zombie gun, and now it was drooling in anticipation of ripping Boris apart.

"Here, kitty, kitty," Boris said with a smile and raised the Makarov PMM.

He decided adding a zombie lion to his kill sheet would be amazing.

~

DMITRY WAS PANICKING, FLAILING HIS ARMS AND THE ZOMBIE GUN to break free from the crowds. He'd been pushed along, swept up in the mass of bodies, and was far away from the front gates before people finally scattered. There were screams around him as the zombies tore into people. He fought to escape.

"The lions and tigers are loose," someone near him shouted.

Dmitry wanted to say "Oh my," for some reason. He'd shot many animals in their fenced in areas and cages after shooting the alpha male squirrel monkey. Now, with his luck, he'd be eaten by a zombie goat he'd turned into a killing machine.

He also needed to calm down, regroup, and keep creating chaos around him. He went to pull out his cell phone to call Ramzan, but his phone had been washed away during the flood of people. He was on his own.

Irritated, he pushed his way to the side of the path and then stepped into the small copse of trees there. He was panting, his heart racing. He checked the zombie gun, making sure it hadn't been damaged. It looked fine. Now what?

Dmitry knelt behind some bushes and began taking long shots with the gun, hitting a few more people and turning them into zombies. They immediately began attacking those around them, and within minutes the area before him was devoid of humanity. He'd cleared a spot, however briefly, and needed to get as far away from here as he could. He needed to remember which way the front gates were, but knew there were a million signs pointing you to souvenir stands, food kiosks and the exit.

The gun had a longer range than he'd thought, and he kept testing it as he walked calmly, stepping over those injured and dead. Animals still in their cages were shot, and anyone he saw in the distance he aimed and fired at.

Dmitry decided he was going to take deep breaths, enjoy the amazing moment—the fresh air, the lovely scenery— and someday Mother Russia would be singing songs about him. They'd erect a monument on this site and perhaps call this Dmitry Zoo in the future world, where America is a weak conquered nation. He would be raised to hero worshipping status. Dmitry liked the sound of that.

Up ahead, heading toward the front gates, was another clump of people being attacked. Dmitry shot several of them to add to the craziness and then decided to find another way out. There had to be a tertiary exit the zoo workers used or a few emergency exits. Regardless, Dmitry wasn't going to escape through the front door. And he knew the Miami PD was now sweeping through the zoo, looking for him, or at least the cause of the disturbance.

Even though much damage had been done, there was still so much more to do. This was a raindrop in the bucket when you got right down to it. This would scare a few jaded Americans but not panic a country.

Dmitry kept shooting, almost bored with it now, and was glad to see after about two hundred feet on the path, the people thinned out. He resisted shooting the few stragglers and those trying to hide behind rocks, benches and ice cream stands. To hit them would only make them attack him. He'd learned that lesson the hard way.

He needed to keep moving. Dmitry hoped Ramzan was still waiting for him on the outside, but had no way to reach him now. He wouldn't know until he got over the fence and waved him down. And got away from zombies and the Miami PD in his way. He was sure the government teams were out there as well, coordinating and looking for the cause of all the excitement.

As Dmitry passed the lion sanctuary he went rigid. The cages were all open and empty. He didn't know how many animals were housed there, but if each cage held only one lion, there could be a dozen currently loose in the zoo.

Yet another good and bad thing. Good because it would create so much more chaos if the police had to battle lions, but bad if Dmitry walked right into the path of one with only a weapon that would get them madder. He had serious doubts about outrunning one or harming it with the zombie gun used as a club.

He rounded the next bend and stopped short.

The lion cub was probably about a hundred pounds and really pissed off. But that wasn't what scared Dmitry the most.

Boris Dragov, one of the most feared men in the SVR and beyond, stood before the lion with his hands outstretched. He was grinning from ear to ear.

And he winked at Dmitry before moving to grapple with the lion.

≈

JENNIFER SANCHEZ STRODE PURPOSELY TO THE POLICE OFFICER clearly in charge. "What are you doing?" she asked.

He turned and grimaced at her. "Who the hell are you?"

"ACES team. I'm sure Chief Alvarez filled you in, so let's cut the crap." Jennifer pointed to the main gates. "Your men are getting in the way. They keep bottlenecking the entry of my team, and forcing innocent people back into the compound, where the bodies keep racking up."

"I'm doing what needs to be done."

"This isn't a hostage situation, and not a standoff. These, um, creatures, aren't hiding from you or shooting back. They're pissed off and running at you. But your men, the ones with the weapons capable of killing them, are blocking the living people. And the living people are dying in droves thanks to you and your men."

He looked like he was about to bark at her, but when Jennifer didn't blink, he backed off. "Fine. I'll pull everyone back."

"Set up a wider perimeter. Check each person as they come out, and set up teams to dispatch the killers. There are many wounded, but right now they are scattered."

"Anything else, ma'am?" he sneered.

"Yes. As soon as it is done, I'm going to need you to assemble a team of men that aren't afraid to shoot. How many tourists visit this zoo on a daily basis?"

"From what I can gather, between two and three thousand could be inside at any given moment. It's the biggest zoo in the southeast. By far. On peak days you might see five thousand. Not to mention the hundreds of workers."

"And all the animals."

"What about the animals? They're in cages," he said.

"Let's hope they stay in cages." Jennifer couldn't imagine the added panic of the tourists if any of the animals got free from their cages. And if this attack was planned in a zoo, she had the sinking feeling one main reason was because of the chaos the animals loose would cause.

"Martin, I need you to coordinate the civilians as they exit. Can you do that yet?"

"I'm doing it now, with Miss Lockhart. We are funneling them into two lines: one for those hurt, and one for those unhurt. But the police aren't being very helpful. They keep pushing them back and forth and we have to fight through when a new attack comes."

Jennifer looked at the police officer.

He grimaced again. "I can't reach them. All the police systems went down."

"Use a bullhorn. I'm sure you can handle it." *Tiene una boca grande,* she thought. This loudmouth might not need the bullhorn. "Just get them to pull back, because more and more people are falling victim."

"Jennifer, we have a new problem," Martin said.

*Of course. Would the bad luck ever end?* "What is it now?"

"There are maybe a hundred of them bursting out any minute. Even with all our firepower, we can't contain this."

"Come again?" she instinctively asked.

"We're about to be in a load of trouble, pretty lady," Dale Comstock said. "And these cops haven't been cooperating with us, so now we've opened the buffet for them and we can only watch as they begin to feast."

Jennifer turned to the officer in charge, who was really in charge of nothing at this point. This was worst case scenario time. "Evacuate your people and everyone else now! Fall back to the road, or we'll have hundreds of dead on our hands. Do you understand me?"

He began shouting to his men nearest him to spread the word, but Jennifer knew it was going to be too little, too late. She made sure her AA-12 automatic shotgun was ready to go. This was going to be a tense few minutes.

Jennifer began moving to the crowds of people, hoping they would be able to save the bulk of them. Hoping the dead she was about to see wouldn't haunt her dreams for the rest of her life.

≈

TIM BAKER WOKE WITH A START, HIS DREAM STILL FRESH IN HIS mind. He was a writer of thriller books, enjoying the open seas on his boat while he tapped away on the laptop, writing about someone named Ike. The dream had turned when he smelled smoke and noticed his boat was on fire, and a host of unsavory characters were on his ship.

Before he could remember the rest, two nurses pushed past where he sat outside David Luciano's room and entered.

"What's going on?"

"Sir, I need you to stay outside," one of them said.

"You can try to make me." Tim moved into the room as the nurse gave up arguing with him.

David was flat-lining. Tim had seen enough death to know what was going to happen. He stepped to the side as a slew of personnel came in, and they began pushing his bed out of the room.

"Prep for surgery," someone yelled. "Move it!"

Tim followed along the hallway but let them go. They banged through the Emergency Room doors and he lost sight of them. A lone nurse stood back and approached Tim.

"He's being wheeled in for surgery. The bullet did more damage than we thought. His vitals are low and he finally crashed, more or less."

"What's the percent chance David will make it?"

The nurse looked away. "You'll have to talk to the doctor about it."

"I'm asking you. The doc seems busy." Tim tensed. He liked David Luciano, and liked working with him whenever he came down to Miami. It would be a shame . . .

"It doesn't look good. He's been comatose since we brought him in, and his vitals have been weak from the on-set. His blood loss is staggering." She smiled. "He's definitely a fighter. Quite frankly, with the injuries he sustained, it's a miracle he is still alive."

"He's a stubborn bastard. I can agree with that," Tim said.

"You might want to get in touch with his family."

Tim nodded. He'd have to get in touch with Jennifer, even though he knew the ACES team was now dealing with the latest attacks. He'd wanted to go but she'd talked him into staying with David in the event he came out of the coma or whoever did this decided to come back and finish the job.

"How long will surgery last?"

She shrugged. "Several hours, depending on what is really going on with his body." She lowered her eyes. "I would make a few phone calls. You are welcome to set up camp here if you'd like, but I can't let you inside for obvious reasons."

"I understand. I think I'll grab a cup of coffee once I can get someone to sit watch for me."

She smiled again. "How do you take your coffee? We have the most god awful coffee here, but if you add enough sugar and cream it will only make you throw up."

"You make it sound so delicious. I take a ton of sugar and a ton of cream. To kill the coffee taste."

"I'll be right back. Hungry?"

Tim sighed. He was just tired and worn out from the past few days. "Not really."

"I'll see if I can get you a club sandwich in case you change your mind."

"I appreciate that."

"My pleasure." The nurse turned away.

"You never did answer my question," Tim said.

She stopped and didn't look back. "Realistically, he might not make it. You need to make those phone calls while I get you some coffee. I'm sorry."

# EPISODE EIGHT
I Shot the Monkey in the Face

**BORIS DRAGOV COULDN'T HELP HIMSELF. HE LOVED A CHALLENGE.**
all his life was about choices, finding the path of most resis-
tance and overcoming it. Boris always put himself in the position to dominate, to not just beat an opponent but to give
them no reason to come back for a second round. He wanted
to annihilate the competition and savor the journey as they
crawled away on broken bones and broken pride, never to
return to the fight.

*It's not the kill, it's the thrill of the chase*, he sang in his head
now, the iconic Deep Purple line ringing over and over.

He saw Dmitry and his intelligence told him to stop what
he was about to do, pull his Makarov PMM, take care of Dmitry and then retrieve the zombie gun.

But the zombie lion cub was set to pounce.

"Dmitry, if you know what is good for you, now would be
the time to give up the weapon and walk away with your life."

Boris smiled when Dmitry pointed the zombie gun at
him. "Pull the trigger and I will enjoy ripping you apart. I
will not stop until you are in so much pain you can no longer
scream for mercy. Is that what you want?"

The lion attacked, sprinting the distance between them
and jumping. Boris was no longer worried about Dmitry. At
this point, whatever happened simply happened.

Right now Boris had a real threat and it bared fangs and
claws.

As the lion lunged, Boris stepped to his right, expecting to
throw the cub past him. But the lion stopped and clamped its
teeth onto Boris' jacket, although it was an awkward attack
and Boris was able to shake loose easily.

He supposed a living, sensible lion cub would take the

time to stalk its prey and go for some posturing. The zombie lion kept on the offensive, jaws snapping and coming back for more. It was now just a slobbering killing machine. There would be no submission, no domination. Either Boris or the beast would die today.

It was on him again and Boris punched it squarely in the nose, but it didn't flinch. Instead, it snapped its jaws and almost took off a couple of fingers.

"You are too aggressive," Boris whispered to it, more for his own amusement. "It will be your downfall."

It lunged again before Boris has time to recover, and Boris went down to one knee. The lion bit into his left shoulder, drawing blood through the clothing.

Boris screamed but it wasn't because of the pain. It was because of his frustration at being bitten and not drawing first blood. To lose this battle meant losing his life. Unacceptable.

The lion clamped down harder and shook its head, spraying blood.

Boris punched it in the face repeatedly, but it wasn't letting go as it tried to sever the arm. It was pulling Boris to the ground and he felt its hot tongue as it lapped up the flowing blood.

Boris dug his free hand's fingers into the mouth of the beast, trying to unlock its death grip, but it was too powerful. His fingers scraped against sharp teeth but he couldn't get into the mouth far enough to attempt to unlock the jaws.

The blood spewing from his arm was covering him and the ground, and he nearly slipped. He decided to use his Gracie Jiu-Jitsu techniques and attack this problem as if it were a human foe, before he went down due to blood loss or a fall.

With his free, uninjured arm, he reached calmly around the neck of the lion and got a firm grip of its mane. He glanced up and was pleased to see Dmitry hadn't moved an inch.

"Pick your chin up off the ground, my friend. I'll be done with this foe soon enough. Then it will be time for us to talk, no?"

The lion's jaws snapped but Boris pushed against the animal, pulling it into his waist. It was still locked onto his arm but he no longer felt the pain. It was now only the rush of the battle and the reality of Boris about to overcome his enemy.

"This must be fascinating to watch, no? The mighty Boris Dragov, using only his strength and will to destroy the deadliest of foes." Boris glanced up at Dmitry. "I hope you will live to tell this story at the next family reunion. I really do."

The lion ripped a chunk of flesh from his arm, and Boris had to concede to the pain. He almost vomited as the throbbing shot up and down his arm, nerve endings screaming.

"You will not defeat me," Boris said and slumped down, eye to eye with the lion. Its eyes were glazed over and bloodshot. This was no more a lion than a raving lunatic or a shark. It was all terror and anger.

His arm came loose from the maw of the lion in a sickening rip, tendons and skin dangling. Boris tried to lift the limb but failed. *Have I suffered irreparable damage to my arm? Have I just ended my career due to my pride?* Boris punched the lion in the face with his good hand to no affect.

Still gripping the lion around the neck, Boris began clubbing it with his wounded arm, but he couldn't seem to make enough impact to stun the lion.

The lion pulled away, quickly coming back and gripping

his arm once more, causing Boris to scream. He felt more blood gush from the wound, coating the hot muzzle of the beast.

Boris felt utter shame at his prideful ways, and knew he'd crossed a line. He'd forgotten about why he was here and what his ultimate goal was today. He'd never backed out of a mission or screwed it up. Yet, here he was . . .

"I need the zombie gun," he said to Dmitry.

The lion continued shaking the wounded arm in his jaw, blood spattering the sidewalk.

Dmitry began backing away.

Boris pulled his Makarov PMM and aimed it at Dmitry, who stopped walking away. Dmitry's face went ashen but he wouldn't turn or plead for his life, which Boris found commendable.

Boris put the weapon to the head of the lion and pulled the trigger three times, blowing its sickened brains out.

Dmitry turned and ran as Boris stumbled to the line of bushes nearby, trying not to collapse until he found cover.

〜

DALE COMSTOCK WAS IN THE ZONE, HIS HK416 AN EXTENSION OF his mind and fingers as he moved, one step at a time, two pulls of the trigger for every step.

If he was a younger man, he might have wasted his time playing 'realistic' combat simulator games. But he knew there was only one way to get him excited: put him in front of a horde of enemies and let him go to town, wiping the floor with them.

Which is exactly what he was doing now. These were the easiest but worst enemies to face, because they simply ran at you without dodging shots or taking cover. But they had the power to overwhelm you in sheer numbers. One false move, one step too many in their direction, and you could be knocked over, pressed to the floor by a host of them, and ripped apart before you could scream.

Comstock watched as Martin kept the same exacting pace close to him and smiled to himself. The man was good. Probably one of the absolute best when it came to taking the shot and getting the job done. Comstock was proud to know he had a hand in it and they were on the same team.

The police officer was beautiful but distracting at Martin's side, but weren't they all? Comstock had immediately read the situation back at Magic Productions and knew the two of them were head over heels. Comstock hoped it wouldn't compromise either of their lives in the future.

"I'm running out of ammo," he said into his headset. "Anybody got some?"

Jennifer came in immediately. "I'm coming up behind you with an extra M4 carbine fully locked and loaded. Interested in trading out?"

Comstock laughed as he took his last two shots and then stopped. "I guess I'll slum it for a bit if I have to. Just hurry up."

He felt her hand on his back and the M4 pressed into his hand as she deftly slid the HK416 from him.

"It's much appreciated, ma'am."

"Don't ma'am me," Jennifer said as she opened fire with her AA-12 automatic shotgun and cleared a path of zombies heading their way. Jennifer cleared her mind, moving her feet in a slow shuffle forward as she took off one head at a time, shooting three more before the first body hit the ground.

"Very impressive," Comstock said. He wasn't being sarcastic. She was that good. Sanchez had a compact swing to her moves, spraying the area in single shots that always found their mark. He wanted to stop her and ask where she'd learned to shoot. But it probably wasn't the right time for that. Besides, if he played his cards right he would be seeing more of Jennifer Sanchez in the near future.

First, though, he needed to join the fight again.

Comstock moved to his right, getting his distance between Jennifer and Martin and shooting into the thick of zombies.

The flow of zombies was slowing to a trickle, and he guessed the sheer magnitude of firepower they were using was almost like a dinner bell to the mindless people. It was like shooting fish in a barrel.

Within minutes they were into the front gates, stepping over bodies, and getting shoulder to shoulder. The path was clogged with the dead. One of the ticket booths had been kicked in, and Comstock pointed the M4 carbine inside and almost pulled the trigger.

"Please don't shoot," the woman, covered in blood, pleaded. "I'm alive."

He made sure he was in no immediate danger of being attacked and checked his weapon.

The woman was visibly shaking.

Comstock helped her out of the booth. There were three bodies inside with her. It looked like she'd covered herself with them in order to hide.

"You're a smart woman. You're alive because of it."

"I didn't know what to do." She started crying. "My husband and children are in the park."

"Let's hope they escaped." Comstock pointed to the swarm of Miami PD entering the zoo. "Go with them. You'll be safe."

"Thank you." She hugged Comstock suddenly.

Comstock watched her walk away, falling into the arms of the nearest cop. He shook his head. It was one thing to be in combat with an enemy military, people trained to kill you or be killed. But he was surrounded by civilians . . . normal everyday people who weren't trained for this kind of hand to hand combat.

He walked away, watching ACES spread out down various pathways, the police joining them. Everyone around him was dead now, bodies broken and torn apart. Women, children, and men.

Another woman limped past him, helped by an officer. She was missing an ear, her shirt covered in crimson. She looked shell shocked.

Comstock didn't blame her and sincerely hoped she recovered. He wished more people were alive. The final body count would be daunting.

Despite what some would think (including his bosses and most military personnel), Dale wasn't a one dimensional killing machine, dropped into a hot zone and opening fire. He knew violence was a necessary evil, but he didn't relish killing just for the sake of killing. He loved his job and career and had no qualms about doing what needed to be done for his country and his freedom, but killing innocents was never in the plan.

He wanted to look away as he walked, but instead committed each face to memory. These people didn't deserve to die and had no real chance of surviving. As these attacks continued, more and more bodies would be littering the streets.

Comstock decided to take some time off once this mission was completed and the zombie gun secured, and do something he'd never done before: train people not as combat killers, but to defend themselves from future attacks.

He smiled, thinking about a line of soccer moms, following his instruction against a zombie apocalypse. He would open the public's eyes and give everyone a fighting chance.

It wouldn't be about the money. It would be about the thrill of women and children being able to defend themselves. And Dale Comstock, American Bad Ass, would become the trainer of soccer moms into defenders of their family.

He smiled again.

≈

MISSY'S MIND DIDN'T REGISTER WHAT SHE WAS SEEING. AT FIRST, she thought all the squirrel monkeys were dead, until a large one sprang at her from above and slammed into the bars of its cage. It hit with such force she stepped back.

"Did he kill the rest?" she asked Martin as he came up behind her.

"He was turned into a monster. Look at his eyes. Whoever did this used the weapon on innocent animals." Martin shook his head. "This is beyond sick."

The monkey kept trying to get at them, hands extended as it shrieked in protest.

"It needs to be put down," Missy said.

"I agree. Make sure you do it in one shot."

Missy turned to Martin. "Me? I don't think so."

"I'm not doing it. You walked up first. It's your kill now."

"No way."

The alpha male squirrel monkey was literally rattling the bars.

"He'll be loose soon. You need to take care of this."

Missy changed tactics and puffed out her bottom lip. "Can't you do it? Please, please?"

"Are you really going to try to sweet-talk me into doing it? Don't you think that's lame? And conniving?"

Missy stepped close to Martin and hid her grin when he involuntarily moved away from her. She had him. "I just need some help. I don't want to kill the monkey. I'm an animal lover. You know what else I love, and love to do?"

She was startled by the shot ringing out so close to her. Martin had killed the monkey with a single shot to the head without breaking her gaze. *This dude is scary*, she thought. *And I am so turned on right now*. "Wow, are you easy. Need to change your undies, big boy?'

"When this is over with, what's the chance you and I can go on a real date?"

*100%*, she thought. "I'm not sure. Let's get through this day. Who know what tomorrow will bring, right?"

Martin grinned. "I'll take that as a yes."

"You're a very positive person, aren't you? I never said

anything close to yes."

"I can tell it's a yes."

"Not even close," Missy said.

"Now you're just plain lying."

Missy didn't want her advantage to slip away. "I'll go out with you once this is over, but on one condition."

"Name it."

"Double date."

"With who?"

"I'll bring my friend Jenny. You bring one of your hot guy friends."

"No fair."

Missy stuck out her bottom lip again. "Ooh, is baby gonna cry now? Fine. Forget the whole thing."

"Nope. It won't be a problem. Not at all," Martin said. Missy could see he looked worried now.

She was going to let him off the hook but decided to bust his chops a bit more.

Martin suddenly grinned. "I'm sure Kostas will love your friend, Jenny. I saw her, right? At the police station? She's hot. He'll be all over her."

"I don't think so."

"I do. We already agreed to it. I shot the monkey in the face. Where I come from, this is considered a verbal agreement."

"Where I come from, this isn't cool."

"Too bad." Martin pointed at the monkey cage. "I shot the monkey in the face."

"You seem to like saying that." Missy smiled. "Fine. This will be the best double date ever. Just wait until Jenny rips into Kostas and his sexist attitude."

"I look forward to it. Now, let's go finish cleaning up this mess."

"After you, kind sir."

"I shot the monkey in the face."

—

**DMITRY THREW UP IN THE BUSHES, LEANING AGAINST A TREE. THIS** was all getting to be too much for him. He still had the image of Boris in his head, facing off against the lion, his arm shredded and bloody, and he couldn't shake it. There was too much bloodshed today and too much violence. And it was all suddenly hitting Dmitry.

He knew he was done in the zoo, and needed to leave before he was caught or killed. His hunger to turn the masses into zombies eroded, replaced by shame at what he was doing. Where was the sport in this? Facing off against an enemy was one thing, fighting and beating them because of superior strength and intelligence. Making them into monsters and watching them kill each other was . . . wrong.

Dmitry would figure out a way to turn the zombie gun over to the ACES team without getting caught. He'd spin a story about being overpowered but escaping. While he didn't necessarily agree with how this mission had gone, he also wasn't stupid. Serving the rest of his life in an American prison, or worse yet in Siberian prison Camp 17, was not going to be an option if he could help it. He knew they would reprimand him and give him some paper-pushing job until he retired. He decided he was fine with it. This crazy subterfuge with Ramzan was ridiculous and Dmitry was caught up in spreading new ideals and a new Mother Russia. He decided he liked the old ways better.

He wouldn't turn Ramzan in or turn on him, but he would distance himself from the radical once they returned home. If he was being honest with himself, he was quite scared of the man.

Dmitry looked back to make sure the zombie lion cub was actually still dead, and Boris was gone. He didn't want either monster sneaking up and killing him. He didn't know which one was worse.

≈

**JENNIFER TOOK THREE SHOTS IN SUCCESSION AND WATCHED IN** satisfaction as all three hit their mark, blowing holes through faces. She tried to ignore the fact she was still killing innocent civilians, but there was no way around it. Until Kim gave her a call and told her to back off, or a magical cure had been discovered, this was the only option.

She wondered how Dale Comstock put himself in constant motion with the way he did things. He was military through and through, and she was turned on and repulsed by it at the same time. She knew intellectually he understood her job and her career and even the life she was leading. No man had ever gotten it. She'd met strong men who wanted her to retire and stay home and cook and clean and have babies while they acted like men. She wasn't wired for domestic life. She couldn't remember the last night she didn't go to sleep with a pile of documents on the other side of the bed, or the last time her television was turned on except to watch a video for work.

Jennifer was in her forties and it was too late for children and domestic bliss and everything associated with it. Her parents harped on her choices constantly, not even realizing her true job and the danger she was constantly in. They wanted to be grandparents and it was understandable.

She just wanted to be happy. And she was. Or had been, until Dale Comstock smiled in her direction and she started acting like a school girl. Now ... she was confused. Did he flirt with every woman he met? Did he have a new girl in every port? Was he just another player, a good-looking jarhead full of himself and brimming with ego? Was the guy married?

Since he'd come onboard, Jennifer had refrained from doing a cursory search of his unclassified records. She could easily find out if he was married, had kids, where he actually lived, and anything else she wanted. All she had to do is show Kostas some cleavage and she could find out Comstock's shoe size and what color toothbrush he used on Thursdays. But she didn't want to do anything like it. She didn't know if she was afraid of the answers, or afraid once she found out he was clean, she'd have nothing stopping her.

"He's leaving as soon as this is over," she whispered as she walked. "It will never work out. Besides, by next weekend he'll be half a world away and I'll be a distant memory. Just another notch he almost added to his belt." She decided to stop this childish infatuation, and focus on her top priority, which was work.

As soon as this was over, she'd shake his hand and tell him courteously but professionally what a pleasure it had been working with him. And then she would walk away, go back to her lonely existence, and wait for the next assignment to cross her desk.

A zombie stumbled from behind the bird building and she stopped and lined it up with the AA-12 before tapping the trigger and watching as the shot ripped right between its eyes. It slowly teetered before dropping to its knees and falling face-first to the path.

*It.* She needed to keep thinking of them as *it* instead of male or female, or human.

Was killing them becoming so much easier now? She shuddered to think she could become so callous so quickly. But it was like every other job she'd ever done. You turn off parts of the brain and simply do what you are told to do. It makes it much easier.

She could still hear the occasional gunshot, but they were getting farther and farther apart. She was glad Kostas was able to divert the news choppers and prying eyes, but there was too much cleanup to be done to contain this for long. With everyone having a cell phone camera, all it would take is one EMT or police officer to snap a shot and have it go viral.

The Miami Zoo was a big place, and walking it as a tourist would probably take an hour. This would end up being a massive undertaking, one she was glad they'd have help on. Jennifer had no idea what spin would be put onto this massacre.

And by rights she shouldn't care. Nothing they ever did really made the news, and that was the point of doing their job well. If the general public had even a small inkling of the day in and day out things they did to keep them safe, there would be mass panic.

Foreign hit-men and weapons of mass destruction inside our 'safe' borders? Our own nuclear and biological weapons under constant threat of being used against us or destroyed, weakening our forces? Cities like Miami, Dallas and San Diego a haven for Russian counter-terrorism groups? Some of your own neighbors really third- and fourth-generation spies? The average person went to work each day from nine to five, collected a paycheck and came home to their spouse and 2.3 children and a white picket fence.

Let them know the white picket fence was built by a communist country and sprayed with anthrax, and you'd have mass hysteria.

But none of this really needed to matter to Jennifer and ACES. What mattered was keeping anything from happening and controlling the small pieces of this incendiary puzzle they were given. You couldn't save the entire world in one fell swoop, but you could spend each day doing something toward the goal.

Jennifer strolled around the next bend, lost in her thoughts but ready, when a man turned and looked at her. He was alive, and she was about to offer him an escort to the front gates, but something stopped her.

He looked confused but not scared. Jennifer watched him turn and saw the pistol in his hand. He wasn't a police officer and he wasn't on the ACES team.

His fingers fumbled with the gun, which she knew was the zombie gun.

Just as he swung it in his hand, not to shoot, but to offer it to her, she fired the AA-12 and put a bullet through his forehead.

~

**JENNIFER WAS DREADING THIS PART. THE MIAMI POLICE DEPART-**ment was still moving through the zoo and eliminating the few stragglers left. The survivors were being treated in the parking lot, questioned and either sent to the local hospitals or released.

The ACES team, having done their principle work, retired to the team van to catch their breath. There would be weeks of paperwork to do and intense interviews, both in person and in an endless cycle of conference calls with the Higher Ups.

Right now it was time for Jennifer to do what needed to be done, both for the team and for her. And she was dreading the latter.

Dale Comstock wasn't around at the moment, which she was glad for. As soon as the weapon was secured, Dale slipped off and started helping with gathering the survivors. Even Martin thought it a bit odd. Not saying the man was heartless, but he usually left cleanup and minor details to the people around him. Dale Comstock was more of a Big Detail Guy. He pointed and shot and someone else cleaned up the body.

"I wonder if your future boyfriend is playing hard to get, or if he suddenly cares about people," Kostas said to Jennifer.

Before she could respond, Martin stepped in. "He cares about people." Martin looked over to the crowds of survivors. "I've just never known him to take an active part in cleanup or recovery. I wonder if this means he found another future girlfriend in the crowd."

Jennifer felt her ears burning. She knew he was trying to lighten the mood, but he'd inadvertently struck a sour note with her. She turned away, catching the amused grin of Missy Lockhart.

"Don't sweat it," Missy said. "He is completely into you."

"I don't care," Jennifer said and shrugged dramatically. "Whatever." She knew she sounded yet again like a fifteen year old, but she couldn't help it. She was hurt he didn't engage her in small talk after, or even congratulate her on recovering the zombie gun and eliminating the enemy threat.

"Yeah, and I don't care about Mike." Missy smiled. "Am I done here? I'd like to get back to my actual job. It was fun, but I need to be a Miami Police Officer again."

"I'll see what I can do." Jennifer shook her hand. "I appreciate the help. I also know my boss, and she'll be calling on you again and again to help ACES."

"I figured as much."

"I know you're teasing me about Dale, but what's the deal with you and Martin?"

Missy shrugged and looked away. "He's all right. Whatever." The women laughed.

"I'll call your chief in the morning and we'll get you back in uniform where you want to be. Remember, though: you always have a spot on my team if you want it. Not front line stuff at first, of course, but I see a lot of me back in the day in you."

"You aren't that much older than me."

Jennifer grinned. "Actually, I am. You'd be surprised. But this job keeps me looking young and fit."

"I see."

"That was a joke."

"But the truth. You look great." Missy looked at Martin. "I guess I'll head out. I hope he talks to you before he leaves."

Jennifer pointed at Martin. "I hope he asks you out finally."

Missy smiled. "He kinda did. We have a date very soon. I even told him he had to bring Kostas for my friend Jenny."

"Wow, Jenny must have really pissed you off."

"See you around."

Jennifer watched her go over to the Miami Police Department side. She was impressed by the woman being able to hang with them, even after this small taste of what ACES was like. They were always trying to recruit from the outside and get someone on the team who wasn't already 'ruined' with years of politics and fighting through red tape until they knew how glacial processes worked. A fresh, naïve approach always worked. Missy Lockhart would make an excellent desk agent and eventually a field one.

Dale Comstock was walking slowly across the parking lot, the M4 carbine over his shoulder, his sunglasses on, and a smile on his face.

Martin and Kostas, both laughing quietly, walked around to the other side of the van but still in earshot.

Dale lifted the M4 and offered it to Jennifer. "Ma'am, here's your weapon back."

"What did I tell you about calling me ma'am?"

"What would you like me to call you?" Dale asked.

"Miss Sanchez . . . Boss . . ." *Call me for breakfast from your bed*, she thought. *Call me lover. Call me . . .*

"Penny for your thoughts," he said.

"I don't think so." Jennifer turned to see Martin and Kostas peeking around the van like children. "Can one of you idiots swap out this weapon for Dale's HK416?"

Martin and Kostas both walked up, Martin handing Comstock his weapon. "Nice seeing you again, Dale."

Dale hugged Martin. "Yes, it was. I hope we can work together again in the near future. It's been too long, buddy. Too long."

When Dale pulled away from Martin, Kostas put his arms out. "Can I get a big hug from the Action Figure?"

"Not a chance. You creep me out," Dale said but shook his hand. He lifted his sunglasses to his shaved head.

Martin grabbed Kostas by the arm and led him quickly away.

Jennifer watched her ACES teammates disappear again. "That was awkward."

Dale suddenly looked serious. "Hey, I was wondering . . ."

Jennifer looked away from his piercing eyes and at his massive biceps. *No, that won't work,* she thought. *How can someone be so beautiful? Every inch of him is sculpted perfectly.*

She looked at the police doing their work and refused to make eye contact but put her hand up. "Please, don't say anything."

When he didn't speak she sighed. *Is this really what I want? Is this really what I need?* "After today, you'll be off to fight another war. I'll be doing paperwork for the next year. I doubt you'll be heading to Miami anytime soon."

"If I had a reason to come to Miami, I would."

"You know as well as I do, we can't take vacation or sick days. We don't get weekends off, and we sure don't get to go where we want to. Especially you."

"What are you getting at?"

"I don't want to make this hard on you. We just met and we've barely spoken. I don't want to hinder your progress through life."

"I don't even know what that means," Dale said. "I like you. I want to see you again. Can't we leave it at that for now?"

Jennifer didn't want to lose her resolve. She decided she was doing the right thing by breaking this off before it even started. "I don't want to be another girl in another city on your tour around the world."

Dale shook his head and put his hand up. "Wait, are you judging me?"

"I'm just trying to be realistic."

"We're both adults. I'd like to get to know you better. I'm in town a few more hours before they ship me off, I'm sure. I'd love to take you to dinner."

"I . . . I can't. We can't do this. I'm sorry." The reluctance was obvious in her voice.

Dale nodded. "I don't understand, but I respect you and your decision. I hope before I leave you change your mind, but if not, I hope we cross paths again in the future."

Jennifer stared at him as he put the sunglasses back on. "Good luck, Comstock."

"Good luck to you, Sanchez. You run a great team here, one of the best ACES squads I've ever worked with. It was a real pleasure. My many, many reports will also support the actions here this week."

"Thank you for saying that. I really appreciate it."

Dale turned away. "If you change your mind, you know how to get in touch with me. I'll be waiting and hoping you call. If not, I hope you find what you're looking for."

"I'm not looking for anything."

"We're all looking for something. Whether we realize it or not. Just don't realize it too late, okay?"

≈

HIS ARM WAS USELESS, A BLOODY STUMP WHERE FINGERS USED to be, his tendons and bones showing through torn skin. A normal man would have passed out from the pain and never recovered, but no one ever accused Boris Dragov of being normal, or even human.

Wrapping his torn shirt around the arm and holding it above his heart to staunch the blood flow, he awkwardly climbed over the wall and fled the scene. With so much chaos still around, it was easy for him to look like another injured tourist running away from zombies.

As he got across the parking lot and slipped over a small retaining wall into the adjoining neighborhood, he stopped and caught his breath. He needed a surgeon and he needed one in the next hour, or he would die from blood loss.

He was dizzy and couldn't remember where he'd parked the car. His head was fuzzy around the edges, and he started seeing spots. Boris decided to climb back over into the Miami Zoo parking lot and commandeer a car, even if it meant having to kill a police officer or an innocent person. He needed to find a doctor, but first he needed to get away from here.

The move over the low wall was painful. The nerves were raw and tingling into his shoulder and chest now. He was close to passing out, knowing the ACES team would find his limp body face-first in the pavement. He couldn't let that happen.

Through his haze he remembered Ramzan was here somewhere. And then he saw the car, with the bullet hole from when he'd shot at Ramzan earlier in the day. He was parked at the end of the lot, away from the police and action, but only a hundred agonizing feet from Boris.

He began to shuffle to the car, blood dripping to the ground as he moved. He placed the Makarov PMM in his good hand and prayed he had the strength to hold it.

*It would be ironic if the damn ACES team mistook me for a zombie and shot me this close to getting away,* he thought through his foggy mind.

Boris shambled to the car on an angle and was able to successfully come up to the passenger door without being seen in the side or rearview mirrors.

Ramzan was in the driver's seat, intently leaning forward and staring out the window at the chaos on the other side of the parking lot.

Boris opened the door with his good hand, still holding the gun, nearly dropping it. Before Ramzan could move Boris had it opened and pointed the gun at Ramzan. "I am going to get into the car, and you are going to take me to a doctor who will not ask questions. Is this understood?"

Ramzan's eyes went wide when he saw the damage to the arm. "What happened?'

"I fought a lion." Boris sat down and put the gun into Ramzan's ribcage. "And I won. Now drive."

"Where is Dmitry?"

"Most likely dead."

"What about the item?"

Boris wanted to shoot him, or at least punch him in the face, but he needed to conserve his strength. "Enough questions. I don't have any answers for you. But f I die today, you will die with me. I told our contact everything, but he is to keep a lid on the information if we both live. Do you understand?"

Ramzan sighed as he started the car. "I need to find you a doctor before you die."

≈

**TIM BAKER'S CALVES HURT. HE'D BEEN DANCING BACK AND FORTH** on his feet for the last few hours without sitting. Every time the Emergency Room doors swung open, he stared at the nurse or doctor exiting, but no one had anything new to report. If he sat down now he would be asleep, and he was afraid to miss anything. He'd sleep tomorrow if he had to.

He knew there were still a few more hours to go before the surgery would be successful, but any news would be welcome. The doctor performing the operation was still inside, which was obviously a good thing.

"Any news?" Jennifer Sanchez asked as she walked up. Martin and Kostas were in tow, all looking battle-weary.

"Nothing yet." Tim smiled. "You look like shit."

"You should see the other guy," Kostas said and sat down in an empty chair.

"We came as soon as everything was wrapped up," Jennifer said, taking a seat next to Kostas. "Now, we all need sleep."

"Go home. I have this," Tim said.

"Not a chance. As soon as the zombie gun was put into a locked box and in the capable hands of our agents, we hoofed it over here."

"Wow. I want to hear all about it." Tim leaned against the wall.

"You'll hear so much about it you'll feel like you were there. I'm amazed Kim hasn't called fifteen times already," Martin said.

Jennifer held up her cell phone. "I turned it off. Accidentally, of course. There will be plenty of time to rehash it over and over in our various reports, and then have someone higher up rewrite most of it and make it into something completely different."

"Where's Dale Comstock?" Tim asked.

"He sprouted wings and flew away, shooting from his bazooka arms and spitting grenades from his ass," Kostas said.

"I would expect nothing less." Tim sighed. "This has been a hell of a few days. I can't wait to go back to boring work in Central Florida. Normal stuff like drugs, gun smuggling and terrorists."

Jennifer laughed. "I guess you are officially released from your duty to the ACES team. Once you fill out sixty-five reports and contact your supervisor."

"If I was smart, I would have been writing them while waiting."

"I can't wait to get back home and sleep for days," Kostas said.

"Just make sure you put the DO NOT DISTURB sign on your door," Martin said. "Because you live in a hotel room."

"I understood the comment," Kostas said. "I just didn't

think it was funny."

Jennifer stretched her arms and legs as she sat. "I want a bubble bath."

"I have a nice bathroom, we can make that happen," Kostas said.

"*Sólo en tus sueños*," Jennifer said.

"Only in my dreams?"

"You're getting so good at Spanish."

"*Me gusta su extremo gordo*," Kostas said.

Jennifer elbowed him. "Watch it."

Kostas leaned back in his chair and dramatically looked at her backside. "Oh, I'm watching it. I'll also be watching it as I slap it from behind."

Tim grinned. "Speaking of ass-slapping . . . why did Comstock leave? I figured he'd stay around, Jennifer." He arched his eyebrows. "Did the future lovebirds have a spat?"

Everyone laughed, including Jennifer. "I have no idea what you are talking about, Mister Baker." She was blushing.

"Whatever." Tim was glad to be joking around and relaxing, even for a few minutes. He was uptight and needed to unwind. But not until David was out of surgery.

"They'll start a long distance relationship, send cutsie e-mails and text messages, then move onto webcams," Kostas said. "From there, it will be sexy texts and pictures of Jennifer in just a thong. Then pictures of Comstock nude."

"Now you're talking," Jennifer said.

"I knew it," Tim added sarcastically. "As long as Comstock isn't in a thong, we're all right."

"I think that man could wear anything and make it look sexy," Jennifer said with a weary smile. Tim knew something wasn't quite right about Jennifer and the way she was talking about Comstock but decided to drop it. Obviously things didn't go quite as planned for the two, or Dale would be here with her now.

The Emergency Room doors swung open and the surgeon working on David Luciano stepped out, wringing his hands.

"How's it going in there, doc?" Tim asked.

The doctor put a hand on Tim's shoulder. "He's gone. I'm truly sorry."

"He's out of surgery?" Tim asked, imagining he'd heard the doctor wrong or misunderstood him. "He's in recovery?"

"I'm sorry," the doctor said quietly. "He was a fighter, but the blood loss was traumatic. We couldn't save him."

≈

**EGOR KOLOFF, SVR FIRST DEPUTY DIRECTOR, IGNORED THE DELUGE** as he stood on the balcony. He was only wearing his uniform and no overcoat, but the cold and the rain didn't affect him right now. His rage was burning and keeping him warm.

His cell phone vibrated in his pocket and he went back into the suite, closing the doors behind him. He let it ring four times before answering with a curt hello.

"Sir?"

"I am expecting good news from you."

There was a pause on the line.

"I understand the zombie gun has been recovered, and now all four have fallen into the American government's hands," Egor said. He pulled his other cell phone out and turned it on.

"Yes, we've been notified of this development."

"You call this a development?" Egor searched his contacts list on his other phone as he spoke. "I call this a major setback, for not only my program, but for the war against the United States. If you've called to be executed, I'm already dialing to make it happen. I suggest you not bother to run."

"No, I have good news."

"Anything less than getting my weapons back is not good news."

"I have information about the current whereabouts of the four items. The fourth, most recently recovered, is en route to the Miami International Airport. They will be shipped to Langley in ten days."

"Go on." Egor paused once he'd found the contact he was looking for, but his thumb held steady above the call button. "Take your time answering, too. Your life literally depends on it."

"This gives us ten days to get them back, don't you see?"

"I see nothing except action. Not hearsay and not what could be. I only deal in what is actually happening. The here and now."

"We have several agents in the area already. They can get the items back."

Egor was not impressed. "The items will be heavily guarded by ACES."

The caller laughed. "They are currently being guarded by airport security and only one minor ACES agent. One we currently have in our pocket."

Now Egor was becoming impressed. "Go on."

"He can assist from the inside at getting a team in and out in record time."

"Can he do it without anyone knowing they've been stolen again?"

"Hmm . . . we can work on it. I just assumed a snatch and grab."

"And alert ACES the weapons are live again? If we can get them in the next twenty-four hours without incident, it will give us an extra nine days to move them to a secure location. Then we sit on them until they are needed. No more wasted incidents and needless killing. Do you understand?"

"Perfectly. We'll get them without incident or death. I just need to know who to send. We have several options."

"Where is Boris Dragov?" Egor asked. He was always the first choice.

"Currently off the grid. I know from my sources he went after the gun at the Miami Zoo, but hasn't been seen since."

"Give him three hours to respond to a call. Then, move down the list. Who else?"

"Ramzan is still at large. My informant let me know Dmitry, who was working with him, was killed with the item in his possession."

Egor smiled. This was the renegade team most likely responsible for the theft to begin with. "Contact him, but don't give him any real information."

"Sir?"

"I want Ramzan eliminated. Is that understood?"

"Of course. There are also Nicholai and Ivan in the field. Both working directly under Boris at this time."

"No longer. Have them promoted. I want those two given this mission. If they succeed, great things will be coming their way. If they fail, I want them both tortured and kept alive for weeks. Is that understood?"

"Yes, sir."

Egor hung up both cell phones.

# EPISODE NINE
Snatch and Grab

**GREGORY RAYNHAM TRIED UNSUCCESSFULLY TO TWIRL HIS 9MM** around his thumb more than seven times. He was stuck on four or five for the last hour, and getting madder with each spin.

There was nothing else to do while he sat in the office of Delta Airlines and waited. And waited. Miami International Airport was always crowded, but you would never know from where he was hidden.

He had no window, no closed circuit television, no radio and no one to talk to. The only time he saw another person was when Sammy came with his meals and a smirk.

Sammy was already at the door, forty-five minutes early, wearing his grin and carrying a greasy fast food bag.

"What are you doing here?" Gregory checked his watch. "It's only eleven."

"So?" Sammy was a big man with a huge beer gut and greasy blonde hair. He also worked for ACES, but was even lower than Gregory in the pecking order: he was a glorified mailroom clerk. At least Gregory had his own cubicle, even if all he did was file old documents. And the occasional baby-sitting job, like now.

Gregory glanced at the open door behind Sammy. "I'm not hungry now."

"I don't really care. I'm splitting early today. I have a hot date."

"No one told me about this change," Gregory said.

"Again: I don't really care. It's not like you're doing anything important. You're sitting in a room with some crates and spinning your pistol like one of my kids. And they're all girls."

Gregory took the bag and put it on his bare desk. "Thanks. Talk to you later."

Sammy sat down on the lone chair. "I'll chill here until I have to leave. So many damn cameras once you leave. I don't want that bitch Sanchez seeing me splitting early."

"You have to leave. Now."

Sammy folded his hands behind his head and put his feet on the desk. "I will leave when I'm ready. What's up your ass today, Greggy?"

"Nothing. I just . . . want you to leave me alone so I can eat."

Sammy got up from the chair. "You eat weird or something?" He pointed at the bag. "I want to see you eat now."

"No. Get out."

Sammy crossed his arms over his sizeable gut. "Nope. I can wait you out."

Gregory needed the man to leave. Now. Before the Russians showed up. He'd promised them no complications, and no one else would be here. They would simply walk in, get the boxes and knock Gregory over the head with a punch or something, and then leave. But what would they do with Sammy here?

Gregory pulled a cheeseburger out of the bag and shoved it into his mouth, gnawing at it and forcing it down his throat. "Happy?" he asked, choking on the food. He pulled the second one out and tried to add it to the first one in his mouth, nearly choking. He was hungry, but this was no way to eat. He could barely swallow the burgers, and suddenly didn't think he would ever order another one.

"You're a sick dude." Sammy looked at the bag. "How do

you eat the fries?"

Gregory started shoveling them into his mouth. "Are you happy?" he asked, pieces of food spewing from his mouth. "Leave me alone." Pieces of mashed burgers and fries were dripping down his shirt and onto the floor. He forced the food down.

"Nope."

They would be here any minute, and they would be pissed. And maybe they'd be mad enough to kill the two of them? Gregory checked his watch again. If they were right on schedule, he had less than two minutes.

He needed this guy gone in the next half a minute or he was afraid to even think about the consequences. As much as he disliked Sammy, and was growing to dislike him more with each passing second, he knew he'd be in trouble for having him in here.

Gregory decided to go for broke. There was only one way to get rid of this jerk, the easiest way to make another dude uncomfortable around you. He hoped it worked, because the alternative wasn't going to be pretty. Or any fun for Gregory.

Sammy stopped smiling when Gregory started unbuckling his belt.

"What are you doing?" he asked.

Gregory held back his smile. "Right after I eat, I pleasure myself into the empty bag. Why, what do you do? Smoke a cigarette?"

"You are the sickest dude ever."

"Yet, you're still here watching me. Who's really the sick one?"

Sammy shook his head but didn't move. "You're lying."

Gregory dropped his pants and reached into his underwear. "Suit yourself." He felt completely humiliated, and knew Sammy would spread rumors about him around Magic Productions. But it was still better than the ACES brethren coming to his funeral. If they ever found all the pieces of his body once the Russians got through with him.

Sammy ran from the room. "There is something wrong with you, dude. I knew it. Everyone said you were like a serial killer, but now this . . ." his words trailed off around the corner as he ran away.

Gregory quickly pulled up his pants and was zipping up when he heard the double knock on the side door. "Damn, was that close," he said quietly. While the main corridors were watched by cameras, there was a way through the airport terminal the government used so they would never be filmed or seen. As an ACES member, Gregory knew about it, though he was never supposed to use it to enter or exit the area.

The big Russian was using it.

Gregory went into the hallway and opened the door, surprised to see two burly men waiting for him. He recognized Nicholai.

The men pushed past him and went down the hall, both smiling when they saw the crates. Nicholai put a hand on the box and stared at Gregory. "There were no complications?"

"None. Everything is in order. I'll be guarding the boxes until they get shipped out." Gregory was quite proud of himself for getting rid of Sammy. It wouldn't be good to mention his close encounter, obviously.

"Very good." Nicholai turned to the man with him. "Ivan,

open the crates and get the items." He turned back to Gregory. "You are sure everything is fine?"

Gregory didn't like the patronizing tone of the Russian. "For the last time, everything is perfect. I've held up my end of the bargain."

Nicholai smiled. "And I intend to hold up mine. You can expect the money to drop into your bank account within the next sixty days."

Gregory was confused. "I was expecting payment now."

"You think I carry attaché cases filled with crisp hundred dollar bills around with me?"

"Well, yeah," Gregory admitted. He assumed when payment terms had been reached, he'd be walking out of the building with a bundle of rolled hundreds stuffed into the empty fast food bag. "We had a deal." Was he being double-crossed by the Russians?

Nicholai suddenly moved, and Gregory found himself slammed against the table, his head hitting the wall behind him. "Did I say you'd get paid today? Did those words ever cross my lips?"

"No, but I assumed I'd have the cash today. I thought it was how this worked."

"And you will get paid. You know what happens when you assume?" Nicholai asked.

Gregory was released and he stood up, shaking and feeling weak. He tried to laugh it off. "When you assume, you make an ass out of you and me."

Nicholai shook his head slowly. "When you assume, my patience grows short. And this leads to me putting a bullet through your left eye. Is that understood?"

"Yes," Gregory said quietly, his voice hitching in his throat. "Sixty days." It was better than death, he supposed. He would accept it but he didn't have to like it.

"We don't want you to get caught, do we? The goal is to get in, get out, and no one will ever know what happened to these items. You are just the monkey standing in an empty room with some crates. What do you know? It isn't like you brought the crates here. They could have been empty already. All your job description says right now is to stand in the room and watch these boxes. No one can blame you for this screw-up, my friend. The government will find someone else to be the scapegoat."

"It might be me." Gregory watched as Ivan put the four items into a shoulder sack. "I'm the one who will take the fall."

"No, you won't." Nicholai offered his hand to shake.

Gregory took it and his fingers were immediately gripped in the Russian's vice-like hand. Nicholai pulled him forward, staring down into his eyes.

"As long as you keep your mouth shut, nothing will happen to you. Why would they blame you? Don't sweat it, as you Americans say. In a few weeks, you'll be swimming in money. You can buy your little daughter whatever she wants for Christmas."

Ivan grinned. "Little Isabella would really like the new line of Barbie dolls. She especially likes the blonde ones. I guess because she has such beautiful golden hair."

Gregory felt like he'd been punched in the chest. "How do you know her name?"

Nicholai squeezed his hand harder. "It's called taking out

an insurance policy, of sorts. We're going to walk out the door, and you are going to do a crossword puzzle or something and look natural. Then play dumb when it's discovered the items are missing. Can you do it?"

Gregory was numb. *They know his daughter's name, her hair color . . . and she collects Barbie dolls. They've talked to my little girl.* "I can do it. Just don't hurt my family."

"Who said anything about hurting your family?" Nicholai released Gregory's hand and turned to Ivan. "Did you threaten this man's pretty little blonde daughter with the dimples and big blue eyes?"

Ivan shook his head. "Why would I do something like that?" He looked at Gregory. "I think he's a smart guy. He's a member of ACES. They only hire the best of the best."

The two Russians turned to leave.

"Wait," Gregory said. "Aren't you going to knock me out?"

Nicholai dramatically rubbed his temples. "Why would we hit you, even though it would be fun? Haven't you been listening to a thing I said? Sit down, shut up and collect your money. Do a nice job and we'll be contacting you again in the future. Think of all the nice things this money will buy you and your family." Nicholai shook his head again. "And clean up the floor. There are chunks of food everywhere. You eat like a slob."

Gregory watched the two men leave before sitting down and shutting up, thinking of the things this new money was going to buy. And trying to push away the thought of these killers knowing too much about his personal life.

≈

**BORIS SCREAMED OUT WHEN THE DOCTOR PULLED THE STITCH TIGHT,** but he refused to pass out and let Ramzan overtake him. The doctor was doing a great job, and the damage wasn't as bad as first thought.

When Ramzan took a step toward the chair where Boris sat, Boris waved the Makarov PMM at his crotch. "Take another step and I will shoot the tip off." Boris smiled. "And I can do it, you already know this."

Ramzan stepped back and put his hands on the wall, like he'd been told. He looked away in submission, which had Boris wanting to laugh despite the searing pain.

Boris casually pointed the gun at the doctor. "I'd take my time and be a little gentler, my friend. If you hurt me again, I just might pull this trigger and splat your brains out on the wall behind us."

The doctor looked shaken but his hands never stopped working. "I understand, sir. You've lost way too much blood. You need to relax the arm. Luckily, nothing important was damaged. You'll have deep scarring but full use of the arm eventually, with proper rehabilitation. The wounds will need to be cleaned hourly and the bandages changed, or the stitches are in danger of pulling out. If this happens, you could literally bleed to death. I need to put it in a sling. Are you sure you won't take anything for the pain?"

As much as he wanted to, Boris knew any drug in his system would knock him out. He needed to rest, but he needed his wits more right now. As soon as he looked weak or passed out, Ramzan would kill him. If he were in Ramzan's position he would do it.

Boris wondered why he didn't just kill Ramzan when the

doctor was done. And then kill the doctor, as well. But he might need one or both in the future. One thing he never did was kill someone on impulse. Well, not often. He kept his eye on the prize, and right now these two men might help him to attain it. And a good doctor with a closed mouth was always hard to come by, especially in a foreign country.

"Ramzan, have you been contacted?"

When Ramzan looked away and mumbled *nyet*, Boris knew it was a lie. It didn't matter. At this point they were both more than likely on another agent's death list. There had been too many screw-ups. The zombie gun was out there, somewhere, and they needed to find it. Dmitry never checked back in. If he was lost, the weapon was lost.

"The weapon was recovered," Ramzan said.

Boris glanced at the doctor.

Ramzan smiled. "The good doctor has been working with the SVR for years. He's handled some important work for us, in fact. Do you remember Gorchenko in the 1960s?"

"Why would I remember that?" Boris asked, annoyed. He was happy Ramzan was talking to him so he could focus on what a worthless man Ramzan was and ignore what the doctor was doing to his arm. He wanted to scream again. The slightest touch caused considerable pain.

Ramzan shrugged. "I thought it was part of your training. Gorchenko told me, before he retired, about our friend here. The good doctor worked on him." Ramzan smiled. "Gorchenko took four bullets, one in each arm and one in both the thigh and shoulder. Granted, no vital organs were hit, but taking four slugs is pretty impressive. Gorchenko was able to walk here, six miles, with all four still lodged in his body.

How's that for tough? He said he refused anesthesia, and walked out on his own two feet twenty minutes after surgery."

"Is this true?" Boris asked the doctor.

The doctor ignored the question and continued his work.

Boris looked back at Ramzan, saying, "The reason the doctor is still alive is because he doesn't talk about things. You might want to learn from this man, before it gets you killed."

"Are you threatening me?"

"No. It's an observation. You'll know when I am threatening you, because you'll be dead."

"I'm not scared of you," Ramzan said. Boris knew it was a lie.

"Are we being pulled from here?" Boris wanted to know. "Do we have a new mission, or are we simply waiting for a bullet?"

"I'm not sure. I get the impression there is something going on without us."

"That would make sense. There are other agents in the field who can attempt to recover the item, especially since we both failed."

"You're probably right."

"Plus, I'm sure they realize you were responsible for the Miami Zoo attack. And they either have Dmitry in custody or he's been eliminated. For your sake, I hope he's been killed. He was always so weak. It wouldn't take much to extract information from him."

Ramzan threw his hands in the air. "I had nothing to do with any attack."

Boris chuckled. "I hope you aren't so delusional to think our bosses don't already know everything you've done. You've been a rogue only because they let you. They obviously see some reason to let you make a mess of this new technology. Perhaps they decided to see if a war could be started or if America would fall into chaos. They gave you the weapon and turned you loose."

"I did it to protect Mother Russia."

"You did it for your own agenda. I suspect it gelled with their master plan, or else you wouldn't be alive right now. I was really hoping my phone would ring and I'd get the contract on your head."

Ramzan pulled his cell phone from his pocket. "You seem to forget I can also get the same call. It would bring me great pleasure to be able to brag about taking you down."

"I'd be quite the trophy, I imagine." Boris grunted when the doctor pulled the last stitch through. "Except I don't run my mouth like you always have. I am much more valuable to the svr than you will ever be. You know why? Because I don't talk and brag about things. I do what I am sent to do, I do it well, and I move on."

"Yet, here you sit, with a ruined arm and a failed mission. I'm sure our bosses will be quite impressed with this epic failure on your part."

"You have also failed."

Ramzan shook his head. "No. I'm a rogue, remember? I was always working on my own, for my own agenda. You said it yourself. I'm here to create chaos and stir the Americans into action. I've done that and more." He pointed at Boris. "You, on the other hand, have failed in your quest. The zombie gun is firmly in the hands of the ACES team. We are agents cut off from any information, and there is a hit squad more than likely en route to shoot us."

Before Boris could respond, the door was kicked open and three men toting pistols entered. The largest man smiled. "Ah, welcome to America, comrades. I'm Fat Tony. I own this damn town."

~

JENNIFER SANCHEZ WAS ANNOYED. IT HAD BEEN A FULL DAY SINCE the attack at the Miami Zoo and she was still buried in paperwork. Kim L was scheduling conference and video chats every four hours with various branches of the government, and Jennifer was expected to be involved in all of them, and read her initial report. She was getting nothing else done, since each call went anywhere from two to three hours.

She checked her watch. She had fifteen minutes until the next call, even though she'd just clicked off from the last one. Her cell phone rang and she cringed. It was Kim L.

"Yes, ma'am?"

"Getting tired of these calls yet?"

"No, ma'am."

Kim chuckled on the line. "Good answer. The CIA is up next, and we need to answer some tough questions from them. This next conference call will be important, so make sure you look presentable. And sit up straight. And keep Kostas out of the room."

"Kostas and Martin are finishing their reports in their own offices and then I told them they could take the night off."

"Ah, Martin having his date with Miss Lockhart?"

*She doesn't miss anything*, Jennifer thought. "I imagine it will be tonight."

"They need to unwind and relax. So do you, Miss Sanchez."

"Eventually."

"But not tomorrow. I need you to get to the Miami Police Department training field. There's a new program the city and the FBI is putting together, a fun thing to get the PTA and soccer moms active in defense."

Jennifer fixed her pens for the tenth time, making sure they were perfectly straight and in order according to the colors of the rainbow. "To defend against what? A self defense class for women?"

"To teach women the finer points of fighting zombies."

Jennifer thought she'd misheard Kim. "Can you repeat that, please?"

"I said zombies. It's been cleared already, and will start next weekend. They'll be making the announcement tomorrow, after you meet with them. This is not a joke, before you ask, and not a Halloween themed party, either."

"Permission to speak freely, ma'am?"

"Of course."

"I don't think me training housewives to fight imaginary monsters is really a good move. We could better serve the public with some promotional material, commercials, maybe a YouTube clip. But asking the common woman to fight zombies isn't really my thing."

"And it won't be. I will, however, ask if you would help in even a small capacity to make sure it goes off without a hitch. And they're no longer imaginary monsters to the city of Miami and the world. Kindly remember that part, Miss Sanchez."

Jennifer knew what Kim meant when she *asked* for something. "I will help in any way I can, but if there is another mission on the immediate radar, I don't want to be caught involved in this pet project. I will not hesitate to help out. I just don't want to miss something because we're hanging out at a luncheon, talking to older women about Oprah and baking recipes."

"Understandable. That's why you won't be running it. We have another coordinator in mind."

Jennifer knew where this usually led to. "I'm not comfortable letting any of the ACES team go for this, even if it is good promo in the community after what we've gone through."

"Right now, the FBI isn't asking for your team to get involved. But you know they will if they see it makes a difference. And it will, whether you realize it or not. After what's been going on the last few days, now is the time to train the people, have some fun doing it and lighten the mood if possible. Plus, make everyone aware this could happen again."

"I hope not."

"The Russians didn't make four of these zombie guns and break the mold. We might be dealing with dozens of them soon. What do we do then? The CIA will be running scenarios in the next month as well, and they've invited every branch of the military to participate. It would be in our best interest to mobilize the citizens in the event of another attack. We got lucky with it being contained in the Miami Zoo this time. What will happen if the airport or a sporting event gets attacked, thousands of people turned into zombies and roaming the streets around it?"

"I guess we're no longer trying to sweep this under the rug."

"It's too big now. We've decided to embrace the potential threat by teaching the public how to defend against the next attack. We're pretty confident another one is coming. Whether or not this one was planned, the cat is out of the proverbial bag. Our enemies will be trying another tactic sooner than later. Panic in the streets and mass hysteria isn't the answer. I think it will be a refreshing move."

"I suppose it makes sense. I just don't like playing zombie-walk with real threats still out there on a daily basis."

"Your participation will be minimal, unless you volunteer to help out, of course."

*That will be doubtful*, Jennifer thought. She was already trying to think of new ways to get as far away from this as possible. While it might help them inadvertently, it wasn't a project she wanted ACES to pour time and energy into unless they were forced. "I'm sure if I have any, I will give all the free time I have."

"I'm sure you will. Are you prepared for this next call? This is the most important. Until the debriefing of the President at seven."

Jennifer sat down. "The President of the United States will be on the phone?"

"Yes, of course. He needs to know what you know."

"What I know?"

There was a dramatic pause, which Kim seemed to enjoy doing. "Yes. You'll be addressing him. He wants to hear it from your mouth. He's not looking for runaround jargon and beating around the bush. He wants to hear everything you know. I am faxing over the list of things you can't tell him, though. It should be arriving any moment."

"Wow."

"I have a quick favor to ask for tomorrow, when you meet with the Miami Police Department."

"Sure." Jennifer was still trying to wrap her head around talking to the President in a few hours.

"I need you to go across the street and pick up Dale Comstock in the morning."

"Why?" Jennifer stood up and put her hands on the desk.

"Isn't it obvious? Comstock will be running the soccer mom zombie defense training."

$$\approx$$

**FAT TONY AIMED HIS PISTOL AT THE RUSSIAN SITTING IN THE CHAIR.** Even though he looked injured, he looked dangerous. Tony hadn't gotten this far without being able to size up the competition in any room and eliminate it. He was, however, curious why the man was pointing his Makarov PMM at his fellow Russian. "Am I interrupting?"

"Fat Tony?" the Russian being worked on by the doctor asked. "I've never heard of you."

"Oh, but I've heard of you and your partner. It seems you've taken control of merchandise I've paid for already. You understand the conflict we have then?"

"Not really." The Russian on the chair slowly turned his gun on Tony. "I am, however, going to ask you to tell your

two goons to lower their weapons. There are too many bar-
rels aimed in my direction. That makes me nervous. When I
get nervous I tend to pull the trigger."

"Ah, you must be Boris Dragov. I've heard quite a bit about
you." Fat Tony didn't want a shootout in the tiny office. He
needed at least one of these men alive so he could find the
zombie gun. He turned to his men. "Lower your weapons,
please."

"That's much better," Boris said. He kept his pistol trained
on the crotch of Fat Tony.

"Wouldn't you rather shoot me in the head?"

"And kill you outright? There's no fun in a headshot. If I
shoot the tip off your manhood, you could bleed out and die
a horrible death."

"He can do it," the other Russian said.

"I have done it."

"Sorry, but I need to keep my dick. It's been a close friend
for years."

"I imagine you haven't seen it for years," Boris said.

"Very funny. I think we need to relax for a moment and
talk."

"I'm not going anywhere for a few minutes. I'm just waiting for the doctor to clean me up so I can get going. I'm feeling hungry. Can you suggest a nice restaurant in the area?"

"I own most of them."

"It would be impressive if this part of Miami wasn't such
a shit-hole."

"Someday this will end up being a gold mine. Trust me."
Fat Tony didn't like the way this Russian was talking to him,
and didn't like the way he was being so casual, even with a

gun trained on him and Boris in a seemingly weakened state.

Boris stood and let the doctor put his arm in a sling and adjust it before turning back to Tony. "I guess you aren't going to shoot me since you let him set my arm. What is it you think I have that you want?"

"The gun."

Boris looked casually at the Makarov PMM in his good hand. "This one? It was a gift from my father when I was born."

Fat Tony smiled. "And let me guess: you shot him with it when you turned fourteen?"

"No."

Fat Tony was starting to realize this Russian wasn't so bad. He needed to turn this conversation around as quickly as possible, get his information and get out. He decided the best way to do it was speaking directly to the other Russian and let Boris know he wasn't impressed with him trying to be the boss.

"He used it to kill his mother when he was twelve," the other one offered.

Before Tony could respond he heard two gunshots, his ears ringing in the small office. His two men slumped to the ground.

Boris lowered his pistol. "They were bothering me. Have a seat, Fat Tony. I think we need to talk about a few things. Perhaps we can help one another. I don't hold a grudge, or feel threatened by many men. Even ones pointing guns in my face. I am smart enough to know when people need to be kept alive. Right now, lucky you, you need to stay alive."

Fat Tony was worried. The two dead guys didn't bother

him. It was the price of dealing with international killers. He had a roster filled with disposable men. But he'd clearly lost the advantage today. "I could say the same thing."

"But it wouldn't be true. We both know this. You can keep pumping up your chest and trying to look tough, or simply sit down, put your gun away, and listen to what I have to offer you for your help."

Now Tony was intrigued. "You need my help?" He smiled. "It looks like you boys have everything under control. Besides the blood everywhere, of course."

"If you are really such a big shot in Miami, we need to know where the ACES team is holed up."

"Wow, that's pretty ballsy. Are you honestly planning on kicking the hornet's nest? Although it would be ironic to turn them into zombies and have them bite people, I suppose. I don't know where they are, but I can find out."

Boris laughed. "You have your ear to the ground, my friend?"

"Yes."

"Then how is it you are the only person in Miami that doesn't know ACES recovered the item yesterday, you idiot?"

"Don't call me names," Fat Tony said quietly. *Recovered? How? When?*

"Can I go now?" the doctor asked.

"Yes. Thank you for your work, and your discretion," Boris said.

The doctor pointed at the broken door. "I trust you'll be paying for this?"

Boris laughed. "Fat Tony, you have all the pull around here."

"I'll get it fixed."

The doctor left without another word, pulling the smashed door almost closed.

"We need to find it before they ship it north." Boris sat back down in his chair and put the Makarov PMM on his lap. "But now it's obvious you don't know anything. I should shoot your dick off just to make a point."

"What's in it for me?"

"Produce the ACES secret fortress headquarters and we'll talk."

"You don't need to know where they're located. What you need to know is where the gun is being held until it gets flown to Washington or wherever."

"Yes, I suppose."

Fat Tony sat down but kept his gun out. "The way I see it, they need a safe place to store the weapon until they cut through all the red tape and are able to ship it without hassle. Something like that could take days or even weeks to get clearance for. There is one place they would need to store and guard it before it can go, somewhere close to the flight, so when they get the okay it can be loaded."

"Miami International Airport," Ramzan said.

"Exactly. I've had guys inside for years, and I know the most likely spot they would hide it. Give me a few phone calls and I'll have it located."

"Then I think we have a deal in place."

"What would that deal entail?"

"I'll let you live," Boris said.

"I'm not too worried about it. I think we both know we could have a long and fruitful relationship in Miami once we get over the machismo and get down to working together. I have no problem helping you get the zombie gun back, but I want to use it as well. I have several enemies I'd love to get rid of, and let them get rid of their friends, and so on and so on. How does that sound to you?"

Boris merely stared at Fat Tony as he continued, "I can find out where it is, but we're wasting time."

"Let's be honest: we're not going to simply hand over the guns and not get killed anyway. I'm starting to see your side of things . . . maybe. The war has begun, and I think we'd be doing Mother Russia a favor by creating even more havoc than before," Boris stared at Ramzan. "With three of us, we can spread out and hit different areas simultaneously. Blanket Miami with zombies and chaos."

"There is no turning back. Once we do this, you will never be able to return to our homeland."

"I might be returning as a conquering hero," Boris said.

"Let's worry about all this fantasy crap once we get this ball rolling," Fat Tony finally said. "We need to get somewhere safe. I have some restaurants in the area. We can get some good food and I can make a few phone calls."

"I am hungry," Boris said. "The last meal I had was a cinnamon raisin bagel with tuna and a coffee."

"That sounds gross," Fat Tony said. "And I eat just about anything."

"It's delicious."

"I'll take your word for it." Fat Tony put his gun away. "I'll get a cleanup crew here as well. Either of you drive? I lost my license."

"Drunk driving?" Ramzan asked.

"I didn't pay a parking ticket, believe it or not. Would hate to get pulled over and get another one."

Boris put his Makarov PMM away. "I guess we're going to do this. It should be interesting. Lead the way, Fat Tony."

Fat Tony held up a finger. "I have one thing to ask: is there really more than one of these zombie guns?"

Boris smiled. "There are four of them."

"This is going to be fun," Fat Tony smiled, and went to search the dead men for the car keys.

$\approx$

**MIKE MARTIN WAS ONE OF THOSE WARRIORS WHO NEVER BROKE** under pressure. In fact, throw impossible odds at him, a limited amount of ammo, no escape route and certain death and he'd walk away unscathed. And he could do it with a satisfied grin and a hope to do it all over again. But next time turn it up a few notches.

Right now, as he slid out the chair at the expensive Italian restaurant and glanced at his three dinner companions—Missy Lockhart, Mark Kostas and Jenny Adams—he thought he was going to vomit. His hands gripped the back of his chair to steady his nerves. He could kill a man at 2,700 yards with a perfect headshot, but in a social setting he was all thumbs.

"You all right, buddy? You look like shit," Jenny said to him.

"I'm fine." As he sat, Martin tried to smile and failed. The ride over had been brutal, with everyone having a big laugh at his expense and obvious discomfort.

Kostas, who was perpetually smiling tonight but surprisingly very quiet, waved for the waitress. "I called ahead," he told her. "Mike Martin."

"What are you doing?" Martin asked, afraid to know the answer. Whenever Kostas used his name for anything, it often meant something borderline illegal or something which would cost Martin a paycheck.

"Nothing much." Kostas smiled at Jenny. "I just wanted to make sure our night went wonderfully. We have two exquisitely beautiful dates here with us, so I took the liberty of a few choices. I hope no one minds."

Waiters brought over two bottles of chilled champagne, positioning them on either side of the women. Dishes of Mozzarella Anacapri and Eggplant Rolatini were placed on the table.

"No wonder the maitre d' smiled so much when I told him I had reservations," Martin said.

"Did you think you had pull in this town?"

Missy was smiling at Martin, and put a hand next to his on the table. *What does that mean? Do I put my hand on hers? Is that what she wants? Or do I play it cool? What if she wants me to do it, but I don't, and she thinks I don't like her? What if . . .*

Missy put her hand on his and squeezed lightly. "This is fun. I'm glad I came."

"I'll be glad when I get some of this wine in me," Jenny said.

"Did you order our main course, too?" Martin asked Kostas, ignoring Missy's hand on his like a teenager. Hell, teenage Mike Martin would have more play than this old loser. He tried to will himself not to start sweating in front of her.

"You mean *secondi piatti*?" Kostas said with a grin. He turned to Jenny. "It means main course."

"*Che è molto impressionante,*" Jenny said. "I spent two years teaching in Rome. I picked up a few phrases."

Missy laughed. "Jenny was a teacher for years, and even a dean at a college."

"Why'd you stop?" Martin asked. He decided to focus on something other than Missy so close to him, and how pretty she looked tonight, and if he put on enough deodorant.

Jenny took a sip of wine. "Butting heads with the administration takes its toll. I got sick of spending more time fighting with them than teaching students. So, I walked away. I wanted to get a temporary job in another field before I went back into teaching. Ten years later, I'm still working for the Miami PD."

"What do you do there?" Kostas asked, leaning forward casually.

Jenny finished her wine and started on the appetizers. "Don't try to be so interested in my life, buddy." She winked at Missy. "It won't take long for you to get some as long as you don't act too stupid."

"Jenny, didn't we have a talk?" Missy asked.

Martin liked Jenny, especially since she was keeping Kostas disarmed and quiet. For all his bravado and machismo, when faced with a woman who knew what she wanted, he was suddenly quiet.

Jenny shrugged. "How old are you, little boy?"

"Uh . . . I'm twenty-four," Kostas said.

"Are you sure? You hesitated there. Are you underage? Do I need to card you?"

"Jenny!" Missy said, a little too loud. Patrons around them glanced in their direction.

Martin leaned over to Missy. "She's fine. She's keeping him quiet, which is absolutely amazing. I think he's met his match."

"She's having fun. And I know by the way she's acting she likes him. Plus, she's a cougar. This will be fun for her to bag a man fifteen years younger." Missy moved closer to Martin. "If she doesn't get bored with him by dessert."

"Good to know." He was enjoying sitting so close to her and didn't pull away. He locked eyes on her and knew he could get lost in her. Too easily. Martin wondered if it was already a done deal, and sighed. He'd never fallen so totally and completely for a woman in his entire life. He'd known plenty of women and boasted of being a player. He was a great-looking guy and women threw themselves at him at times. But this . . . this was something he'd never felt before, and he wanted to kick his own ass for it.

"What are you staring at?"

"You're very pretty," Martin said.

"I know." Missy laughed at her joke but didn't move back or break his gaze. "Guys tell me that all the time."

"I'm sure they do."

"Usually, I'm handcuffing them and tossing them into the back of my car."

"Damn criminals."

"I have no idea if they're criminals or not. I'm talking about when I'm off duty."

Martin laughed. "Funny."

Jenny took the wine bottle from Kostas and filled her glass.

"Keep these coming, buddy. I'm off tomorrow." She piled her plate with more food. "Are you going to be the gentleman and order my meal?"

Kostas looked confused. "If that's what you want."

"Order another bottle of wine and I'll show you what I want." Jenny looked at Missy and frowned. "Yeah, yeah, I know: Jenny!"

Martin didn't know when Missy took her hand off his, but he suddenly wanted to grip her by the hand, spin her around and kiss her. Like he was fifteen. He kept his composure as the waitress came back to take their orders.

"How is it getting back to police work?" Martin asked once they'd ordered (and Kostas ordered for Jenny).

"Boring, if I'm being honest. Traffic stops don't hold the same attraction as they used to. I had to fight just to get back on a shift today. Thank Jennifer for me, by the way. Chief Alvarez said she created quite a stink about me not getting back to work."

"I'll let her know." Martin sipped his wine. "You know, there is always a place on ACES for you. They don't offer the invitation lightly."

"I appreciate it, I really do." Missy picked up her wine glass but kept it hovered near her mouth. "Some of the people at work are treating me differently now."

"How?"

"A few are subtly hostile about me being gone for, what, a few hours? I think I missed two shifts. They act like I bailed on them for bigger and better things."

"Professional jealousy."

"Of course. Then there are the ones who suddenly want

to be my best friend, thinking I can get them into ACES and a better job. They think just because I worked with ACES for 48 hours, I'm suddenly on the government's payroll and I'm getting a big paycheck."

"Actually, wait until you see the check. Jennifer put you in for a week's pay, which is quite substantial. We get paid very well. Of course, with all the red tape and hoops you need to jump through, it'll take six months to get. But it is worth it. Trust me."

"Really?" Missy asked. She sipped her wine and then cocked her head at Martin. "How much?"

Martin grinned. "Maybe I shouldn't have said anything. I don't want to tempt you back over to the Dark Side, especially when you were so adamant about getting away from ACES."

Missy frowned and Martin felt like an idiot.

"I didn't mean it quite the way it fell out of my mouth. Let me rephrase it."

Missy cocked an elbow on the table. "Oh, this had better be good, big boy. Begin your groveling. I'm waiting."

Martin looked at Kostas and Jenny for help, but they were involved in a side conversation, talking in low whispers. He supposed they were talking about him and Missy.

"Cat got your tongue?"

"No, I just don't want to say another stupid thing. Give me a minute." Martin picked up his wine glass, but it was empty. Now he was beginning to sweat.

Missy, clearly enjoying herself, poured him another full glass of wine. "If I were you I would gulp it in one shot. Liquid courage, big boy."

"Stop calling me big boy."

"Why, big boy? Does it bother you?" Missy leaned against him again and smiled. "You know I'm just teasing you, right?"

"Yes."

"But I still want to hear about this Dark Side you are trying to lure me into. Does it include dental?"

"Yes, and a nice 401k, as well as life insurance."

"And life insurance might come in handy, especially with terrorists trying to shoot you and zombies trying to eat you. I imagine hazard pay, too?"

"That's pretty much the huge paycheck part of the equation. You're too busy counting your money to worry about the bullets whizzing by overhead."

"Nice." Missy leaned even closer. "Did I mention I'm happy I came tonight?"

"I'm not sure. To be positive, you might want to say it again."

Missy leaned in with a smile, staring into Martin's eyes. "I'm really, really, really glad I'm here tonight with you."

"I'm glad, too." Martin started to close his eyes and move his lips forward. He didn't care about a restaurant filled with diners, or Kostas and Jenny. He wanted to kiss her and fall into her completely. He wanted to . . .

Jenny stood up. "I'm going to the little girl's room." She looked at Kostas. "If you have any balls, you'll meet me in stall number three in four minutes."

"Jenny!"

"I'm kidding, I'm kidding." Jenny winked at Kostas. "Meet me in six minutes. I'll start without you."

# EPISODE TEN
Zombie Killing Soccer Moms

**JENNIFER SANCHEZ GRIPPED THE WET TISSUES IN HER HAND, NO** longer of any real use to dab her teary eyes. She looked across the funeral home and admired the huge turnout for David Luciano. His family and friends were congregating upfront, paying their respects.

ACES team members were in and out all night, introduced to his family as co-workers for the movie production company where they all supposedly worked.

Dale Comstock came up next to Jennifer and nodded, moving to her side. He looked incredibly sexy in a charcoal gray suit and deep red tie, his head freshly shaved and his eyes sparkling. It was a rush to pick him up from the airport this morning, and they'd spent a busy day together. A trip to the Miami Police Department to set up a demonstration for tomorrow afternoon, paperwork, a briefing of foreign agents still active in Miami, and miscellaneous duties kept them close together but apart.

Martin and Missy came up, Missy hugging Jennifer.

"How're you doing?" Martin whispered as he hugged her.

"I'll be fine. David was one of the good guys. I wish we'd spent more time training him."

Martin shook his head. "Don't go there. He had excellent training, and knew all the risks of this job. He didn't make a mistake and neither did you. He just went against someone with knowledge and more skill, and luck."

"And that someone is Boris Dragov," Kostas said as he walked up. "I just got the word. They found the body of his second, Andre, floating in the bay."

"It makes sense, with Ramzan in town and Dmitry running around with the zombie gun. I wonder how many more players are involved, though," Jennifer said. "We'll reconvene in two hours at Magic Productions and go over everything."

Dale stepped forward and smiled. "If I can make a suggestion, Miss Sanchez: why not get some sleep tonight and look at this fresh in the morning?"

Jennifer knew he was right, and she knew he had an ulterior motive and would ask her to dinner or maybe more . . . and she decided she would. Being around him was exciting her. She'd been around plenty of strong men in her career, but Dale exuded such raw animal magnetism. "I agree. This is a pretty emotional time. We'll meet at oh-six-hundred."

Martin glanced at Missy. "We're going to say our last respects and leave." He glanced at Dale. "Have a great night."

They left hand in hand. Jenny came up and wrapped an arm around Kostas and kissed him on the cheek, which clearly embarrassed him.

"I guess we'll be heading out," Kostas said.

Jenny suddenly hugged Jennifer and put her mouth near her ear. "Please, honey, tell me you're going to climb the Comstock Chocolate Mountain, or I will."

Jennifer laughed and squeezed back. "Jenny, I sure hope so."

Kostas shook Dale's hand silently.

"It was great meeting you, Jenny," Comstock said. He shook her hand but then didn't look surprised when she hugged him.

When Jenny pulled away she shook dramatically. "Jeez, I think I just had an orgasm." She turned to Jennifer and winked. "Tell me all about it. Every last detail."

Kostas looked annoyed and steered her away and out of

the funeral parlor.

"That leaves just the two of us," Dale said with his charming smile. "I'll see you at the soccer field after your meeting."

"Sure," Jennifer said and faked a smile. Now she was confused. "Feel free to stop over at Magic and help with my debriefing. We still have a threat to deal with, finding the Russians responsible for the attack. We could use your help. I'll do the paperwork and let Kim L know you're going to assist us."

They started walking to the door but Comstock stopped. "I can't."

"Too busy with the soccer moms?"

He laughed. "Actually, I am." He held the door open for her. "I retired."

"Is that supposed to be funny?"

"I put in the paperwork, despite about twenty people telling me I was insane."

"I make twenty-one." Jennifer couldn't believe what she was hearing. "There is no way the CIA or FBI or the President would accept your resignation. Not to mention every other branch of government. I'm sure they're also living in fear you'll merc out and come back to haunt them."

"I'm still going to work for the good guys, but I'm devoting myself to training civilians and doing something other than killing."

"You'll get the itch again."

"If I do, I'll shoot Kostas."

"Win-win. I don't think a man like you can handle hanging out with annoying soccer moms, drinking beer and getting fat while watching sitcoms until you pass out each night."

"It beats getting shot at and sleeping pinned against a cold rock in the desert."

"Does it?"

Comstock laughed. "No. I'm sure I'll get the urge to shoot live targets soon enough. Kill some bad guys. Fun stuff."

"Did they give you this gig when you retired?"

"Actually, I came up with the idea at the Miami Zoo. I told Kim I was going to do it, with or without their help. Once they approved it, I sent in my letter."

"Stuff like this takes weeks to do," Jennifer said. She was at her car, keys in hand, and hoping he'd notice and invite her out to dinner or a drink. "There's no way you pushed this through so quickly."

"I'm very persuasive. You might not realize this, but I am kinda important," Dale said with a grin. "They didn't really have a say in anything."

"I might hire you for ACES, just to get things done for me. If I have to file another fifteen requisitions for changing the toilet paper, I'll scream."

"The finer points of bureaucracy. I'm so glad I went into the part where they tell you to point and shoot. It's easier pretending you're just another weapon to them. Once they see you can converse, they start talking to you. I wanted no part of that."

"And now you'll be in the thick of training and doing things you never thought you'd be doing." Jennifer punched the button on her keychain and unlocked her car. *Make your play, Dale. Say the word and I'm yours tonight,* she thought.

"I'm going to do it on my own terms. They know this, and they know how I am. I also know you aren't ready to step down from ACES and work with me, but I want to formally make the offer to you: if you ever need a change of pace and something a bit more relaxing and fun, I'd take you with me in a heartbeat."

"I appreciate it. I really do. Maybe someday I'll take you up on the offer," Jennifer said. *Or any offer tonight.*

"I'm excited to have you onboard helping me with this first run. Miami was the obvious place to begin this, and also an excuse to see you again."

Jennifer smiled. "I was glad to see you, as well. Today was awkward."

"Yes, all around."

Jennifer leaned against her car. "So, uh . . . what are you doing now?"

Dale smiled. "I'm going to my hotel room and getting some sleep. I have a big day tomorrow." He stepped close to her. "And so do you."

She looked at her watch. "True. It's still early, and I'm hungry. Can't go to bed on an empty stomach."

"I guess not." Dale leaned forward and kissed her on the cheek. "I'll let you get some food. I have to get some sleep."

Jennifer was stunned when he turned and walked to his rental car. *This isn't how this is supposed to go down tonight,* she thought. *Not tonight.* She glanced back to the funeral home as people kept coming and going for their fallen brethren.

Dale was fumbling with his keys as he glanced back at her and smiled, giving a wave.

Now Jennifer was pissed. She was sick of him controlling the situation. Dammit, she was the boss when you were in Miami! How dare he come back so soon and then play with her like this?

"Hey, Comstock," she growled as she walked up to him.

He was still smiling when she grabbed him roughly by his huge arms and pulled him to her. "Where do you think you're going?"

"There's a hard hotel bed calling my name."

"And there's a warm Latina female who wants to moan your name," she said, amazed but happy she'd said something so bold to him.

"Didn't you give me a speech about this not 48 hours ago?"

"Are you going to hold me to my word, or follow me back to my house?"

Dale kissed her softly on the lips. "Are you sure?"

"You are a beautiful man, but you talk way too much. Shut up and follow me."

~

**GREGORY RAYNHAM MUST HAVE FALLEN ASLEEP, BECAUSE WHEN** he sat up in his chair drool was slipping down his chin. He wiped his bleary eyes and yawned.

"Have a nice nap, Gregory?"

"Who the hell are you?" Gregory was at attention and reaching for his pistol. His holster was empty.

"Looking for this?" The large man said, twirling the pistol around and around his finger. Six, seven, eight, nine times . . .

"My record is seven," Gregory said, still groggy but trying to remain calm. The big guy didn't scare him as much as the two crazed Russians with him. He'd dealt with enough of them to know, and he also knew beyond a shadow of a doubt the one with his arm in a sling was the dreaded Boris Dragov.

"Gregory, we seem to have a problem and we'd like your help in solving it. Would you do that for me?"

"I don't want any trouble. I'm just here to guard these, uh, crates."

"The empty crates?" the Russian in the sling asked. "Where are the zombie guns?"

"Zombie guns?" Gregory asked. He decided the best defense right now was to play dumb. "I just guard whatever is in this room. My day is spent standing here and making sure no one gets in. I guess I fell asleep and someone snuck in."

"I would say not likely, but we waltzed right in and got your gun and checked the boxes. And we weren't even quiet about it," the big guy said.

"I've always been a deep sleeper. Was I snoring?" Gregory didn't know these guys, but if they were affiliated with or as bad ass as the last two, he was in trouble. Especially since they wanted what he'd already sold.

"Let's cut through the chit-chat. You look stupid, but not quite that stupid." Boris pulled out his formidable weapon. "I'm going to count to three and then I'm going to shoot the tip of your dick off."

The other Russian laughed. "I'm beginning to suspect you have an unhealthy appetite for shooting men's dicks off."

Boris wasn't laughing. Or smiling. He was pointing his gun at Gregory's manhood. "One . . ."

Gregory covered his groin area with both hands, knowing it wouldn't block a bullet. But he was still trying to survive.

". . . Two . . ."

"Okay, okay, don't shoot it off." Gregory waved his arms. "If I tell you who took it, will you let me live?"

Boris lowered the gun. "I won't shoot you."

"How can I trust you?"

"You really can't." Boris put his Makarov PMM back in its holster. "Again, I will not shoot you. All I want is the information and then I want to leave as quietly as when I came in here. I don't think you want me to put a bullet in your heart, right? That might hurt."

"I'm getting bored," Fat Tony said. "Start counting again. I want to see this douchebag's head explode on the wall behind him. He doesn't know anything."

"I already got the count to two." Boris put his hand on the gun.

Gregory decided it wasn't worth the effort or his life to play dumb anymore. "Fine, I'll tell you. But they look pretty mean. I need protection for my family."

"Tell us their names."

"How do you know it isn't just one guy?"

"You said they." Fat Tony smiled and put out his hands. "How long do you think I can keep him from shooting you?"

"He promised he wouldn't shoot me."

"If you told him the answer he was looking for."

"There were two big Russians."

Fat Tony nodded his head. "Was that so hard?"

"Did you get their names?" Boris asked and once again pulled his pistol.

"The one I dealt directly with was Nicholai, but I don't remember the other one's name right now. If you stop pointing the gun at me, I might remember."

Boris put the pistol back. "I know him. And Ivan was with him."

"This can't be good," the other Russian said.

Boris shook his head. "This means we've been pulled off the mission and left for dead. Or, more than likely, an added bonus to the plan: eliminate the two of us. Nicholai was always looking to move up and over me, so it makes sense. I'm sure Ivan is just going along for the ride. He's loyal to Mother Russia first and foremost."

"I'm putting this next part in your hands," Fat Tony said. "We need to get the weapons back, and if you know where they ended up, so much the better."

"The problem is going to be getting them back before they go into storage," Boris said.

Gregory casually shuffled his feet toward the door, hoping the three men would be distracted enough so he could escape. There were too many people who knew the items were missing, and he would be taking the fall. Worse, he was still in fear of his life.

"I wonder what they know," Boris said. "If we disappeared off the radar of the SVR, we might be able to work this out in our favor. What have you heard, Ramzan?"

"It looks like you aren't in play anymore. I'm a rogue and they've put the word out to dispose of me, actually. I guess Nicholai took your spot in the pecking order. Ivan will be getting a promotion as well, I imagine."

"Then I guess the first order of business is making it known I'm back in play, but only to Nicholai. I need to figure out the proper way to get him to keep his mouth shut when I call him."

Gregory was at the door and trying not to listen to the men as they made plans that no longer concerned him. He wanted to get home, pack up his things and get his daughter from school. Maybe he could drive out to Colorado and spend time with his brother. He'd stop at the ATM and clean out his bank account. All $800 or so. Not nearly enough to get from Florida to Denver and have money to live, but he'd get as far as he could and then figure it out. He was sure his bro would be cool with them staying for a few days or weeks. He hoped so, anyway.

He felt the big Russian's hand on his shoulder and spun around.

"Going somewhere?"

Gregory tried to laugh and act casual. "I was just going to stand in the hallway until you boys were finished chatting. I don't want to get in the way. I'm sure you have a lot to talk about, so I'll be out here."

"I don't think so. Come back inside."

Gregory tried to keep from having a panic attack. He decided against sitting down in case he needed to flee. He loved his job and had probably blown it. He thought of an angle to keep him from getting fired or arrested. "I don't mean to interrupt, but can I ask a favor?"

Fat Tony smiled. "Of course you can. After all, this is all about you. Don't worry about the fact we're trying to get something done. We want to make you comfortable. Ask away."

Gregory figured he was being sarcastic but ignored it. "Can one of you knock me out?"

Boris laughed. "What?"

"If you guys come and go without knocking me out, I'll get fired or arrested. But if you hit me in the head, I can say I was attacked and the guns were stolen. See? Then I won't be questioned."

"None of what you just said makes sense. When they question you, what's to stop you from mentioning us?"

"Money." Gregory was trying to figure this out as he went along, but he'd need cash. Now. "For a few thousand, I can point the finger at the other two guys."

"That sounds reasonable. Can I give you a check?" Fat Tony asked.

"I'd prefer cash."

Boris shook his head. "Enough of this. We're wasting time. Let's get out of here." He turned to Gregory. "I have something for you as payment for letting Nicholai and Ivan in here."

Ramzan grabbed Gregory from behind, covering his mouth with one hand and getting him in a half-nelson hold.

Boris pulled out a large curved blade from his boot. "I promised I wouldn't shoot you, and I am a man of my word. But it will give me great pleasure to carve you up."

≈

**KOSTAS WAS BUSY PLUGGING GADGETS INTO WHAT LOOKED LIKE A** soundboard when Martin walked up. The field just west of Miami was nothing more than an enclosed swampland the military covertly used for training and shooting exercises.

"You're sure we're allowed to be here today? I thought we needed clearance," Martin said.

Kostas smiled. "I got clearance."

"Legally?"

"Sure. I can get past a padlock in seconds."

Martin shook his head. "I'm not getting in trouble for this."

"You worry too much. What's the worst thing that can happen? We get escorted off the grounds by some stiff uniform pointing a rifle at your head?"

"Why at my head?"

"Because you're the big alpha male of this group. You are the obvious threat. Not little old me. I'll start crying if I have to. I can't go to prison. I'm too cute and fragile."

"Whatever." Martin placed his carry bag on the table and unzipped it, placing his four favorite rifles before him. "What are you shooting?"

"Nothing. I'll control the targets."

Martin had another sinking feeling about this. "Why is it every time you invite me for something simple, it turns into this grand thing? Why can't we set up a few glass bottles and shoot at them?"

"Where's the fun in boring targets?" Kostas pulled a small metallic helicopter out of his bag and placed it next to the rifles. He pulled out several more, one at a time, and lined them up in a row.

"I'm afraid to ask what we're about to do."

"Anyone can hit a stationary target from a couple thousand feet, but who is skilled enough to nail a flying target the size of a model airplane?"

"I'd say Mike Martin, but you'll come up with a sarcastic answer."

"Me? Never. I was going to say Dale Comstock, but you're a close second."

"Dick. I'm not even going to ask where you got them from."

Kostas added the tenth one to the table. "You might not want to know. In the small chance they are found to be missing, I'd hate for you to go down with me."

"I'm going home."

"You might as well stay. You're already considered an accomplice after the fact."

"After the fact you stole government property so we can shoot them into pieces?"

Kostas began pulling out the wiring on the first one. "Exactly. It's called destroying the incriminating evidence. I need to rewire them. It will take me a few minutes to sync them with my radio control. Feel free to set up some boring bottles and shoot at them."

"I can't believe we're doing this."

"Sure you can. I think we've done some worse things together in the short time we've known each other. It's no fun if we follow the rules. Hell, I'm on ACES because I never followed the rules. I have a great job, nice paycheck, and all the government toys I want to steal and play with."

"And now you have a girlfriend," Martin said with a smirk. Kostas had been very quiet since their double date. Jenny was a funny and blunt woman, but for all her bravado and sexual innuendoes, she didn't seem easy. She enjoyed the game more than the actual end result, and it was clearly throwing Kostas off his supposed game.

Kostas stopped working on the helicopter but didn't look

up. "She's not my girlfriend."

"I figured after her subtle hints about sex in the bathroom, you two were quite the item."

"Nope." Kostas shook his head and went back to work. "If we can be serious for a second, I need to talk about it."

Martin couldn't help but laugh. "Are you coming to your older brother for sex advice?"

Kostas closed his eyes. "Maybe. Nah, forget it. Let's shoot things."

"No way. This is too easy. Should I clear the guns off the table so you can lie down?"

Kostas was silent as he pulled a second helicopter from the rank and began manipulating it.

Martin had never seen the smart ass this quiet, and it was amazing. He couldn't wait to tell Jennifer how deeply this woman was affecting him. "I'm done with the jokes."

"Are you sure?"

"Let me explain the birds and the bees to you, son."

"I'm going home now."

"Sorry. What's the matter? Jenny seems very interested in you. Very."

"Yes, she does. And she is, I guess. But . . ."

"Just say it. I'm listening," Martin said, trying not to chuckle and get him quiet again. He was really enjoying how Kostas was squirming right now.

"I can't figure her out. She's all sex talk and jokes when we're together, but in the short time I've known her, we've, uh . . . kissed. That's it so far."

"Have you made a move?"

"Not really. I'm getting a vibe from her about pacing, and

she sets the damn pace. She is totally in control, and I don't feel like I have any say in when or if we're going to have sex."

"Sounds like you haven't even gotten to second base with her yet."

Kostas shook his head. "I came close last night."

"Cool. Maybe after algebra class you can make out under the bleachers."

"Jerk."

"Why not make the move? You know, you talk a big game but it seems like you met your match. I'm really enjoying this."

"I'm sure you are. Me? Not so much. She's really hot. She has a great ass."

"Maybe someday she'll let you touch it."

"I hope so." Kostas grinned. "Jerk."

"Have you actually talked to her? It's only been a couple of days. Why are you so hung up on her already? You always act like such a player. All you do is brag about the strippers, models and hot chicks you date."

"I know, and I don't ever lie about it. I might exaggerate but I'm not making up stories. But Jenny is different . . . she's . . . I don't know. When I met her, I thought she was going to be another notch on the bedpost, but she's really keeping me on my toes. When I tried to talk to her this morning about us, she cut me off. She didn't want to look ahead. She asked if we could just enjoy the moments we have together."

"When are you seeing her again?"

"Tonight." Kostas started on the next target. "I can't stop thinking about her. She is so unlike any woman I've ever been out with."

"I think I know why that is, and what her speech to you meant."

Kostas stopped working and looked at Martin.

"She's obviously a lesbian."

"Sometimes I hate you."

"Seriously, why are you getting all tangled up already? Enjoy the ride. She seems like an awesome girl. Missy says nothing but great things about her, and I find her to be cute and funny. Her not having a filter when she speaks is amazing."

"Unless you're trying to have something more than casual sex."

"How's the casual sex so far? Oh, right . . ."

"I'm getting sick of calling you a jerk in this conversation. Just pretend I keep saying it." Kostas leaned against the table. "Man, it's only been a couple of dates, but I'm already head over heels in love with her. Is that possible?"

Martin thought of his own feelings for Missy. "Yes. I can relate."

"Can you?"

"Missy is awesome but disarming to me. She's not exactly playing a game, but she is another one who keeps you guessing. She is a ball-buster and won't let anything you say slide, but it's a good thing. I think I fell in love with her right from the first look. There's something special about these two women."

"I guess now we just need to not blow it. That might be our game: following along and staying out of trouble."

"Like stealing model planes to blow up?"

"Not blow up." Kostas picked up his remote control.

"We're going to shoot them. Let's put one in the air and see if you're really as good as you think you are."

"I think I'll start with the old standby until I get into a groove," Martin said and lifted his Tac-338 McMillan tactical rifle off the table.

"This should be interesting." Kostas controlled the helicopter, lifting it above their heads. "I'll take it easy on you. How about a thousand feet to start?"

"How far can you fly it?"

"I can get them about six miles without trying. Can you shoot it from six miles away?"

Martin aimed and fired in one fluid motion, smiling when his first shot blasted the helicopter into pieces. They fell to the ground.

"Wait until I get it in position. Damn. That was only five hundred feet."

"A twelve-inch moving target at five hundred feet is a good warm-up. I'll let the next one go a thousand."

"I only have a dozen of them. Let me get it up and move it around before you kill it. You know how long it took me to get them?"

"Can you put up two at a time?"

Kostas snorted. "I can get all of them airborne at once. But the sky filled with targets for you is cheating. I want them to be a small speck on the horizon. Offer you a challenge."

"Pull," Martin shouted. Twelve targets? He'd only need twelve shots. As he watched the next helicopter get smaller and smaller, he began to focus. He needed to forget about Missy Lockhart and his own feelings, and get back into the groove of honing his skills and shooting things out of the sky.

〜

**NICHOLAI AND IVAN PUSHED THEIR PLATES AWAY AT KUNG FU** Kitchen and Sushi. The restaurant was busy, and the two men were seated in the far corner watching as people came and went, piling food onto their plates.

"I can't remember the last good meal I've had," Nicholai said. "I generally hate this American bastardized version of food, but this place gets it right. I'll come back here if I can."

Ivan closed his eyes and leaned back in his chair. "I could take a nap."

"I agree. I'm glad you suggested we get away and get a real meal. Drive-thru hamburgers and bad room service were starting to get on my nerves."

"I need to pick up some Pepsi before we head back to the condo. You drank the last of it and didn't tell me."

They'd secured a condo in a gated community on South Beach, but there was no food stocked. Instead of ordering delivery takeout pizza and Cuban food, they hid the zombie guns in the attic and went out to eat like normal people for once. In this line of work, a sit-down lunch without an agenda was rare, and they wanted to take advantage of it.

Now that the mission was wrapped up, they were simply on hold until a drop off point for the weapons was given to them, or the zombie guns were picked up by another party. It didn't matter. They were both being promoted and they were going to get bigger and better jobs now that Boris Dragov was gone.

Nicholai genuinely liked the man, even though he was tough to work with. His thinking was never straight-forward.

He liked to play a game of chess with the enemy and show off his intelligence and superior skills. Nicholai decided to just get the work done quickly and efficiently and move onto the next one. This wasn't a game to him, and it wasn't about being clever or letting everyone know how good he was. It was about finishing what you started.

"I also think a box of Oreo cookies are in order," Ivan said. "I'll be hungry in an hour. I've also been meaning to try some of the American sitcoms everyone raves about. I might even fall asleep on the couch for the first time in months."

Nicholai nodded. "I think cookies will be nice, but I want to get a gallon of vanilla ice cream and crush the Oreo cookies on top."

"They make Oreo cookie ice cream, you know."

"Really? We need to stop at a supermarket on our ride home. I want to see and taste this ice cream."

"I'm ready when you are. I'll leave the tip," Ivan said.

"I don't agree with tipping."

"Here we go again. I've heard this argument from you over and over. These people are trying to earn a living, just like we are."

"I don't get tips."

Nicholai was startled when his cell phone rang. He pulled it from his pocket and looked at the number and smiled, putting a finger up. "This will be interesting. Hello? Boris?"

Ivan dropped a few dollar bills on the table and the two men left quickly.

Ivan pulled out his cell phone.

Nicholai leaned against the sedan. "How are you, my friend?"

"Let us cut through the niceties, Nicholai. I know you have the weapons, and I want to be involved in their safe return."

"I'm sorry, but you know as well as I do what the consequence is for failing a mission. I've completed mine and you have not. Boris Dragov, of all people, should know what the penalties for this are. You've eliminated quite a few operatives for failing to comply with strict orders."

"Then bring me in."

Nicholai was confused. "I don't think I heard you."

Ivan gave him the thumbs up as his call connected. "Keep him talking until I get an answer," Ivan whispered.

"You heard me just fine. If I stay out here as a rogue, they'll send men like you and Ivan to hunt me. Eventually, somewhere down the line, someone will get lucky and take me down."

"As always, you are quite humble."

"It's not arrogance if it's the truth. I don't want to run. I want to face our bosses in the SVR and plead my case. Let them know I am throwing myself at you. In fact, be the hero and say you talked me into coming in. Whatever it takes for you to get me safe passage back to Mother Russia."

Ivan smiled. "We just got another job. See if Ramzan is with him."

Nicholai matched his partner's smile. "How do I know this isn't a trick? Where is Ramzan?"

"He's with me, but he really has no choice in the matter."

"Meaning?"

"I've captured him. He is the real rogue in this operation, and the one who our bosses will be interested in interviewing. This runs deeper than you can fathom. Killing the two of us won't make sense, especially when you find out how intricate these traitors have sunk their claws in the hierarchy. It would be in your best interest to bring me in alive. While I failed my mission, I think the bigger picture is more important. These zombie guns exposed a weakness in our defenses against the Americans. Men like Ramzan have their own twisted agendas, but he is a small part of the equation."

Nicholai was intrigued. If he could bring in both men alive, and it led to crushing a rebellion, he would indeed be a hero. He would move right up in the rankings. The man who brought down Boris Dragov would be powerful. "I will call you back in one hour with a neutral site to meet. I want Ramzan secured, and if this is a trick, I will gladly torture you myself for information."

Nicholai disconnected the call and turned to Ivan. "We're bringing the two of them in."

"We have word to eliminate them."

"Call him back. Once he realizes the information we can get from these two, they will change their mind."

"Should I ask for backup?"

"Why? So someone else can share in the glory?" Nicholai opened the car door. "This is our chance to rise to the top. We need to get to the warehouse district and find a suitable place to take them down. Even if they aren't trying to trick us, they are quite dangerous."

"All the more reason to get help," Ivan said. "We've worked under him for a long time, and we both know what he is capable of."

"Are you scared, Ivan?"

"Very much so."

"Good. So am I. We need to use this fear of him to our advantage, and not get sloppy or make a mistake."

≈

**JENNIFER WAS GETTING MAD, AND SHE TRIED TO FIGHT IT BUT WAS** losing.

"This is a great turnout this morning, and so many lovely faces," Dale Comstock said to the women in attendance. There were perhaps thirty women, ranging from early twenties to late forties, and dressed like they were going to the gym. They giggled like school girls at every word from Comstock, and it was grating on Jennifer's last nerve.

Especially after the amazing night they'd shared.

"I want to have some fun today, but teach everyone here a few things if I can."

"You can teach me a few things," one of the women said loud enough for everyone to hear, and they all laughed. Except for Jennifer.

Dale was wearing camouflage pants, a tight sleeveless gray T-shirt and his sunglasses perched on his shaved head. His Springfield .45 pistol was in his shoulder holster. He stood in front of a soccer net, with a table of common everyday items displayed next to him. "All kidding aside, I was expecting a few people to turn out today. This is just a rough sketch of how the program will work. The Miami Police Department did a great job of getting the word out so quickly. I thought I was coming here this morning to talk with them about setting up the program. I didn't know we'd already started it."

"Did you kill zombies?" one of the women asked him.

Dale stopped smiling. "Yes, ma'am. Killing isn't a fun thing to do, but when there's a monster between you and your loved ones, you need to make a split second decision. In the movies and TV shows, you see these buff heroes with an MK-19 40 mm machine gun strapped to their back and arms with muscles on top of muscles."

"Like you?"

Dale smiled. "I don't think I can carry a big gun like that on my back."

Jennifer rolled her eyes when all the women started laughing a bit too loudly for the cheesy joke. She knew she was getting catty now. *Maybe it's time I took a walk or got another cup of coffee,* she thought. Before she started punching soccer moms in the face.

She relaxed and circled the group but stopped when she realized she was sizing each woman up like they were an enemy soldier and she was about to pull out her AA-12 automatic shotgun and spray them with bullets. *What is wrong with you? One night with Dale, and now you're acting like a jealous girlfriend.*

"I'd also like to introduce a member of an elite task force that keeps Miami safe from foreign attack. She was instrumental in coordinating both the military forces and the Miami Police Department officers during the recent tragedies. Ladies, please welcome Jennifer Sanchez."

There were a few sporadic claps for her from the women, which only infuriated Jennifer more. Now she wished she had her shotgun with her. "This is a great turnout today. It has been my pleasure to work so closely with Dale Comstock," she said and purposely curled her lip in a smirk. When most of the women caught her meaning they looked pissed. It made her happy. "I hope to learn quite a bit from Dale, and hope he learns from me as time goes by."

Comstock looked at her funny but smiled. "Thank you, Miss Sanchez."

Jennifer nodded at him and felt foolish. While they'd spent an amazing night together, what more was it? She woke up in his arms and felt alive for the first time in forever. But breakfast was spent with small talk about the upcoming day. He didn't ask her about her family, or anything important. Looking back, he had avoided all conversation about the two of them and the future. She wasn't even sure how long he intended on staying in Miami. If the program took off like she thought it would, he would be traveling across the country with it. And leaving her behind.

"I have a few things on this table I'd like to show you. But first . . ." Dale pulled out his Springfield .45 pistol and made sure a round wasn't chambered. "In the event of another attack, I might use this baby in a pinch. I am a professional, and have many different weapons at my disposal. I've also been trained to fire under pressure and know what to do in most situations."

Dale walked around the table and put a hand on a frying pan. "What is this?"

"A frying pan," one woman said.

"No, this is a heavy blunt object you can use to strike a zombie in the head." Dale picked up a cereal bowl. "Another striking object, even to buy yourself some time and not get bitten."

"Aren't zombies really slow?" Another woman asked.

"In movies they are. In fiction books they shamble around, but in real life, they move fast. You've all seen the news footage, and I was there. It's scary, ladies, let me tell you. It is a normal person trying to kill you because they are so incensed. Look at the person next to you. She could be infected. How would you keep her from getting at you?"

"By using whatever you had on you? But what if it's just a set of car keys? I took self defenses classes when I got divorced," a buxom blonde said, smiling at Dale. "Since I'm now single and don't have any kids, I'm home alone every night."

*Why don't you just pull your fake boobs out and smack him with them?* Jennifer thought. *This isn't a dating event, you bimbo.*

"Where is your purse?" Comstock asked her.

"Under the table."

"Get it for me and I'm going to show you how many weapons you carry with you. We'll get into what you have in your home in a little bit. Right now, let's pretend you are walking down the street, minding your own business, when a deranged zombie suddenly appears down the sidewalk and charges at you."

The woman held up her large purse.

"Do you mind if we go through it in front of everyone?"

She smiled. "Not at all. I'm Angela, by the way."

"All right, Angela. Pretend I'm a zombie and I'm trying to bite you."

Angela laughed. "I hope I don't accidentally let you get your hands on me."

*I hope I don't accidentally get my hands on your plastic body and crush it,* Jennifer thought.

Dale glanced at Jennifer. "I know we're having fun today, but I need everyone to focus for a second. This is life and death. It could be the difference between saving your children or having to kill them."

Everyone got quiet.

"I hope that sobering thought sinks in. This isn't a discriminating thing. No one is immune to it, and no one is safe. It doesn't affect the weak or the old or the young or by race. It affects everyone and everything. Whoever is in the crosshairs of one of these weapons is in trouble."

Dale paced twenty feet from Angela and stood before her. "I'm going to run at you, so get ready and pull out whatever you have in your purse to use as a weapon but please don't attack me with it until I say so. Let me know when you're ready."

Angela put a hand on the zipper of her purse and smiled. "I'm ready."

Comstock charged her at full speed and Jennifer could see Angela panic as she fumbled with the purse, not even getting it open before Dale stopped short of crashing into her. He put his hands on her shoulders and leaned forward. "Right now, I am biting your neck."

Angela smiled.

"And severing your carotid artery. You will be dead within minutes of blood loss."

"Oh."

"I'm going to try it again. This time relax, breathe, and focus on the task at hand, Angela." Dale went back into his set position twenty feet away. "Ready when you are."

"I'm ready," Angela said but she was no longer smiling, instead staring at Dale as he began to charge her.

She unzipped her purse and reached in, pulling out a long cylindrical item and almost planting it in Dale's eye as he veered away from her.

Jennifer and everyone else laughed.

Angela, clearly embarrassed, held the silver vibrator in her hand.

Dale tried not to laugh but couldn't help it. "Well, that's one way to stop me in my tracks."

"I think I'm going to die," Angela said and put it back into her purse. "I can't believe I just did that." She started walking away.

Dale took Angela by the hand and pulled her close, whispering a few words to her. She started laughing and joined the group.

Jennifer leaned forward, trying to hear what he was saying and knowing how stupid she was for doing so. But she couldn't help it. This wasn't healthy, and she knew it. *Too much, too soon, get your feelings in check before you blow this,* chica.

"I guess I can safely say anything in your purse can be used as a weapon. Car keys can gouge out eyes, lipstick and mascara tubes as well. If you have one of those monster wallets packed with receipts, it can be hurled or used to hit them. The point is you need to fight back. You need to keep them from getting their hands and mouth on you, and you need to get away to safety."

"What if there are a bunch of them?"

"Good question. Your first line of offense is a good defense. I'm not here to teach you how to start fighting the zombies. I'm trying to protect you from them. If you are cornered or find yourself needing to protect a loved one, these are some basic things you can do. In later classes I'll teach you actual techniques for working in a coordinated group and keeping several of them at bay at once."

Dale waved his hand at the table of items. "This is a visual to let you know there are many weapons at your disposal. No matter what room you find yourself in, or where you are, there are ways to protect yourself. And ways to survive." Dale looked at Jennifer. "Miss Sanchez will be helping me with her own expertise on these matters in the coming sessions as well. Now, are there any last questions?"

Jennifer's cell phone rang and she answered as she walked behind the soccer net. "Hello?"

It was Martin. "We have a major problem."

"What is it?"

"The zombie guns ... they've been stolen. All four of them."

Jennifer dropped her cell phone and turned back to Dale Comstock and the group of women, knowing these lessons would be useful in the next few days. Because the world was about to make another turn for the worse.

# EPISODE ELEVEN
## The Four Rogues

**NICHOLAI STOOD IN THE CENTER OF THE ABANDONED WAREHOUSE,** turning slowly to make sure he wasn't ambushed. Dust and debris covered most surfaces, the windows coated in grime. If nothing else, Boris had picked a great moody place for this meeting.

He heard a car pull up outside, but knew it was for show. He knew Ramzan was likely already in position in the rafters, but so was Ivan. They would play this one by the book. Nicholai hoped it didn't go south, or he would be in trouble. He had no delusion he could take down Boris in a fair fight. Besides the man's legend as a Gracie Jiu-Jitsu master, he was simply an animal. Boris would rip people apart for disrespecting him, or even a perceived slight. Nicholai shuddered when he remembered all the jobs he'd worked with Boris, and the ones where the man had taken great glee in torturing people when he thought it was called for.

The side door opened and Boris walked in with his arms spread out and a smile on his face. "Nicholai, it's been so long since I've seen you in person. Have you gained weight?"

Nicholai grinned. By weight, he immediately knew Nicholai had an extra weapon on his person. The man missed nothing. "You can never be too heavy, am I right?"

Boris stood exactly twenty feet away from his former henchman. "It seems a few days have changed our places. I find it interesting. I always knew you and Ivan were meant to move up to bigger and better things. It was the reason they paired you with me, you know. To train you and smooth out the weak spots, to make you both into killers who could be entrusted with the might of Mother Russia against the Americans. I wonder how well I did."

Nicholai refused to be baited by Boris. He knew what the man was doing because he'd watched him do it to foes over and over, subtly taunting until they were caught off-guard. One minute they were smiling and looking relaxed and the next Boris had his hands around a neck and his Makarov PMM pressed to a temple. "Still carrying the Makarov?"

Boris patted his jacket. "Of course. It's still my main piece. I've never forgotten it was you who bought it for me." Boris laughed. "I would greatly dislike having to use it on you."

"That would be ironic." Nicholai patted his own jacket to let him know he was also armed, if only for show and to play the game. "Where is Ramzan?"

"I was just about to ask you where Ivan is hiding."

"More than likely they have weapons trained on one another right above our heads."

"It makes sense. They were always loyal to the cause, and to doing the right thing. I just wonder right now what you think the right thing to do is, old friend."

"The mission given to me." Nicholai didn't know where he was going with this, and he didn't like it one bit. "The one you failed to complete."

"I've decided to look at the bigger picture. We keep being used as pawns in this chess match, but we never get near the real prize."

"What is the real prize?"

Boris spread his hands. "Defeat of our enemies. However it needs to be done. This one move at a time is not working, and we have a chance to tip the balance in our favor. Burying the zombie guns is not going to get anything done. It will put us right back to square one. I say we use the weapons and begin to destroy the Americans, before they can recover from the destruction created by a single gun. Can you imagine Miami, in the grip of panic as the zombies close in from all four sides? We could level this town and send a message. We could create worldwide chaos, but we need to act on it now."

Nicholai wasn't impressed. "I leave those things to better people than you and I. My mission is to keep the zombie guns hidden until it's time to use them. It might be tomorrow, or it might be ten years from now. But that isn't my call."

"Why not?"

Nicholai shrugged. "If you came here to turn me into a rogue, you are wasting your time. I'm here to bring you in and let the SVR deal with you and Ramzan. While I respect you as a mentor and an agent, I can't allow you to walk out of here to spread this insanity."

"I didn't expect you to." Boris looked up. "Ramzan, it's time for us to go and face our bosses."

"They wanted me to execute you and Ramzan. I talked them out of it. You both still might be valuable to the SVR, and I felt I owed you at least this much. However, you do know once I turn you over, it will be up to you to survive."

Boris nodded. "I appreciate the sentiment. I think I'll be fine. I've gotten through worse situations than this, don't you think?"

"I was there for a few," Nicholai admitted with a laugh. The man was indeed charming, and he'd miss working with him in the field. He had no delusions. Boris would be summarily interrogated and killed once he returned to Russia.

Ramzan climbed down from the area above and Ivan came down from the opposite direction. The two men joined Boris and Nicholai in the center of the warehouse.

"Now that we're all here and reunited, I think it's time to leave," Nicholai said. "Arrangements have been made to slip the both of you out of the country before anyone is the wiser."

Boris turned to Ivan. "You've heard what I've said. Now is the time to take a chance and strike, while the Americans are still reeling from these small attacks. We can end up as heroes today, or we can tow the company line and die anonymously."

Nicholai put up his hand. "Do we do this job for the glory, the praise? No. We do it because we love our country."

"We do it to better our country, too. We don't blindly follow orders. We hope we make a difference." Boris pointed at Ramzan. "We all thought he was a madman, but I've seen the light. He is more patriotic than all of us combined. Ramzan sees the big picture, and he's willing to sacrifice himself to make sure Russia comes out the other side of this strong. What do you think you are doing? Really? All of us? Killing a person here and there isn't going to change anything. I'm not talking about revolution. I'm talking about helping our homeland. We don't want to destroy the government, we want to help it to progress without all the red tape or so many opinions as to what we need to do to be the powerhouse we used to be. A strike against the United States will show the world we mean business. How many Middle Eastern countries are trying to take credit for the attacks? How long before a splinter group who wants to tear down Russia steps up and does just that?"

Nicholai shook his head. "This is none of my concern. I

don't want to change anything. I want to do my small part and do it well. Right now it means getting revolutionaries in check. I'm sorry, old friend, but I can't let you do this. Someday you will see you are wrong." He pulled his pistol slowly from his holster and saw Ivan did the same. "I think we're done here."

"You are making a mistake," Boris said.

Nicholai was waiting for him to go for his Makarov PMM but Boris didn't move. He simply shook his head.

Nicholai felt a sharp pain in his temple before his head exploded.

≈

BORIS DIDN'T KNOW HOW TO REACT. HE WAS EXPECTING THE shot to come from above, where Fat Tony was hidden. If he shook his head, Fat Tony would shoot Nicholai. Ivan would be forced to tell them where the zombie guns were hidden before he was executed.

But Ivan stood with the pistol still in his hand and pointing at where Nicholai was formerly standing. The shot was still ringing in the acoustics of the empty building. Nicholai was dead, half of his head missing and blood splattered across the concrete floor.

Ivan lowered his weapon to his side. "Tell me more."

Boris laughed. "I wasn't expecting this move, Ivan. You caught me off guard."

Fat Tony came stumbling from the shadows, breathing heavily. "No fair, that was my shot," he said through the wheezing. "I almost killed somebody."

"I did." Ivan pointed his gun at Nicholai. "I just effectively cut myself off from the SVR." He looked up at Boris. "I've gone into battle with you more times than I can remember. I've done jobs I didn't agree with, and neither did you. But we did them for the common cause. I agree with Ramzan and looking to the future. If we get hanged as traitors in Gorky Park, so be it. I will still be dying for my country."

"I don't intend to die," Boris said. "I intend to stay under the radar. Once the SVR sees what we are about to do, they will send teams out to stop us. The ACES group will pull out all the stops as well. We will have some major heat breathing down our necks." He put a hand on Ivan's shoulder. "Are you sure you are willing to join us?"

Ivan nodded. "Yes. Just tell me what we're going to do and I'll do it."

"We need the zombie guns."

"Not a problem. They're hidden in the condo. We were supposed to rendezvous with a team shortly, to turn over the zombie guns and the two of you. I know Nicholai had the best of intentions in mind, but we all know you would have returned to Russia a corpse."

"How were they going to get us out of here?" Ramzan asked.

"Narco submarines in the area. These, in turn, would move us and the guns to a safer and bigger ship. But once they realize we aren't coming and aren't going to be signaling them tonight, the hunt will be on for us and the guns."

"I am going to ask once more: are you sure putting yourself in danger with us is what you want? I'd hate to force you to do something you haven't thought over," Boris said.

"I'm sure." Ivan glanced at Fat Tony. "I'm not sure who this gentleman is, but I imagine this is now a foursome. There are four zombie guns, so I take it as a good omen. I'm also sure if you weren't 100% sure about me and my involvement, he would have gotten the head shake and taken me out."

Boris smiled. "As long as you know. We need to be quick and begin this, before ACES follows out path and catches up."

"They won't. We snuck the guns out from right under their noses. We had a man inside," Ivan said.

Fat Tony smirked. "After Boris took care of him, he won't be telling anyone who took the guns. He won't be telling anyone anything, in fact."

"So much for the element of surprise. I'd say we need to get this going now." Ivan led them outside.

"I'm hungry," Fat Tony said.

"I had Chinese buffet not too long ago," Ivan said.

"There's a Dunkin Donuts not too far from here. We need to stop there. They make a great cinnamon raisin bagel with tuna sandwich," Boris said.

Ivan wrinkled his nose. "That sounds disgusting."

"Don't knock it until you try it."

≈

**"THIS IS IT,"** JENNIFER SAID. THE FIRST CALL CAME OVER THE POLICE band. "Lock and load. We'll take two vehicles for the drive over and spread from there. I've already gotten the police chief coordinating with us so there isn't any problems. We get there and we take charge. We knew it was coming."

As Jennifer, Comstock, Martin and Kostas went to get

into vehicles, Martin put up his hand. "We have a problem." He pushed the small radio receiver into his ear. "There is a second hotspot on the other side of town."

*Great.* "Then we split into two groups. Martin and Kostas to the new location."

Just as Jennifer opened the door to the van, Martin shouted. "At least four spots now, all over the city. You gotta be kidding me."

Jennifer didn't want to believe it. "All at once? This can't be happening."

"It is. I'm guessing we have four shooters coordinating an attack. Chief Alvarez needs to call in the cavalry on this one."

"We are the cavalry," Comstock said. "I need a set of car keys. Are we taking other ACES members with us?"

"I had them heading to the first one if they were in the field." Jennifer pulled out her cell phone. "Follow the police radios and head out. Comstock, drive due west. Martin head east and Kostas head north. I'll take whatever is to the south."

"The rest of the team in Magic Productions will either be coordinating from here or following behind. I'll take the van and make it our home base for now," Kostas said.

"I hope you bring an actual weapon and fight," Comstock said with a grin. "All your fancy technology packed into the van isn't going to help us much. This thing is beyond worrying where it is. It's everywhere, and all at once. I'd stop hiding behind a computer screen and pick up an M4 carbine, buddy."

Kostas grinned. "I have just the weapon: a remote controlled flyer that will help us get some air coverage and kill some zombies."

"We're wasting time." Jennifer pointed at Comstock. "You want the Prius or the Harley?"

Comstock laughed. "What do you think?" He hefted his weapons bag over his shoulder. "Good luck." He pointed at Martin. "Keep track of kills, and no cheating."

"Then you can't cheat," Martin said and took the keys to the Prius. "I don't need a fancy ride to get out there."

"I don't either." Comstock got on the Harley and started it with a grin. "But I look damn good getting there."

~

BORIS KNEW HE WAS SOMEWHERE IN NORTH MIAMI AT A PARK, and he didn't need to know too much more. After his initial attack, he planned on driving due west and shooting as many people as he could.

The park was packed with families having picnics, a group of twenty-somethings tossing around a football, and several dog walkers.

The zombie gun didn't have a long range for accuracy, so Boris decided to back into a spot with easy access to the exit. He stepped out from the air conditioning into blistering Florida heat, even though it was getting later in the day. He was sure he looked odd wearing a dark suit jacket, but there would be other things to worry about soon enough.

A jogging woman, her German Shepard trailing her on its leash, ran by on the sidewalk. Boris shot the dog and watched in fascination as it turned on its owner, biting her on the calf and bringing her to the ground, where it continued the attack.

Several people nearby came to her rescue, but the dog attacked anyone who got close. Boris shot another two people in the group but quickly moved away to seek new victims.

He walked slowly up behind moms sitting on a park bench, watching their children on the swings. He zapped them and jogged away before they noticed him and gave pursuit. Boris figured another few zombies would do the trick, especially in such an open area. If some of them escaped into the residential areas behind the park, they could wreak havoc and be harder to find.

"We're really doing this," he whispered. "We're making history."

They'd all kept in touch via cell phone and started the four attacks in four different key spots in Miami at exactly the same time. This would assure Miami PD, ACES and anyone else would have a heck of a time trying to put out so many proverbial fires.

This would not be controlled. Miami would become a war zone, and it would spread like a disease as some of the zombies moved unchecked into other areas. Boris smiled, envisioning the beautiful Florida Keys covered in blood.

As the group of football players joined in the fray to help, Boris stepped closer and shot two of the bigger ones, watching them stop and begin biting their fellow playmates.

It was amazing to see how quickly someone could change into one of these monsters, their demeanor changing rapidly from concern to anger, immediately attacking the nearest person and trying to rip them apart. Pretty intense and scary.

Boris kept moving, circling around the park but keeping his eye on everyone infected and making sure none of them saw him. The last thing he wanted was for a mob of them to see him and give pursuit. He had the Makarov PMM on him, but it would be a shame to waste a shot of the zombie gun and then have to kill them. Ramzan told the men about the limitations of the battery packs and they didn't have unlimited shots before the zombie gun would run out.

He hid behind a tree when two of them looked in his direction, but they were in pursuit of a woman running past. The park was clearing out and he guessed he'd only turned a dozen people so far. He needed to create more, and was glad he still hadn't heard police sirens. He'd be able to drive out of here and go down the road.

As he got back to the car, one of the zombies ran at him from the parking lot. He had no choice but to shoot it in the head. "What a waste," he thought. "Killing a perfectly good zombie."

Boris drove out of the lot and rolled down the window. If he saw anyone unlucky enough to be walking, he'd turn them and drive away. He had a lot of ground to cover if he wanted to saturate this fourth of Miami, so he drove quickly, only slowing down when he saw a group of senior citizens power walking out of the park.

He shot the two women in the back of the pack, but didn't stick around to see how the attack ended. He needed to keep rolling.

At the next intersection he turned right randomly and stopped at a red light, where he shot the passenger in a convertible and patiently waited for the green light before he drove off, ignoring the screams of the driver.

He heard the siren before he saw the police car, but it was

behind him and heading in the wrong direction. Boris didn't know how close Ramzan or the others were to him, but he supposed the first call had already come in. As the cop rambled past it was joined by another. Boris slowed down and let the police cars by, taking the moment to shoot a couple as they walked along the road.

The zombies ran in opposite directions, looking for flesh. Boris was glad they didn't simply attack each other in a rage, and wondered why not. It would make sense for them to blindly bite anyone and anything in their way, yet they acted like the other zombie wasn't even there. If Boris got out of this alive and the SVR didn't assassinate him, he would try to find out the answer.

On the next corner was a pizza place, so he pulled into the parking lot without stopping and shot a teenager as he was entering, sure it would create chaos inside. As he pulled back onto the main road he heard the first scream and smiled.

The target areas needed to be busy, but Miami was so spread out and it was so hot most people were hiding in air conditioned houses and eateries or had the car windows rolled up. He decided to test the accuracy of the zombie gun through car window glass at the next light.

There was a family of four in a mini-van. The wife in the passenger seat glanced out at Boris and he smiled before shooting her with the zombie gun. It worked perfectly, and she slammed her face against the glass to get at him. He drove away, knowing she'd set her sights on the family at any moment.

Boris picked up his cell phone and dialed Ivan. "This thing works through glass, you know."

"I just found that out. The police are coming at me, so I have to move west. Will meet you at the safe house."

With this information in hand, Boris decided it would be even easier. He stopped at the next light at a busy intersection and shot into a coffee house, happy when the man he'd aimed at began lunging over the counter.

He heard more police sirens and wasn't surprised when the first helicopter crested behind him, en route to the park, he imagined.

Boris drove and shot, weaving in and out of the business sections and the residential areas that butted against it, finding plenty of victims to add to the devastation.

＝

THE MIAMARINA WAS FILLED WITH TOURISTS AND AVID BOATERS, A picturesque scene. The breeze coming off the water pushed the oppressive heat away, making it bearable. Ramzan went to his boat, which had sat idly for days. With Dmitry gone, Ramzan went through his items and inventoried the many weapons hidden around the hold.

But he didn't need handguns and the two rifles, because the zombie gun would do the necessary work. Ramzan knew he wasn't going to get away once the attacks began and the city was turned into a seething mass of biting monsters. He decided to prepare the boat quickly for an easy escape, because he'd need to get away. Did he trust Boris, Ivan and Fat Tony? Hardly. Right now they shared the same common goal, but Ramzan knew the men had been easily persuaded and could be turned right back to the other side at the first obstacle.

A smart agent always had a backup plan, and Ramzan always tried for several. He knew the SVR would take him down at the first opportunity. While he was sure this attack on Miami would force his countrymen to take up arms and continue the fight against the Americans, he would still be punished at some point in the future. Regardless of the outcome.

Ramzan didn't do this to be a martyr. He did this because it was the right thing to do, and he needed to do it for his love of Mother Russia. If he paid for it with his life, as long as he changed the balance of the world order, he would die with a smile on his lips.

And if he could live to fight another day, so much the better. If he made the right moves today, he could stir up the entire area and then sail away and watch Miami burn from the comfort of the pleasure boat. He had no long-term idea where he would head, but he decided he'd let the wind take him. Ramzan had new identities waiting for him in several countries, but they were all tied to the SVR. He'd taken the liberty, right before he'd decided on this mission, to set up an account and life in the Bahamas. He would sail there and secure everything he needed before setting his sights on another place to regroup and set his next move into play, whatever it would be. It would depend on what happened in the next few hours.

Satisfied the boat was ready to launch, he calmly walked down the docks and away from the boat. His first stop would be across the street at the sporting arena, where he figured a crowd was always convened for one event or another.

He smiled as he went, greeting the families out for a stroll or getting ready to launch their boats on this late, sunny afternoon. His happiness wasn't like theirs, however; he was about to turn their world upside down and he relished the thought. Innocent people needed to die in order for people to get angry and take action. Weak people reacted to these situations, while Ramzan acted to create them. This first ripple would spread for years to come, maybe even decades.

Just as he thought, the area around the arena was crowded with people waiting to enter to see some high priced athletes play a children's game, or perhaps some innocuous musical ensemble playing their brand of drivel. It didn't matter to Ramzan, because the outcome would be the same.

He found a spot just off to the right of the entrance closest to him and stood near a palm tree, casually pulling out the zombie gun and shooting half a dozen people standing in the back of the lines.

When those people attacked those in line in front of them, it was like a wave. As people began to see what was happening and run, Ramzan shot those thinking they'd get away.

He began walking, catching as many fleeing as he could and watching as they attacked others. Ramzan decided to churn up the area, like being in shark infested waters and chumming. Soon, there were two score zombies ripping people apart, and he kept pointing and shooting. When security guards came out of the arena, they were hit and joined the fray.

Ramzan decided against wandering the streets in the area and shooting people. He'd leave the widespread panic to the other three men, and concentrate on clearing this area and hoping the zombies ran out of fresh victims and moved outward to other areas on their own.

He casually crossed the street, back to the Miamarina. He shot as he went, careful to only hit those people not in direct line of him. He didn't want to be attacked, but the zombie gun had a decent range and he was an accurate shot with it.

The screams from the arena were starting to reach the docks, and Ramzan stopped and hit a few people as they began to stir from their false revelry. A couple on a nearby boat stood from their chairs on the deck and Ramzan shot the woman and watched as she bit into her lover and the two went over the side into the bay.

He kept shooting, the world around him swirling in chaos. Ramzan smiled when he heard the police sirens. If he could eliminate the Miami PD as they came, there would be no way to control the destruction.

Ramzan turned away from the safety of his boat, moored only a hundred feet down the line, and with a smile, went in search of better prey.

≈

IT WAS JUST ANOTHER SUNNY DAY IN OPA-LOCKA. FAT TONY SAT in his car in the air conditioning, not looking forward to what he had to do. Turning people into zombies and watching them kill their neighbors and family members wasn't the problem. It was getting out of the car in this oppressive heat. He wished he'd brought a couple of sodas with him. Fat Tony couldn't leave his jacket in the car because his two shoulder holsters would be visible.

Sabur Apartments was the perfect starting point, since it was packed densely with gangbangers, drug dealers and prostitutes. Fat Tony knew from experience this late in the day the courtyards would be teeming with riff-raff looking to score and deals to be made.

He'd often sent his men here to get information or hire a thug for a job, but he'd only been here personally once.

"Might as well do this," he said and exited the vehicle. He decided against bringing any of his men with him, since they wouldn't understand what he was doing and why. Plus, with more men toting guns and getting in the way, he might not be able to escape.

Fat Tony's ultimate plan was simple: help the Russian cause and be rewarded for it once America fell to the Commies. They'd probably slice up the States, and he wanted to control one. This one. He could already imagine being the big boss, and having thousands of people under his rule.

But first . . . on this side of the street there were two levels of the Sabur Apartments, but it ran back on either side behind it, with the courtyard in between. Fat Tony decided to cause a little chaos on this side before going around.

Sitting outside the main office were three black teens, wary eyes watching his approach. One stood up and met him halfway across the parking lot, keeping his distance. "You lost, fat man?"

Tony smiled. "I'm looking for an old friend, Marcus. Can you let me know which apartment is his?"

The teen snorted. "Man, Marcus and Tiny got whacked."

Fat Tony frowned. "That's disturbing. Who shot them?"

The teen looked confused. "Who shot them? No one shot

them. I didn't say they were shot, man. I said whacked." He started twirling his fingers around his head. "High as kites, man. They got stoned off their asses and bit each other and shit. Blood everywhere, it was insane. This place swarmed with cops." He narrowed his eyes. "What did you want with them?"

"I'm Fat Tony."

The teen laughed. "So what?"

Tony smiled. "If there is anyone that took over the family business from Marcus, he'll know exactly who I am. And then, when he tells you and you have to come crawling back to me to apologize, I'm going to watch your two friends there break your fingers. Is that understood?"

"Are you threatening me, fat boy?"

"Making a promise. Go run along and tell your boss his boss is here."

The teen hesitated, but ran up the stairs to a second floor apartment and knocked. The door opened and he went inside.

Tony decided to settle a few scores before the real fun began. As much as this complex helped him with his activities, it was still more trouble than it was worth. Besides, once the Commies were carving out their new empire, this place would be small potatoes. It might even be harmful to Tony, so why not raze it to the ground now?

A Cuban man stepped outside the apartment and grimaced. Fat Tony knew him as Hector, a nobody gangbanger that obviously took control as soon as Marcus was no longer holding the reins. He recovered and smiled, motioning Fat Tony to come up.

"I'd rather you joined me down here," Fat Tony said and wiped his brow. "It's too damn hot for this, and I'm not going to climb up those rickety stairs."

Fat Tony made a show of walking to the office and casually turning his side to the group of men. As he did so, he pulled the zombie gun from his pocket.

"I'm glad you came over, because there are a few things you and I need to discuss," Hector said. He was almost down the steps, with the teen in front of him and one of his lackeys following behind.

Fat Tony whipped around and aimed at the teen's face, pulling the trigger before turning and doing the same to one of the other boys sitting near him.

Hector was pulling out a pistol. "Got the safety on your toy gun?" He aimed at Fat Tony. "Is this some stupid joke?"

Hector's gun went off when the teen bit into his neck suddenly, knocking him to the ground. The lackey behind him was stunned at first, but then drew his handgun. Fat Tony shot him with the ray.

The two teens were now wrestling on the ground, one trying to bite his pal while the pal tried to draw his weapon but keep teeth from digging into his face.

Tony slipped past the ruckus and around the building before he was attacked, coming to an entryway and walking into the courtyard. There were dozens of people standing around in various cliques, doing whatever it is they did each warm night.

He aimed the zombie gun and began the chain reaction as far away as the ray would venture, and before long the courtyard was teeming with screams. Tony walked across to the opposite exit, shooting along the way. People were coming out of their apartments, and they were shot as well.

Fat Tony calmly circled the building, hitting another few people before getting back into his car. He was covered in sweat as he pulled out onto the main road, cranking the air conditioning and driving the three blocks to the nearest fast food restaurant. He needed a few drinks before he continued his journey of destroying Opa-Locka.

He laughed when three police cruisers sped by in the opposite direction.

≈

MIAMI INTERNATIONAL AIRPORT WAS CROWDED AS USUAL. IVAN didn't need to get past the parking lot before he was deluged with people coming and going. All he had to do was roll down the window and begin shooting random people as they exited vehicles or went to get into their parked cars.

He rolled up and down the aisles, watching in his rearview mirror at the scene he was creating. People were slammed against trunks and onto the pavement, yelling and running. Ivan put his arm out the window and tried to hit everyone in his sight that wasn't too close to his sedan.

Unfortunately, the people had scattered too soon, either getting to safety or as zombies off to find another victim.

When he got close to the airport entrance he parked and exited the vehicle.

"You can't park there," a security guard yelled from down the line.

Ivan shot the two women that happened to be standing

near him, and they distracted the guard by assaulting him.

The automatic doors opened when Ivan walked up. He didn't bother to enter, preferring to point and shoot as rapidly as the zombie gun would let him. He stepped off to the side as the doors closed, but he could hear the screaming. Ivan smiled.

While this scene was being played out across Miami, Ivan decided he wouldn't spend too much time here. Let the others take the fall for this monumental attack. He would be happy to return to Russia in one piece and with a cover story for why he alone escaped, and why he had a zombie gun in his possession. He would tell of the betrayal of Ramzan and Boris, and how he was able to wrestle one gun off of Dmitry's dead grip but no more.

He'd be promoted. With so many dead agents, he would move right up in the ranks. He might even become the go-to player, and he'd have a staff of men to do his bidding. Ivan had no delusion this attack would create a new world order and another world war. It would blow over, and within six months everything would be back to normal.

It was easier to go along with the madness, get a zombie gun, and create some trouble before getting out alive. If he was being honest, he wanted to also see how this weaponry worked at full capacity. The knowledge would prove useful in the future.

And he was glad he did, because it was amazing to see the rapid change in those you hit with it. Of course, he wouldn't admit to actually using the gun, insisting he battled the men for it and then escaped.

The doors opened again and three men ran out screaming.

Ivan shot the last one in the back and watched as he began chasing down the other two, who were unaware they were about to be knocked down and bitten.

Before the doors closed again he took another few shots inside. Then he turned and began shooting at anyone standing out on the sidewalk still unaware of what was happening. Ivan walked back to his car and got in.

He knew he should drive away and make his escape, but he wanted to see more zombies. And if all this chaos the four men created actually did work, he might be rewarded. He could play both sides of the fence if he needed.

As he pulled away from the curb he shot another woman, and then decided to make a pass through the parking garage before heading out.

There, he found people trying to get to their cars and drive away. He shot a few stragglers as they came down the stairs and stomped on the brake when the elevator door opened and five people came running out. He shot three of them and watched as they attacked. The next level down he found a woman huddled with her kid next to a car, and pulled the trigger.

As he exited the parking garage and shot the two guards sitting in the little booth, he heard the police cars coming up the road.

Ivan remained calm as he drove away, doing the speed limit. He didn't need to draw attention to himself right now. He needed to get to South Beach before nightfall and get away.

He pulled his cell phone out and dialed. "This is Ivan. There are some issues, but I have one of the zombie guns with me. I'm heading to the rendezvous point right now. I should be there soon, at which point I'll call back. I will explain everything when I get there."

Ivan smiled when he disconnected. This was all going according to plan, and the adrenaline rush of shooting all those people with the zombie gun was still coursing through him. As long as he could get through whatever the others were creating between the airport and South Beach, he would be fine.

He glanced in his rearview mirror and frowned. One of the Miami police cruisers hadn't stopped at the airport. Instead, they were following him as he exited.

Ivan sped up and put the zombie gun on his lap.

# EPISODE TWELVE
## Mission Accomplished

**DALE COMSTOCK FOLLOWED THE POLICE CARS AS THEY HEADED INTO** Opa-Locka, but he quickly sped past them with the Harley. He didn't have any more time to waste and he didn't have to follow protocol. He needed to kill zombies.

He listened to the police band on his headset as he weaved in and out of traffic and figured out where he was going. *Back to the bad part of town,* he mused. These guys weren't playing very fair. But it didn't matter to Dale because he would rid the streets of this horror once again. And then he'd be off, doing his thing . . .

Dale silently prayed Jennifer would be safe, even though she was the toughest chick he'd ever met. By far. Yet, she was sweet and loving and tender and beautiful.

Up ahead he saw a police cruiser stopped, lights flashing and the officer out of the car but running away. Dale saw why as he parked the bike. There must have been twenty zombies running down the road toward the police car.

Dale pulled out his HK416 and started firing into their midst, cool and calculating shots that ripped through skulls with abandon. The officer ran past him without questioning why he was shooting, which was just as well. Comstock wasn't about to stop to have a chat with the cop. He was too busy keeping the zombies in front of him at bay.

He switched to his Springfield .45 pistol and finished off the last handful before stopping and reloading. When it was obvious there were no more in the immediate area summoned by the shooting, he got back onto the Harley and began cruising the streets, looking for more enemies and the Russians.

Twice he stopped, balanced the bike with his legs, and

fired at zombies, bringing them down. He kept weaving in and out of streets, looking for more of them.

He stopped at an intersection where three bodies were splayed and bloody, a zombie biting and ripping flesh. A man with a camera stood nearby, filming.

Dale drove up slowly and shot the zombie in the head when he looked up.

"Wow, that was cool," the man said and kept shooting footage, now trained on Dale. "Are you a super cop or something?"

Dale pulled right next to him with a smile and punched the camera, driving it into the guy's face. As the guy fell Dale reached out and caught the camera. "Nah, I'm the American Bad Ass."

Comstock slammed the camera to the pavement and stomped it with a boot.

The man's face was a bloody mess. "You bloke my noth," he mumbled.

"If I were you I would go home and lock your doors. And feel lucky I found you before he got tired of biting dead people. Idiot."

Dale turned and shot another zombie as he came running down the street at him, before climbing back onto the bike and riding off again.

Two blocks away he encountered another zombie, which he shot with the .45 without slowing down. He made a left at the next intersection since there were stopped cars ahead but no immediate danger from zombies, and sped down the block.

The police radio crackled about another cluster only a

few streets away, and the sighting of a dark blue sedan with a large driver that might be the cause.

"Gotcha," Dale said. He would change tactics and try to find the car, only shooting zombies if he ran into them. His goal had changed. If he could stem the tide of people being shot, the police would be able to clean up the mess.

Another six zombies were shot as he cruised, but the police were in the area and shooting them as well. He decided to save his bullets and focus on the sedan.

He didn't have to wait long, as the car crossed his path two blocks up, heading east. Comstock sped up and saw the tail lights as the sedan took a hard right ahead.

There was another seemingly random turn and then Dale was only a hundred feet behind. The driver was definitely the culprit because he shot a man running, turning him into a zombie. Dale shot the man before he had time to take a step in his direction.

The longer the Russian kept moving, the more victims he would have. Dale didn't want to keep this up and see more and more innocent people die. He decided to do something about it now.

At the next long stretch of street, Dale shot out the two back tires of the sedan with the .45 and slowed down as the car jumped but kept straight, sparks flying underneath as it bounced on the two blown tires.

He was expecting it to come to a stop or flip, but the driver was good. He kept it straight and steady, although he wouldn't get far riding on the rims. The car made a sudden left turn and went over the curb, but it kept moving and Dale kept back when the sparks were flying in his direction.

"This guy is going to kill someone," Dale thought right before the car slammed into a parked police car on the next block.

The driver, a heavyset man, got out and began to lumber down the street. He was bleeding from a cut on his forehead and cradling the zombie gun.

Dale parked the Harley and turned off the engine. Once he was sure the man was more interested in escaping than shooting at him with the zombie gun, Dale sprinted down the road and caught up quickly. Still jogging, the man turned and tried to lift the zombie gun to fire, but Dale unarmed him, slapping him across the face with the weapon.

The big man stumbled but kept upright, still running, blood splashing from his face and down his chin.

Dale simply ran next to him, then turned backward and kept pace. "I can run a lot longer than you can, buddy. The gig is up, as they say. Anytime you're ready to stop this ridiculousness, you let me know. I once ran sixteen miles with a hundred pounds strapped to my back, and no water. You think you can get away?"

The man seemed to think about it for a few minutes before he stopped, hand covering his heaving chest. He went down on one knee, trying to catch his breath. "I ... give ... up ..."

"I thought so." Dale searched the man, taking his weapons away and helping him to his feet. "You need to catch your breath, because I'm not carrying you."

Fat Tony sat down on the curb and nodded as Dale Comstock radioed in and asked for a squad car, letting everyone know one of the zombie guns was off the street.

≈

**JENNIFER PULLED UP TO THE MIAMARINA AND PARKED, REMAINING** calm even though there were bodies everywhere. She made sure there weren't zombies around the van before exiting, leading with her AA-12 automatic shotgun.

She saw the massacre which had occurred in the immediate area and across the street at the arena. There was a single zombie biting a prone woman. The zombie stood when he saw her but she put it down from long range with a shot to the head.

The streets and docks were eerie. She'd been here not too long ago, with people bustling about and having a great time. Now, it was desolate. Creepy. She didn't know where to go first.

Two squad cars pulled up and she notified them who she was and directed them to circle the arena and look for survivors and zombies. "I guess it's settled now," she whispered. "I'm going to check out some boats."

The first boat to her right was covered in blood. "Hello?" she yelled. She wasn't going to do a search of each boat, and figured the quickest way to get the zombies moving was to make her presence known.

It worked, because three of them began running toward her from the farther dock. She methodically took them down. Targets which didn't bother to duck or dodge a bullet were more than easy to deal with.

She did a cursory check left and right of each slip as she moved, but she didn't see another zombie or another living person. A good portion of the slips were empty, and she hoped it meant people had escaped.

The sound of more police pulling up comforted her. She imagined this hot zone was now cooling off, and she needed to follow the trail of bodies, whichever way it went.

Jennifer heard gunshots across the street and went to investigate, figuring more zombies were in the area and the police were taking care of it. When she heard someone yell to stop, her interest was piqued.

Coming around the front entrance of the Miamarina, she instinctively ducked down and lunged to the side, getting behind the garbage cans. The gunman ran past, shooting over his shoulder at the police.

Jennifer held back from taking him down when she saw he carried the zombie gun. If she could follow him to the others . . .

This was obviously one of the Russians who'd come in on the boat not too long ago. In all the excitement she'd forgotten they were still around, but it made sense they would be involved.

He slipped onto the boat.

Jennifer waited for the police to catch up, but when they didn't she looked. They were currently occupied, as two of their number had been turned into zombies and the rest were currently fighting them.

She knew the rest of ACES were busy putting out other fires around town, and she didn't think she had time to waste. As she began moving down the dock she heard the boat engine turning over.

She thought the Russian was alone onboard, and he was already pushing slowly away from the dock. Jennifer leapt onto the stern and almost slipped. Her AA-12 came up but the Russian was already ducking down.

"It's over. Come out and I won't shoot you," Jennifer said.

He slipped a hand around the entryway to the canvas cabin and pointed the zombie gun in her direction. Jennifer slipped down and to the side. She didn't see rays emanating from the gun but she wasn't taking any chances. The light on top kept flashing like a children's toy.

"Last chance," she yelled. She didn't want to kill him, but he wasn't cooperating. The boat was now shooting out into the bay with no one at the controls.

He yelled something incoherent over the engines and tried to angle the zombie gun to shoot her, but she slid across the stern onto his side, forcing him to move as well.

*Is he really going to do this? He's hiding behind a canvas wall. But if I move on him, he'll turn me into a zombie. I'll give him one last chance, or else he goes down.* Jennifer sighed. She knew how this was going to end. "Last chance again."

"You said that already," he said as he blindly aimed in her general direction.

Jennifer tried to aim low when she pulled the trigger on the shotgun, but the movement of the boat as it sped along jerked her second shot high. The first one ripped through the thin canvas and hit him in the thigh, but the second one hit him in the neck.

Before she could recover and go to him, he was wind milling his arms, blood spurting from his neck, then he pitched over the side of the boat. He was quickly lost as the boat continued to speed along.

Jennifer ran to the controls, noticing with relief the zombie gun, covered in Ramzan's blood, sliding around on the deck. She slowed the boat down and turned it around, but his body was already gone under the waves.

≈

MIKE MARTIN SHOT FOUR ZOMBIES IN THE PARKING LOT OF THE fast food restaurant. He'd been following the police scanner reports and the trail of bodies and zombies, but had no idea if he was moving toward or away from the gunner. Despite Comstock mocking him, the Prius wasn't a bad car to drive. He pulled from the lot and drove slowly down the road and away from the park where he'd begun and the first calls had come from.

Miami was crazy, and the calls were coming in so fast Martin couldn't keep them organized, but he started picking out the reports close by and got an idea where the zombie gun was heading.

Twice he had to jump the curb in order to get around stalled vehicles, and both times he stopped and had to shoot zombies in the head. It was slowing him down but he still had a job to do. Clearing the streets was the first order of business.

Plus, the gunfire brought more zombies to him. He never had to go too far, but it was a losing battle to him. The farther he got from the gun, the more zombies he'd have to kill. This wasn't a video game. This was real life, and it was getting frustrating.

Martin heard about a scene roughly six blocks from his current position and immediately headed there, because an officer asked for backup and three cops had been turned into zombies and there was a man firing at them. It had to be one of the Russians.

He hoped Missy wasn't involved in any of this, but knew she would be. She did her job well, and she was heroic. And he missed her right now, but he pushed his feelings aside and refocused on the task at hand.

Martin circled the block the battle was raging on and got out of the Prius. He ran as fast as he could, taking out another zombie as he moved. As he made it back to the original street from a different angle, he had to shoot and kill three police officers who were now zombies.

He saw the sedan and the Russian squatting behind it. The car was riddled with bullet holes and the tires blown out. There were a dozen cops firing on his position, but the Russian looked calm as he moved back and forth, using the car as a shield and picking off the cops one at a time, turning them into fighters for him.

"Back up," Martin yelled. "He's turning you into zombies."

The police shot another of their former fellow officers and heeded Martin's warning, switching to a new position across the street. Another of their number was hit and immediately took three bullets in the chest before he attacked.

More bullets flew across the street, punching out the car windows and slamming into the side of the car, but the Russian was still up and shooting back with deadly accuracy.

"Boris Dragov, give yourself up," Martin yelled. He knew as soon as he saw the Russian they were dealing with a strong opponent. Martin was actually quite envious of the man, and a big fan of his Gracie Jiu-Jitsu matches he'd seen online. The man was a killer, and one of the many enemies Dale Comstock and Martin had often spoken about.

Now, he was across the street, and turning innocent people into zombies.

"Is that the famous Mike Martin I see?" Boris yelled back. "I feel honored." He shot again and Martin sighed as he shot a man nearby in the head before he attacked.

"You are surrounded. Come out with your hands up and place the zombie gun on the car hood."

"I don't think so." Boris shot again. The police were down to four men now. "How about you walk away and I don't turn you into a zombie?"

Martin didn't know what to do. Boris was too smart to let himself get shot and too accurate with the gun to get near him. And they were sitting ducks out here with someone as good as Boris in control. Martin decided to change tactics.

"Is this the legacy you want to be known for? The great Russian warrior, shooting innocent and weaker opponents from long-range?'

Boris shot three people as they ran down the block, forcing the police to kill more civilians.

"Do you think your petty argument is going to stop me from my mission? You are even weaker than I thought." Boris suddenly stood and pulled the trigger. Three of the remaining cops were hit.

Martin shot them and screamed for the last police officer to back off before he was next. "It's just you and I, Dragov."

"Then give up now. I can do this all day. I'm having fun."

Martin stood and placed his Tac-338 McMillan tactical rifle on the car in front of him. "I'm just going to be sad when

I put a round between your eyes." Martin knew he was gambling but didn't want this game to last any longer, and had dealt with men like Dragov long enough to know what they really desired: a worthy opponent. "And I'll be really sad because I didn't get to finally meet you one on one and kick your weak Commie ass with my fists."

"Is that supposed to get me to lose my advantageous spot and drop the zombie gun?" Boris said and stood, aiming at Martin. "I really don't think I want to do that. Would you, if you were in my shoes?"

"If I were you I wouldn't, because you know I can beat you."

"I doubt it," Boris said and laughed. "You and your mentor have always been afraid of me. Word spreads in the Gracie Jiu-Jitsu community, no matter what continent you're on."

"How ironic, since we heard the same about you," Martin said. "In fact, I know from reliable sources my challenge to you has gone ignored for years." It was a lie but Martin didn't want to get turned into a monster.

Boris waved his finger but still pointed the zombie gun at Martin. "You know that's a lie. In fact, if you had thrown down the gauntlet I would have accepted it, if only to destroy you and at the same time show Comstock what a bad job he's done with his star pupil."

"I'm doing it now. I put my weapon down." Martin stepped out from behind the car and into the street. "There's only one way to settle this. If I beat you, I take you in. If you beat me you can run away and keep shooting people with your cowardly gun."

"Why would I do that? I hold all the cards." Boris stepped

out from behind the car. "If I were you, I'd start praying or thinking of all your friends and family you'll soon be biting. It was nice to finally meet you, though. I'll make sure when I turn Comstock into a zombie I mention I got you, too."

Martin had gambled and lost. He thought he could overcome the Russian by messing with his ego, but the man was better than he thought. So be it. "Then pull the damn trigger, you weakling coward. At least I know I was the better fighter than you."

"Whatever helps you sleep at night." Boris laughed. "Oh, wait . . . there won't be any sleep for you after this." Boris pulled the trigger but the light on top of the zombie gun didn't glow.

Martin laughed, relieved. "Is there a problem?"

Boris kept pulling the trigger but nothing was happening.

"I can't believe you tried to take the easy way out. And it failed." Martin took a step forward and started stretching his shoulders and loosening his hands. "You'll have to live with it now. I don't know if you believe in God, but I think he just taught you a lesson. I'm about to teach you another one."

Boris dropped the zombie gun and took off his jacket with a grin. "No matter. I'll enjoy breaking your body with my hands. I've done it to much better opponents than you."

"We'll see." Martin moved and met Boris in the middle of the street. "I just wish Comstock was here to see me crush the mighty Boris Dragov. I guess I'll just have to tell him all about it."

Boris lunged and the two men locked up, gripping each other's shoulders and trying to push the other off-balance. They grappled for several minutes with neither getting any kind of advantage.

"You're weak. I can feel it when you grab me, but mostly I see it in your eyes. If you have watched my matches you'll know I can crush you at any moment. Are you ready to feel such excruciating pain, Martin?" Boris fought with everything he had, despite his injury. He was no longer wearing the sling, his arm burning with pain. But he would never show his weakness.

"I didn't realize you talked to your opponent until they were bored to death. I have to admit, it is an ingenious move on your part. What you lack in obvious skill, you make up for in weak trash talk. I've seen your matches from when you were much younger, and they were impressive."

They locked up again.

"However, now you are rusty and a little fat around the middle. Too many American cheeseburgers and milk shakes, Commie?"

Boris executed a sudden lunge to his right but Martin over-adjusted, and Boris slipped his left foot around his ankle and drove Martin to the pavement.

Martin found himself underneath Boris, but didn't panic. He'd been in this position many times during matches and in actual combat. He put his elbows next to his body so Boris couldn't move up as he sat on top of him, and slipped his right hand across his body, gripping the wrist of Boris.

"You think it will be so easy to flip me?" Boris asked, and struck Martin suddenly in the face, breaking his nose. Boris kept striking with his free hand.

Martin tried to execute a reversal but Boris was too good, and held his position on top, hitting Martin at will.

"I am disappointed. I thought you were such a great foe, but you are an amateur," Boris said.

Martin was getting light-headed from the hits, his head banging against the ground with the force of the blows. His hand slipped from Boris' wrist.

Boris rose up with a grin and raised his hand for a final strike. "Good bye, Mike Martin."

"At least I know I won."

Boris hesitated. "I'm about to kill you."

Martin smiled through his bloody lips. "I beat you. You pulled the trigger. The only reason we're here is because you failed. You chickened out. You knew I could beat you in a fight, and you tried to take the easy way out. I hope you can sleep with that thought at night."

Boris looked incensed. "I beat you."

"Not yet."

Martin grabbed his wrist again, hooked his foot with his, and lifted his pelvis, deftly reversing positions in the blink of an eye. He began punching Boris in the face, deciding he didn't need to say another word until the Russian was down and out.

Boris was a bloody mess, his eyes rolling around in the back of his head.

Martin didn't stop punching until he was sure his knuckles had been broken and Boris was not getting back up. "I can't wait to tell Comstock this." He also couldn't wait to see Missy again. He prayed she was safe.

**MISSY LOCKHART DIDN'T BOTHER RUNNING THE LICENSE PLATE.** She'd clearly seen the man with the zombie gun leaving the airport parking lot. Instead, she radioed into dispatch to let them know the plate number and make and model so she could get back-up.

She wasn't surprised to hear there was no help on its way, since the entire city was being overrun at the moment.

"It's all you, rookie," she said. *It's time to earn your paycheck, and show* ACES *hiring you for a temporary job hadn't been a fluke or a poor choice.* She decided, when this was all over, she'd formally request a sit-down with Jennifer Sanchez about coming onboard the ACES team permanently.

And it had nothing to do with Mike Martin. Well, not everything. If she were being honest with herself... but now was not the time to dwell on her future. Live in the moment. Seize the day. Any other cliché to keep her head in the game.

He was heading due east toward South Beach, but she could only follow along and hope he would get blocked off at some point ahead. Maybe if there was enough chaos, his car would get blocked in and she could approach without getting shot.

Missy passed the ACES team van and saw Kostas driving. "Kostas, I need back-up. One of the weapons is in the car I'm following."

"Roger that."

Missy felt better having Kostas joining the chase. They were heading down the Dolphin Expressway and the Russian weaved in and out of traffic and shot right through the toll plaza. Missy and Kostas were right behind him, careful not to hit another car and get left behind.

*The man can drive,* Missy thought. *But so can I.* By the time the Russian was on the MacArthur Causeway, the traffic had thinned out. She hoped South Beach was clear, or evacuated. But not filled with zombies.

The Russian made a right onto Alton Road, heading south. There was traffic ahead but it wasn't heavy. Missy kept pace when he began to weave in and out but she heard an explosion behind her and looked in her rearview mirror.

The ACES van had been sideswiped by an SUV.

"I'm on my own again," she said, refocusing on the pursuit.

He turned onto Inlet Boulevard and sped up with a straight stretch of open road until he came into South Pointe Park, where he began driving over the grassy field at top speed.

Missy kept up, the police car jumping and slamming as she went, her head smacking against the roof of the car. She was disoriented and almost slammed into his parked car, sitting on the beach.

"Damn, where did he go?" she moaned, opening her door and drawing her handgun. She shook her head, clearing it. His driver door was open but she didn't see him.

Missy walked slowly to his car, keeping it in between her and the open door so if he were inside he wouldn't have a clear shot at her. Her police training kicked in, and she crouched as she got next to the rear of the car. She did a quick peek but he wasn't in the backseat. Gun still trained in front of her, she slid around to the driver's side. He wasn't there. A look around her surroundings didn't show him, either.

The beach was deserted, but there were many places for him to hide. Now she was starting to doubt he was in the car.

Had he gotten out that quickly? Was he sneaking up on her right now?

She did a 360 degree turn but he wasn't around. The only noise was the waves and their never-ending slip onto the sand. He had to be in the car.

Missy took three steps back, toward the water, and then to her left. If he was in the car he'd be in a prone position and wouldn't be able to shoot her. She hoped, at least.

But he wasn't in the car.

She heard the splash in the water behind her and turned just as Ivan sat up on one knee and pointed and fired from the surf.

Missy pulled the trigger, her mind registering she hit him in the weapon arm.

Everything went red for Missy Lockhart.

≈

KOSTAS DROVE THE BATTERED ACES VAN AS FAST AS THE BLOWN rear tire would let him, following the obvious path of Missy and the Russian through the park.

The squad car and the sedan were on the beach. Kostas parked away from them at an angle and exited the vehicle, his 9mm in hand. His clip was loaded and he was scanning all around him, especially the water. He knew the Russian could be anywhere if he was alive, and since Missy hadn't called out to him and she wasn't in sight, he figured she was either down or a foot chase had begun. He'd find their footprints in the sand soon enough.

Both cars were empty and he didn't see anything in the

water, but there were structures on the beach and the tree-line for people to hide.

Kostas frowned when he saw the zombie gun, bloody, washed up on the shore. He retrieved it, waiting for an ambush. There was blood everywhere, but no Russian and no Missy.

He found a single set of tracks heading to the south and followed.

Kostas was sweating even though it would be nightfall soon. The water was peaceful and could lull you into a sense of security. He kept an eye on the water. And the tracks as they veered into the palm trees.

He was exhausted but knew the containment of the problem would be coming soon. He had that much confidence in the ACES team, and his fellow members. He even liked Comstock and hoped the man would stick around. He wanted nothing more than to take Jenny to dinner and try to understand the woman, but knew he'd need more than another dinner date to unravel her. He also hoped Missy was safe, wherever she was.

"Missy?" he yelled when he saw her walking ahead through the trees. She might be hurt or disoriented because she was moving so slow.

Missy Lockhart turned and stared at Kostas with unabashed anger in her eyes.

"No."

She began running toward him, hands held before her in pursuit of his flesh.

Kostas raised the 9mm and pulled the trigger.

~

**CHIEF ALVAREZ SMILED AT JENNIFER SANCHEZ. "I WANT TO ONCE** again thank you for your efforts today."

Jennifer shook her head. "It's the men and women under your command who did the bulk of the work. They kept in constant contact with us and led us straight to the four zombie guns."

Everyone had checked in so far, and all four weapons were recovered. Comstock was already here with her in the police station parking lot and Martin was en route to the hospital. Kostas was driving back with the gun in tow. All in all, the mission was a success, although the body count was unreal.

Jennifer sighed and went back to sit on the hood of her car. Night had fallen but it was still warm, and she felt gritty. She needed a shower. She glanced at Dale as he came up, talking on the phone with someone.

Dale hung up and frowned. "I'm leaving."

Jennifer was stunned. "When?"

"Right now. There's something going on in the Middle East and they need me."

"Tomorrow they need you."

Dale wrapped his big arms around her and kissed her on her head. "I have to go."

"I thought you were retired?"

He laughed. "Did you think Kim L or anyone would accept it? They have a private plane waiting for me."

"I'll drive you," Jennifer said.

"No. I don't want to say good bye to you. I'll take the Harley. Have someone pick it up when you get a chance." Dale pushed away from her and kissed her gently. "I'll be in touch. This isn't the end for us, it's just the beginning."

"I want to believe that."

He put a finger on her lips. "Then just let me ride away. I want to remember your perfect face before I go."

"I want you to remember this," Jennifer said and passionately kissed him.

~

"YOU LOOK LIKE SHIT," MARTIN SAID FROM HIS HOSPITAL BED TO Kostas. "Where have you been hiding?"

"While you were playing your kung fu crap, I was recovering a zombie gun."

"I did it the hard way. I heard you found it in the water. That isn't much to brag about, buddy." Martin pointed at his broken nose and battered face. "I took a beating to get mine. It will make for a cooler story when we're out with the girls tomorrow night."

Kostas turned away. "I have something to tell you, and you aren't going to like it . . ."

~

THE NARCO SUBMARINE FELT CLAUSTROPHOBIC TO IVAN, BUT HE WAS glad to still be alive. The bitch cop had put a bullet through his arm and tore through his side and the salt water stung on his wounds.

"Tell me again what happened," the sub commander asked.

Ivan grinned. "I'm not telling anyone anything until I get some medical attention. I'm going to bleed to death, and once your boss hears what I have to tell him, you'll get a medal for helping me live. Do I make myself clear?"

The commander frowned. "I am . . ."

Ivan put up his good arm and waved the man off. "I don't care who you are. Just help me with the pain. By the time you get me out of American waters and back to a safe haven, I'll be ready to talk. Until then, leave me alone."

Ivan was in tremendous pain, but he also needed time to formulate a proper story to keep from being hanged for his rebellious actions, and if he played his cards right, he'd be the top agent used by the SVR in the next planned attack. And he knew after what they'd just done, another one was imminent.

Ivan smiled as he closed his eyes and tried to sleep, cursing the commander for taking so long with his medical attention.

He'd live to fight another day, and to tangle with ACES in his own time.